DEAR UNIVERSE

FLORENCE GONSALVES

LITTLE, BROWN AND COMPANY
New York Boston

For Daddy —FG

Little, Brown and Company
Hachette Book Group
1290 Avenue of the Americas, New York, NY 10104
Visit us at LBYR.com

First Edition: May 2020

Little, Brown and Company is a division of Hachette Book Group, Inc. The Little, Brown name and logo are trademarks of Hachette Book Group, Inc.

The publisher is not responsible for websites (or their content) that are not owned by the publisher.

Image of peach emoji on page 45 copyright © Arizzona Design/Shutterstock.com. Image of wind emoji on page 45 copyright © Carboxylase/Shutterstock.com. Image of stars on page 343 © hircus/Shutterstock.com.

Library of Congress Cataloging-in-Publication Data
Names: Gonsalves, Florence, author.
Title: Dear Universe / Florence Gonsalves.
Description: First edition. | New York; Boston: Little, Brown and Company, 2020. | Summary: "Seventeen-year-old Chamomile struggles to bring together her two universes of school, filled with the hype of senior year and future plans, and home, where her father is living with a terminal illness, until she meets a fellow student and hospital volunteer who helps her understand both worlds as one"—Provided by publisher.
Identifiers: LCCN 2019022199 | ISBN 9780316436731 (hardcover) | ISBN 9780316436748 (ebk.) | ISBN 9780316436762 (library edition ebk.)
Subjects: CYAC: High schools—Fiction. | Schools—Fiction. | Best friends—Fiction. | Friendship—Fiction. | Parkinson's disease—Fiction. | Sick—Fiction. | Family problems—Fiction.
Classification: LCC PZ7.1.G65219 De 2020 | DDC [Fic]—dc23
LC record available at https://lccn.loc.gov/2019022199

ISBNs: 978-0-316-43673-1 (hardcover), 978-0-316-43674-8 (ebook)

Printed in the United States of America

LSC-C

10 9 8 7 6 5 4 3 2 1

What you seek is seeking you.
—RUMI

I want a private supply of shooting stars.

I want crackers.

I want someone to come along and love me.

I want cancer.

Just kidding.

I want someone to open the notes on my
phone and realize I'm a goddamn wonder.

I want better nipples.

I want alien familiars (don't ask).

I want to be taken someplace golden, like a field or
the back seat of a car, and kissed so softly I sneeze.

I want to feel safe against another person's body.

I want to be gorgeous behind my face and stuff.

I want to know what to do about my dad dying.

I want a car.

I want a teacup pig named Betty.

I want an STD test, just in case that dream
I had involving Eugene Wolf was real.

I want an ask-cute to prom so adorable it cuts
me open and I crawl out of myself and find the
space I left growing a paper flower instead.

Prologue

Days 'til prom: Eons

YOU KNOW THAT MOMENT WHEN IT HAPPENS? AND YOUR LIFE goes from one long snore-fart to hell-freaking-yeah? That moment happens for me in, of all places, gym class.

It's the second month of school and I'm running like a goddamn hero, flag in hand when, "GOTCHA!" someone shouts, ramming into me and tackling me to the ground. They follow up with "Oops, sorry." It's a two-hand touch.

"It's okay," I say, with a mouthful of grass and the weight of another person compressing my lungs. I roll over as the sun is rising over the portable classrooms that are so run-down a raccoon fell through the ceiling our freshman year. I'd just transferred to Gill School then, and all I knew about the place was it had uniforms. Plaid skirts and small mammals with hand-paws? No, thanks. But when you get kicked out of public school, you can't really be choosy.

"I didn't hurt you, did I?" the boy asks, and that's when I get a look at him. He's wiry, with dark hair and a few pimples and these great bluish-gray eyes that I picture swimming across.

"No, I'm fine," I say, and I am. I'm still clutching that triangle of highlighter-orange fabric, hardly able to breathe, but I'm better than fine because a boy is finally on top of me.

"Okay, good," he says, jumping off quickly.

"Come on," someone from my team calls as they run by. Everyone's returning to their sides, which means the gym teacher must have blown the whistle, but I didn't hear it.

"You're a fast runner," he says.

"Thanks." I wipe my brow. "There's a lot of stuff I can't let catch up with me."

He laughs and then we look at each other. You know. *Look* at each other. Our eyes are like BAM! *You're a body with sex-parts. Let's get to know each other.*

Abigail says she watched the whole thing from jail (she always makes a point to be captured first) and it was a meet-cute like no other.

"I'm Gene-short-for-Eugene Wolf," he says. "You're Chamomile, right?"

I nod. "Yep, like the tea, only not as hot."

He laughs and we walk back to the center of the field,

where the team with pinnies (his) is facing the team with stale, wrinkled gym shirts (mine).

"You're funny," he says, and I smile. *Funny* is a new thing for me. Until everything started happening with my dad a few years ago, I didn't really have to be.

As we walk across the patchy field I try to envision what he sees when he looks at me: long hair that always borders on frizzy, two individually nice but asymmetrical eyebrows, a nose that's never been pierced. "I was thinking you should come running with me sometime." He looks over at me and I look back at him, our eyes pleasantly locked.

"I don't really run," I say, like the dolt that I am.

"Oh, you should try it." Then he lists all the reasons: college scholarships, teammates, heart health (which may or may not be true, given that people croak during marathons all the time). "Plus, then we could see more of each other."

Boom, bang, pop. Heart fireworks. I smile and he grins and Gene-short-for-Eugene Wolf has one of those melting grins that makes you heat up, then drip.

"Okay," I say as the whistle blows and he puts his hands on his knees, facing me with faux competitiveness across the imaginary line we're about to cross. "I guess I'll come running with you."

So we run. He picks me up outside my house before school, while it's still dark and the birds are black shapes against a sky that's very slowly starting to lighten. We run all over the place—through the woods, around the ice-cream place in town and the drive-in movie theater, and we stop at the playground for a drink of water, and then one time he kisses me there. Our mouths are still wet with water that tastes like a penny died in it.

"Race me?" I say after. I'm breathless because the closest thing I've had to being kissed before this was a gross encounter with a really friendly dog at Petco, but from then on we're a threesome. Not me, Gene, and the dog, but me, Gene, and running. Running before the world even wakes up. Seeing the sun rise over the roofs, like someone making breakfast in the sky, the egg cracking and then light. Over the next few months he shows me something to love, and that's why it's so hard later to let him go.

But why do I have let him go, you ask? Because I'm about to be bitch-slapped by the universe.

1

SECOND HALF
OF SENIOR YEAR
{JANUARY}

Days 'til prom: 103

I'VE GOT MY NOSE LODGED IN A RACK OF OTHER PEOPLE'S clothes when my best friend taps me on the shoulder frantically.

"How about this one?" Abigail asks, shoving a dead cat into my arms.

"Ew." I jump back and nearly knock over a row of vintage dresses with yellowing sleeves and a certain old-lady smell to their armpits.

"Relax, Cham, it's rabbit." Abigail sniffs the collar and wrinkles her nose. "Or *was* rabbit."

"You can't wear a fur shawl to prom," I say, throwing it back to her with a quick Hail Mary because I have a moral compass, thanks for asking.

"Why not? It's basically a winter prom, given that the end of April is as cold as a dead guy's ball sack."

I cringe and Abigail laughs. She loves disgusting me with her taste in just about everything.

"Besides." She pokes me in the ribs. "It's our debut into society. The end of high school! The precipice of Real Personhood! I can wear whatever I damn well please."

"Yeah, which is exactly why you don't want to wear a dead animal as a shawl." I continue browsing the racks of orphaned clothes just waiting to find the right home. "It could be the best night of our lives. You don't want pictures of you with a carcass around your neck."

She checks herself out in the mirror. "Fine, you're right."

"Does this make my neck look ostrich-y?" Hilary calls from a dressing room at the far end of the store. Sometimes I pretend Hilary isn't there, and then I actually *forget* she's there. There's nothing wrong with Hilary, but it comes down to numbers. Two is perfect. Three is one-of-these-isn't-like-the-others.

"Hilary, you have a slender neck that necklaces throw themselves at," I call to the row of dressing rooms, each with a different mirror and feather boa decorating its door. "Please don't make me strangle it."

Behind Abigail, I spot a white lacy dress on one of the mannequins in the window. Because it's on display, it's probably a million dollars. Or a size impossible.

"All the pressure is going to be off once prom rolls around." Abigail sighs as I slide past the woman who just walked in to check out the dead-grandma dresses. "Just about everyone who didn't do early decision will know where they got into college, so we can finally all relax—"

My hand stiffens on the neck of the white lace (I swear I'm not trying to strangle a mannequin). Abigail looks at me skeptically. "You *did* start your applications, didn't you?"

"Of course I started," I say. "I'm almost done, but can't we enjoy this glorious last leg of high school without obsessing about college?"

"You don't have a future unless you plan one in advance," Abigail says.

"Well, there's still a whole two weeks before regular applications close. And after that there's rolling admission, so basically the amount of time I have is forever. I've been waiting for this moment since I was a freshman. I'm gonna *savor* it."

"Okay, I think I found the one," Hilary says, sashaying over to us in an emerald-green ball gown. She recently dyed her hair a cool blue that makes her dark eyes look even darker.

"I love it, Hil," I say, patting one of the ruffles awkwardly. *Love* is maybe an exaggeration.

"Right?" She checks herself out in the mirror next to the door, and the woman behind the counter nods in approval.

"Very eighteen-hundreds chic," the woman says with absolutely no intonation in her voice.

Hilary reaches around to check the tag. "And I can even afford it! The world isn't always on board with your girl's financial-aid budget, but Willa's Closet knows how to deliver."

"Amen to that," I say.

"I'm just worried that we're shopping too early," Hilary says, moving from her reflection in the mirror to her reflection in the window because sometimes mirrors don't tell the truth. "What if my style changes in three months?"

My eyes linger on the white dress for another second before I tear myself away. "Nothing's gonna change in three months except we're finally gonna be free of high school and parents and Mr. Garcia quacking at us to stop making out in the hallways."

Abigail looks forlornly out the window of the shop. "Can you believe three months are all that's left in senior year? Are we ever going to meet your parents before we graduate, Cham?"

"I've told you eight million times: They don't really live in this universe."

"Yeah, yeah, they're aliens, or they work for the CIA, yadda, yadda yadda," Abigail says. "I'm just realizing all the things we still haven't done."

"Don't get too sentimental too soon," Hilary says. "You

have to save some of that for your valedictorian speech, which you *will* beat Josie for." I nod distractedly, the white dress catching my eye again.

"Did you want to try it on?" the woman behind the counter asks me. She has her laptop open, and it has all sorts of stickers on it. When she gets up, I realize she's not really a woman, she's more of a girl, but that always confuses me. I thought I'd be a woman when I started buying tampons and face cream, but now that I've passed those milestones, I'm starting to think I'll never be a woman. Or worst of all, I've actually been one all along.

"Here," the woman/girl says. She jumps up into the window display and takes the dress off the mannequin. When she holds it out to me, its shoulders slump.

"That's okay," I say, averting my eyes from the naked mannequin totally exposing herself to the center of town. "I don't think it'll fit. Besides, I'm gonna pass until my boyfriend secures the deal and shows me the tickets."

"*You* could ask *him*," she says, with just enough judgment in her voice to piss me off. *You're a shit feminist*, the line of her mouth adds.

"Nah," I say coolly. "I asked him to officially be my boyfriend. Now it's his turn to make a move."

"Well, are you sure about the dress?" She holds it out to me and I notice the cup size. Grapefruits, at least. I look closer. Scratch that. Watermelons.

"It'll never work." I point to my chest. "Tiny-tits committee."

Abigail comes over and hits me in the arm. "We're being body positive, remember? It was our New Year's resolution."

"It's never the new year," I say, drifting toward the rack of shoes. There's a pair of lace-up combat boots almost identical to the ones I'm wearing. "By the time it's the 'new year,' it's just *the* year."

"Oh, shut up, Cham. I put up with so much shit from people about how fat girls can't dance, and I just keep shaking my ass anyway." She starts party-girling around Hilary, who laughs.

"I know, I know, I'm sorry." I put the boots back and look down at my boobs. "I'm sorry for underappreciating you, my itty-bitty titties that last grew in seventh grade." I pat the top of my bra, which always drifts away from my chest like a sailor going out on a whim.

"Good girl," Abigail says, now shimmying in front of the mirror, and Hilary shimmies against her back too. Neither of them has any qualms about dancing in public. I stand beside them and run a hand through my dark, frizzy hair until a knot stops my fingers.

"Shouldn't you be at dance practice anyway?" Hilary asks, turning to a rack of "special-made" denim items. *How do we live in a world where recycled jeans cost more than nonrecycled jeans?* "Or do you get to skip because you're a captain?"

"It got canceled," Abigail says, frowning at the jeans on jeans on jeans.

While she tells some story about how practice got canceled because her coach's pug had a panic attack at doggy day care, my phone dings. I look down at it, stepping out of the way of the only shopper in the store besides us, who seems completely unfazed by the recycled-jeans scam as she piles a pair over her arm.

"It's Gene," I say a little too loudly. The woman looks over at me judgmentally, but it's not my fault that seeing his name on my screen creates a little lightning storm in my belly.

"And how is Eugene Wolf?" Hilary asks in the British accent she frequently catches from a mysterious airborne virus. She tries to get her chin over my shoulder to read my text, but I clear my throat and turn from her because I try not to encourage other people's character flaws. "He says, *I have a surprise for you!*" I feel a huge grin take over my face.

"There she goes," Hilary says, crossing her eyes at me, and Abigail laughs. They call it the Cham-in-love grin, but it's actually the Cham-in-like grin, because until Gene says it, I'm not admitting anything. There's nothing worse than being in love with someone who's only in like with you. Not that I know that for sure, but I'd rather not find out.

"Maybe the surprise is a prom ask?" Abigail says. She selects a few dresses from the nearby rack while I pretty much entirely lose interest in shopping.

"I *hope* it's a prom ask," I say, looking down at my phone and wondering which cute-but-chill thing to respond with. "I mean, I definitely want it to be a massive romantic gesture, but I also don't know if I'm properly prepared for that. I need to wax my mustache before I get a surprise like that."

"That's so cheesy," the woman/girl says. She's appeared out of nowhere with a box full of hangers. She slaps her hand over her mouth. "Oops, I didn't mean to say that out loud."

I laugh and pocket my phone. "What's wrong with cheese? I love a good stinky blue."

She collects more hangers from the rack and adds them to the box. Her ponytail is high on top of her head, and her big hoop earrings look like they weigh a whole person-hood. She shrugs. "I've just never been that impressed by anything a guy has surprised me with."

"It's probably sex," Abigail hisses, then heads for the dressing room that has a hexagonal mirror and a bright pink feather boa on the door.

"Nah, I think I'm gonna save that for prom."

"Prom sex! Prom sex!" Abigail chants.

"Shh, Abigail! We're in public," Hilary says. When she tugs at a knot in her hair, a few blue strands come out.

"Guys, help me respond," I say, catching a glimpse of myself in the mirror: asymmetrical eyebrows, the skeletons of two pimples, and teeth just straight enough to justify the orthodontic hell of my middle school years. Yup, I'm on my game today. My phone dings again. "He says, *Come over*," I report.

"Do it," Abigail calls. That's all the permission I need.

"But we just got here," Hilary pouts.

"Sorry, gotta go," I say, heading for the door. "But don't buy your dresses without me! If we don't buy them at the same time, it'll be bad luck, and that is *not* the sort of luck I'm aiming for on prom night."

"What if we find the perfect ones?" Hilary asks.

"Yeah, sorry, Cham, we're not making any promises," Abigail says. She comes out of the dressing room in a short, sleeveless dress, her fantastic boobs doing fantastic things below her gold necklace. I feel a jab of third-wheely-ness, but I'm trying to be less paranoid lately. Just because they both applied to state college (along with 75 percent of our class) doesn't mean they're going to get in.

"Good luck with your surprise," the woman/girl behind the cash register says as I pass her. "And finding a prom dress."

I smile, pushing the door open into the cold January sunshine. "I'm kinda hoping it's gonna find me."

Dear Universe,

These are the possible theories for Gene's surprise:

- Cotton candy. A room full of sweet perfection, and we spend the whole night licking the walls and the furniture and each other. Blue tongues. Pink tongues. Sugar kisses.

- A quick trip around the world on a very fast plane positioned such that we're always one step ahead of the sun, where it's never tomorrow, living in the perpetual limbo of the last minute of every day.

- Doing it? Doing the dirty? Making love? Sexing on each other together? (If I can't even pick a term for it, I probably shouldn't be doing it.)

- Watching a movie and falling asleep on Gene's shoulder while drooling on his track zip-up...

- Yeah. The last one.

Going to see Gene involves a thorough washing of all the parts of my body that touch him. I, for one, like my smells, but I can understand why others might prefer Fresh Ocean

Breeze to Cham-Hasn't-Washed-Her-Armpits-Since-Her-Eight-Mile-Run Breeze. When the cleaning ritual is complete, I go to my room/mini-universe, where the walls are painted black and a projector casts stars all over the ceiling, my bed, and the floor. With my best outfit on (leggings), I add a little mousse to my hair. It takes the frizzies from brainwashed misfits to rebellious corkscrews with excellent personalities. Even though I spend a fair amount of time in the mirror, I think what I really want is the sort of beauty that has nothing to do with what I look like: beauty that's always there, even if no one's around to see it.

Downstairs, all the lights are on in the kitchen. I hurriedly take a mint from the drawer full of things that aren't mine and keep an eye out for my parents. The counters suggest that Mom was in the middle of making dinner—a box of rice, a pan half filled with water in the sink. Cooking was my dad's domain before Mom took it over. At first I tried to get her to play Elvis in the morning and whip up pancakes for dinner, but it didn't feel like home when it was forced.

"Hey," I call, pulling open the sliding door that separates my parents' part of the house from all the other parts. "I'm going to Gene's!"

I used to ask them before I went places, but they kept saying no, so now I just offer my plans up as facts. Or prophecies.

"Wait," my mom yells. Her voice is muffled by a closed door and whatever else separates us that we can't see. "Come here, Cham."

I drag myself down the hall, which is lined with proof of all my awkward stages: fifth grade with the four-braid situation; seventh grade with the braces so big you could pretty much straighten a leg; and freshman year of high school, where I basically look like I do now except I hadn't mastered my Gill School uniform yet, so I had it buttoned up to my lower lip. Suddenly it smells so strongly of pee I have to breathe through my mouth.

"I was just saying that I'm going to Gene's," I say again, my voice sounding nasally as I pause outside the bathroom, where my mom's bright yellow bucket of cleaning supplies waits. I think she and the bucket are in a codependent relationship, but I guess the lavender-tinged-bleach smell isn't the worst thing to have seeped into our lives over the past few years. My mom opens the bathroom door, fully exposing my dad on the toilet: pants down, toilet paper in hand, everything private decidedly un-private.

"Judy!" my dad cries.

I slam my eyes shut as he pulls a hand towel over his lap. "Can you guys keep the door closed when you're coordinating bathroom stuff?"

"Sorry, Cham!" my dad hollers from somewhere in the great abyss of relieving oneself. More quietly to my mom, he hisses, "You always forget about my privacy."

"It's okay," I say with all the okay-ness I can muster.

"I'm sorry, Scott, but I wish you had waited," she says to him in a voice I don't think she means for me to hear. There's a prickly feeling in my throat and my stomach. I think I swallowed a young porcupine. "You have to stay in your chair and wait until—"

"So can I go to Gene's?" I ask, vision still a little scarred.

"Just a second, Cham," my mom says impatiently.

I turn my back to her and the bathroom and the entire situation. On the wall behind me, there are younger versions of ourselves. In one picture, the three of us are outside when my dad was still landscaping. I'm naked as a duck playing in the hose while my mom cuts the heads off petunias in her garden. My dad is pretending to mow her flowers down and she's laughing; they're in their own world together, while me and the hose are getting along just fine in ours. I don't know who took the picture.

"Cham, have you ever noticed how clean the cracks between the tiles of the bathroom floor are?" my dad asks. "Your mom does a stupendous job."

"Yeah, stupendous," I say, nibbling at my fingernails impatiently. I hear the toilet flush and a paper towel rip.

"Well, sounds like you guys are pretty busy in there," I say, tiptoeing away backward. My feet have a feathery presence even on something as hard and unforgiving as the floors of our house. "I'm gonna leave you to it and head to Gene's, okay? Thanksloveyoubye."

I'm out of the hallway and through the sliding door like a comet. In the dark, overly ordered mudroom, where my mom basically alphabetizes our jackets, I put my sneakers on. That's how it's been going lately anytime I could be in trouble with my parents. I'm not complaining. If you think about the solar system and which part you'd like to be, you'd probably say the sun, but if you think about it *better*, you'd realize the sun blows up eventually, destroying everything and ending life as we know it. Planets like little old Pluto just drift out of the solar system and get forgotten.

2

Days 'til prom: Still 103

ONCE MY BODY REGISTERS WE'RE GOING TO GENE'S HOUSE, every electric current in my human system speeds up: My heart takes over the drums, my thoughts are all past and future and what it was like when he kissed my shoulder during gym class when I was wearing a tank top and what it will be like when we see each other tonight.

"Hey, you," Gene says, opening his front door and grinning. His hair is actually combed and he's wearing a pink bow tie, which he adjusts with a totally adorable look on his face. Our eyes connect, triggering the smile response, the heart response, the thought response, and every other human response.

"You're wearing a suit!" I say, and the light from the

house makes him glow like the best boyfriend I've ever had. (Read: He's the *only* boyfriend I've ever had.)

"Not a full suit," he says, pointing to the blue jeans he always changes into after school. "Just a fairly decent shirt and this great polka-dot thing I found in my mom's closet." He steps closer to me, and his head shades me from the blinding porch light. There are thousands of winter moths flying around it, just trying to catch a hot break. He crosses his arms. "Damn, it's cold."

"I'll warm you up." I wrap my arms around his neck, sandwiching myself between him and the half-open door. It's taking all my energy not to be like, OMGWHATSMY-SURPRISE?!

"So is this some sort of preview for prom?" I ask casually, sniffing at his bow tie. I get a little too into it, and a snort escapes my nostrils. The whole thing ends up being a bit more animalistic than I intended.

He laughs and links his fingers in mine. "Prom is like three months away. Everyone needs to chill." *Uh-oh. I don't like the sound of that. I don't like the sound of that one bit.* "Doug has a whole chart of people he could ask and where he wants to order his suit from," Gene continues, blowing into his hands, "and I just think we all gotta relax about it. It's not supposed to be stressful. It's supposed to be sawweeeet."

"For sure," I say, though I'm much less *sure* than *for* implies. "So about that surprise." I peer into his house.

His moms are joking around in the kitchen, touching each other in a way that's cute for parents, like my parents used to when they'd make breakfast for dinner. I look away. "Your house always smells like lasagna or some cousin of linguini and red sauce, so I'm guessing the surprise doesn't have to do with the moms' cooking."

"Okay, about the surprise," Gene says. He ducks into the house and comes back with a big envelope. He drum rolls against the rich red door, and the golden numbers rattle in their screws. "I got in."

He beams and holds the envelope so close to my face that my nose comes up against its manila wall. It's a better college than State. And a lot farther away.

"W-wow," I stammer. "That's so huge, congrats!"

It's a fight to keep the smile on my face from turning into a grimace of panic. I really have to get those college applications in. "I'm so happy for you," I add. My cheeks hurt from smiling. I wish I could take the envelope out of my face, but what if it's too heavy for my hands to hold? Do you ever get the feeling you can't handle the weight of something, no matter how much it *actually* weighs?

"Close the door, you're letting all the heat out," Gene's mom Ma calls, appearing in the hall with a stack of cloth napkins and silverware. "There you are, Cham! I'm so glad you could celebrate with us tonight."

I smile even bigger. "Wouldn't miss it!"

"Come on in!"

Inside, the house is warm, and all the noises are safe noises of people doing stuff you take for granted: stirring a pot on the stove, carrying silverware from the drawer to the table, following the hockey game that's playing on the TV in the living room.

"Hi, Cham," Gene's other mom says as she adds pasta to the boiling water on the stove. "Isn't it incredible news?"

"Yeah," I say, taking in the long wooden table with its twelve empty chairs and two unlit candles. It's so hot in here I think I'm going to be cooked alive. Or maybe steamed, if my sweat doesn't evaporate fast enough.

"Well, the rest of the family will be here any minute. Why don't you guys take care of drinks?" she says.

Gene steers my shoulders to the cabinet. "On it."

As he and I carry glasses to the table, I take in the decorations strung around the room for this momentous occasion: streamers from the ceiling with Gene's new college colors, a pinny on the door, and a large cake on the side table waiting for everyone to face-stuff its *Congratulations!*

"So the surprise is celebrating you getting into college? With your family?" I whisper when we're alone in the room. I'm trying not to sound like an incredulous asshole, but c'mon. I think my assholery is justified.

Gene wraps his arm around my waist. "I promise that's not all. We get to chill after, and I can have a party Friday night as long as everyone turns in their keys. And"—he pauses dramatically—"Mom and Ma said you can sleep over. Like in my room."

I blink at him, waiting for him to continue. When he doesn't, I say, "Oh, great!" and plant a kiss on his cheek. The doorbell rings, giving me a chance to regain composure.

"Be right back," he says, jogging to the door with his long legs and big feet that you'd never expect to be good at running, but humans do experience miracles regardless of their anatomies. *I guess a slumber party with a boy is an okay surprise?* I duck away toward the stairs.

"Hey, Josh," I say as I pass his younger brother, who's in the middle of a video game at the foot of the stairs. He doesn't say anything because he only likes to say something when he's interrupting Gene and me in the middle of *our* playtime. Don't let them fool you: Kids suck just like the rest of us.

"Let me get this straight," Abigail says when I've gotten her on the phone. "He didn't ask you to prom?"

"Nope."

"And the best night of your life was actually just the night Gene got into college and subjected you to dinner with his whole family?"

"Yep."

"That you're now hiding from under his bed while he eats gluten-free tofu-pigs-in a-blanket?"

"Correct."

I can almost see her rolling her eyes. "You're a weirdo, Cham, and he's an asshat for telling you he has a surprise for you that's actually about him. Can you and I just date? I'll teach you how to code and never offer you the best night of your life unless I figure out a way to get Elvis back from the dead."

"I do love me some Elvis." I pick through a few crusty shirts under Gene's bed, really hoping it's Elmer's glue on his sleeve and not...something else. "I guess the surprise is that we get to have a sleepover after his party Friday night?"

"Yeah, I got the text a few minutes ago. I can't believe he invited the *whole* senior class. It's gonna be wild." I hear her unzip her backpack, which she always has stocked for various occasions, from the end of the world to impromptu parties. "We need a freaking break from homework and AP classes and college decisions and blah blah blah. I just want to shake my ass someplace where people can watch me."

"Same, except where no one can watch me." I bang my head on the wooden plank supporting Gene's mattress as I crawl from under it to stare out the window forlorn-cat style. There's a certain darkness to eight PM in suburbia, like does anyone really *choose* to end up here? I sigh. "Maybe he'll ask me to prom Friday night with an arrangement of beer bottles and everyone watching."

"Maybe," she says doubtfully.

"Well, I guess I should get back to it," I say, walking into Gene's bathroom and pausing in front of the mirror.

"Godspeed, little one."

"You always say that," I complain, "and I never know what it means." She's already hung up.

After a long dinner, during which I pretend not to imagine what "after high school" looks like for me and Gene—beyond Senior Volunteer Trip to Nicaragua—he pulls me into the closet at the end of the hall.

"I wanted to do this all night," he says, drawing me toward him and the rack of clothes. It smells a little bit like shoes and soggy umbrellas, and I fall against a cushion of puffy jackets as he kisses me. There's a softness to his lips, and when our tongues touch, it's like he's licking the inside of my whole body. Our breathing gets faster. And then my phone goes off.

"Ugh," I say, looking down at it and using one of the hooks in the closet to steady me. "My mom wants me home now."

"No," he says, grabbing me playfully. I groan into a large leather jacket to my right. We only have a few seconds left to cram our bodies into each other, so I pull him toward me. His fingers travel up my shirt. Every new place he touches makes it harder to breathe. Either that, or I'm slowly suffocating in this cowhide pocket.

"Do you want me to run back with you?" he asks, then

kisses the back of my neck, which now holds all the nerves of my body.

"You don't have to," I say. *But like, yeah, I do.*

"It's okay," he says, and gives me one more kiss. He smells peppery, like he does when he's starting to sweat. "I want to."

Once he's put on the eight layers required to go running in Massachusetts in the butt of winter, we hold hands and walk outside. He talks about how excited he is to start training right after Senior Volunteer Trip because preseason starts in the middle of June. I don't say anything. I don't really know where *we* comes into all of this.

"Race you to the corner?" I ask suddenly, then take off, feet hitting the pavement, body revving up. I pump my arms and legs faster, breathing more quickly to create a rhythm. I hear him behind me, sneakers slapping the sidewalk, so I cut across a lawn and then the road to beat him. Some lungs crave oxygen. Mine crave the lack of it, and the strain for more.

I force everything in my body to work harder as I approach the red octagon, my orange sneakers blurring with the dark pavement, and the curb of the sidewalk shaking back and forth. Just as I'm starting to taste iron in my mouth, I reach it. With a grunt and a jump, I slap the top of the stop sign and run a bit past it as my legs slow down.

"You win," Gene pants, slapping the stop sign too. He jogs over and pretends to bump into me. "Excuse me, excuse me," he says.

"You let me win," I gasp, and push him toward the road. A car goes by and catches us in its headlights, kissing. The kissing makes it kind of hard to breathe, but breathing easy is boring anyway.

"Come on," I groan, grabbing his cold spandexed butt and taking off.

For a few seconds I'm ahead of him, charging toward the traffic light, but then he catches up with me, a few strides here, and then he's ahead of me.

"Wait!" I call as the light turns green and the stopped car drives off and the pom-pom on Gene's hat bobs away. "Wait," I call again, but I can't catch up, so I just keep running as fast as I can after him.

3

Days 'til prom: 100

ON THE MORNINGS WHEN MY HAIR IS OBEDIENT, I HAVE EXTRA time before school to tend to the thing under my bed. Don't worry; it's not a monster. Maybe I am too romantic, but since that day with Gene in gym, I've been keeping a cardboard box there for all the sweet debris of senior year: movie stubs, the moldy daffodil Gene got me for my birthday in November, Polaroid pictures Abigail took of us, the fangs Gene and I wore trick-or-treating even though some old man said we were too old to be trick-or-treating, a Milk Dud, some sample perfume, and an unopened condom with red flames on it that says *In case things get hot*. It's not that I'm a pack rat or a scrapbooker or a hoarder. It's that right now we kind of have a kingdom here in the universe of rare and regular high school experiences. Maybe I'm too sentimental, or maybe one day when I'm old and life is bankrupt of adventures and my memory is even worse than a goldfish's with Alzheimer's, I will take this box out and remember. I'll touch the black Ticonderoga and know what it was like to be bored out of my freaking mind in Calc until Gene walks by and throws his pencil at me and suddenly every bacteria in my gut is alive. I'll remember how it felt to make videos with Abigail and laugh until we wet her bed. Maybe the deep purple paint on the box will be chipped and the glow-in-the-dark stars will be peeling off, but I'll look inside and know that every single moment of senior year mattered.

Obviously, I haven't told anyone about this. The only thing more embarrassing than having something like this is having something like this that is mostly full of notes I've written to myself. This is the note I wrote in August that started it all:

Dear Universe,

I was sifting through the catalog of potential high school experiences, and I've decided to place an order for something just a little amazing. I want a yearbook signed *you rock, don't change* by everyone except for my best friend, who basically writes my living eulogy, and my high school sweetheart, who runs out of pages with his x's and o's. I want to go to prom with said high school sweetheart, and he will remember to get me a corsage. I want to get invited to a party. I want to spend most nights with Abigail, eating pizza and looking for stars in her driveway. (Not with Hilary. Hilary can find a new friend, thank you very much.) I want to look back and remember like four things from senior year: the first beer I drink (which is bound to happen soon, right?), the first boy I kiss (also bound to happen soon, right?), the entire month abroad wreaking havoc on the world under the guise of charity during Senior Volunteer Trip, and that sweet, sweet time (prom night?) when I do it. I have a feeling sex is one of those things that just lifts us up. And with prom and graduation and everything happening, *we* are happening. This is it, you know? What do you need from me to make something just a little amazing happen, Mama Universe? A PO box?

Post-breakfast text exchange with Abigail, Hilary, and me, even though I should be at the bus stop freezing my sweet little nips off:

 A Friday with a party attached to it is literally orgasmic.

Please don't literally orgasm at his party. C

Ya...remember when Danika got really drunk on Halloween and took her clothes off and sat in the middle of Doug's kitchen?

Poor thing.

My brother got us alc btw!!!

What kind?

Who cares as long as it gets us drunk?

Quick survey: Is Gene gonna ask-cute me to prom?

Honestly girl I doubt it

How about will we do it?

Def more likely

Nah, I think you're saving it 'til prom

Hehe

Can't the school day just be a freaking pal and finish with itself already

Patience, young grasshopper. Good things come to those who wait.

And those who carry a red condom?

Selfie in the hall between Calc and Spanish that totally encapsulates my mood for the year: Abigail's sunglasses covering seven-eighths of my face, Gene's striped tie wrapped on my head like a bow, Mr. Garcia in the background with his mouth open, about to give me a warning for (a) dress code violation, (b) cell phone violation, and (c) chewing gum in school.

#senioritis

~~

"Hurry up, everyone," Evelyn, our English teacher, says as Abigail and I just make it to our desks when the bell for last period finally rings. We always sit in the front row at Abigail's request, I guess so she can pay attention or something. For the most part I watch the water stain on the ceiling develop into something that looks like a piece of toast with Jesus on it.

"Speaking of sex," Evelyn starts, even though no one was speaking of sex. She's interrupted by a bright red tutu that squeezes through the door and nearly knocks her over. It's attached to Brendan, the guy who always dances around like it's *Swan Lake* up in the Gill School.

"Pardon meeeee," he sings as he bounces in and takes his seat in the back, the tutu standing out over his uniform like a mighty plea for fun in this penal institution called school.

"Try to be on time." Evelyn grimaces, closing the door with a loud click. Her hair is freshly buzzed, and her bright yellow pantsuit makes her look like that guy Curious

George is always running from. "As I was saying, sex." She pauses dramatically with her hands on her hips. "Drugs," she adds with a devious eyebrow wiggle. "And rock and roll. Can anyone tell me what's missing there?"

"Sounds like everything to me," Abigail says, and people laugh.

"PHILOSOPHY!" Evelyn exclaims, then grins maniacally. The thing to know about Evelyn is that she's actually a thirty-year-old piece of quinoa who thinks students and teachers are "equals." This is why she lets us swear and call her by her first name and talk about things like sex, drugs, and rock and roll.

"But, Evelyn," Evelyn says, with mock wonder, "what do risky business and illicit substances have to do with pondering the meaning of life?" She whips a piece of chalk out of her breast pocket and faces the moldy olive chalkboard, a relic of the Gill School's early days that Evelyn couldn't part with when it made its way to the dumpster. Twice. "Contrary to public opinion, philosophy did not expire in ancient Greece. If you get philosophy down to one of its basic definitions—" She takes out another piece of chalk and scrawls: *study of knowledge, reality and existence*. "We're just thinking about thinking and living: how we know what we know, what human experience really is, the birth of an existential crisis, the death of God, et cetera."

"Rest in peace, God," Brendan sings from the back corner.

"Shut up, loser," someone mutters from the side of the room.

"Who said that?" Evelyn's eyes dart around. We all look at one another, knowing no one is going to own up to it. "If I hear anything else, everyone will have a detention," Evelyn warns. We shift in our seats and she lets it go. It's not that Brendan's a bad singer—I actually secretly like his voice, from the falsetto to the husky low notes—but it's annoying that he's not more self-conscious. *Play by the rules of social convention, dammit.*

"Pondering life is a big order, so we gotta start somewhere smaller and more manageable," Evelyn says, leaning against the board. "We're gonna start with ourselves. What we believe, what our motivations are, how *our spirit* is." She rests a hand over her heart. "How amped are y'all?" There are unenthusiastic sounds from the rows of people behind us, but particularly from the guys in the corner who have hockey practice before school. They mostly just grunt.

"Evelyn, this is so boring," Travis from the hockey team complains, his face smooshed so far into his hand that his words come out a little muffled. "Who wants to think about this stuff? You said we were gonna talk about sex, drugs, and rock and roll."

Evelyn makes her way over to the other side of the room, then faces us. "All right, Travis, since you asked, here's how we're gonna connect the two. If the ethos of the seventies was sex, drugs, and rock and roll, what's the ethos of today?"

She scans the room with her eyes wide, probing us for answers, or maybe hoping that we'll give a shit. "What does *ethos* even mean?" Travis asks.

"The spirit and the beliefs of a time," Abigail says, doodling absentmindedly.

"Uh, do we even have one of those?" Danika asks, and everyone laughs.

"Yes, great question!" Evelyn says a little too excitedly. "This is what philosophy's all about! You know what? Everyone, get into groups of four," she says, clapping her hands together. "We're going to start talking to each other and asking this question. Is there a spirit or a belief today in your generation? This is how great philosophy starts! Quickly, now, everyone up!" Evelyn says, urging us up with big waves of her hands. "What are the spirit and the beliefs of today, or even just of the senior class, your friend group, *you*. And if it *is* sex, drugs, and rock and roll, please say *I have a friend*... so I don't get fired. Go, go, go!"

The classroom erupts into a cacophony of metal on floor. I scoot toward Abigail like a dog rubbing its butt on the carpet, and we're joined by two more desks: on the left, a skinny boy named Marquis, with a tuba case by his chair; on the right, a guy named Jared, who Abigail used to have a crush on.

"How is this English class?" Jared whispers with disbelief.

Abigail leans into the circle and lowers her voice. "Evelyn gets away with subjecting us to her college major because the Gill School loves her." Then she puts her arm around me. "Just think of what you would've missed if you hadn't been kicked out of public school for explosive anger that bordered on—"

"Definitely tell everyone my life story, Abigail," I say sarcastically.

"She punched a bus window at a girl and almost blinded her," Abigail says matter-of-factly. She can't help herself. She loves having an audience.

"That's pretty badass," Marquis says, fingers twitching like he's playing an invisible tuba that none of us can hear. "What'd the girl do to deserve your fist?"

Abigail laughs. "Wait, I never even asked you that, Cham. I just thought it was hilarious that you got kicked out of public school."

I sit on my hand to keep it from twitching with muscle memory. "She was just being an asshat," I say dismissively. *Do you have a PhD in the field of neurological medicine, Ava-of-the-complicated-orthodontic-situation? Then maybe don't spend half of our field trip giving my dad a dismal prognosis of Parkinson's disease that ends with* and then he'll die!

I feel someone behind me, so I turn around. Brendan's standing between our cluster of desks and the cluster of desks next to us. Unfortunately, that's what happens when there's an odd number of people: Someone gets left out.

"Here, join this group," Evelyn says to Brendan, and they both walk over to us.

We move our desks around to make room for him, and Evelyn points at me. "Take it away, Cham. What's the ethos of the time?"

"Um." I preach to the high heavens about running socks on Twitter, but ask me to tell someone something in real life and I have laryngitis of the soul. "Compost?"

She laughs. "Okay, I'll take it. Now, let's go smaller. What's the ethos of the senior class?"

"Work hard, play hard," Marquis pipes up. He shakes his head, and his braids fall over his face.

Evelyn nods, then looks back at me. "How about you personally? What's your ethos? What makes your life really good?"

I picture Gene's lips. *Making out.*

"Cham likes running," Abigail prods.

"All right, I'll stop torturing Cham. What's your ethos, Abigail?"

Abigail chugs her arms, and her fabulous boobs move around in her blouse. "Dance like a mother-effing—"

"I hope Mr. Garcia doesn't walk by," Evelyn interrupts. "Anyone else? We're running out of time." She eyes the clock and mutters something about the fallacy of linear time. "Has everyone had a chance to say something?"

"Brendan hasn't gone yet," Jared says, gesturing toward Brendan in a friendly way, as if he didn't just throw him under the bus. "Did you want to say something, dude?"

Brendan undoes his elastic and fixes his man bun, which he grew over the summer. When senior year started, hardly anyone recognized him. I think it kinda suits him.

"My ethos is to get weird and stay silly." He rubs his hands on his tutu, and the fabric crunches together. "I wanna heal the world with laughter."

I look up from my desk and we accidentally make eye contact. His brown eyes are all parts confidence, no parts self-doubt. None of us say anything. The silence in our group is heightened by the noise of the groups around us packing up their bags before the bell rings.

"That's beautiful, Brendan," Evelyn says, clapping her hands and addressing the whole class before she lets us out.

"Good work today, " she says. "We'll keep going next class. Oh, and for the few of you still writing your college essay for rolling admission, I need a draft in two weeks." She makes ominous eye contact with me. "I know rolling admission doesn't have a specific deadline, but I do need a finished assignment from you. Can the people who signed up to tutor please raise their hands?"

Brendan puts his hand up and so does Abigail. "God help you," I whisper to her.

"No, God help *you*."

"Great, thanks," Evelyn says, brushing some chalk off

her hands. "Reach out if you need essay help. Everyone else, be working on your independent book projects. And, oh okay, fine. Have a great weekend," she says, surrendering to the sound of the bell and the whole room hopping up. I've almost tasted sweet freedom when she waves me over. "Can I talk to you for a second?"

"Sure." I zip my bag and join her at her desk.

"I just wanted to give you some more feedback on your essay. Did you get a chance to work on it since we last talked?"

I look down at my combat boots, which are my "single item of chosen sartorial individuality" that Gill School allows on Fridays. "Um..."

"Never mind, don't answer that." She takes a folder from her desk drawer, then hands me the printed copy of my essay. It's floppy in my hand, and each sentence is so covered in red ink she might as well have slaughtered the alphabet. God, it's mortifying to reread myself, but I can't *not* read it.

Dear College Admissions Person,

It was just a minor setback, getting kicked out of public school at the end of eighth grade, but I've definitely come out on the other side of it.

"It's a good start," Evelyn says, leaning toward me. Her amorphous squiggly metal earrings jangle against her second set of amorphous squiggly metal earrings. "But I don't know that you really want to open with a misdemeanor. Also, the essay can't end a few paragraphs later with *And everything's good now.*

She points to a particularly ink-gory paragraph, and I nudge my essay away from her. I pretend to examine it, but I know exactly what it says. It includes the phrase *overcame my anger amidst a pit of stress balloons.*

"It's great how you learned to be in control of your emotions," she says gently, "but your essay doesn't really go anywhere. There's no *lesson* here." She leans back in her rolling chair as if we're two friends shooting the shit. In reality we're one teacher and one student who can't seem to give a shit. "The college essay can be about tapioca pudding as long as it shows you, the real you. What makes you *different*? What are you *passionate* about? What have you *learned* in the past seventeen years?"

She peers into my soul. I peer at the clock. "Ummmm, I guess I don't really know."

"Would you be opposed to choosing a new topic?" she asks hesitantly. "Maybe getting some tutoring?"

"Yeah, good idea," I say, unzipping my backpack and carefully placing this little number in the one binder I put all my schoolwork in.

She purses her lips. "I'll send you some of the Common App questions," she says. "Maybe you can work on it this weekend and send me the first paragraph?"

I stand up with a sigh. "Honestly, Evelyn, I just can't bring myself to do homework on the weekend. It crushes my soul," I say with a hand over my heart. "And given the fragility of my soul in the first place—"

"Cham," Evelyn says in a warning tone. "You know you have to pass this class to graduate, and go on Senior Volunteer Trip and move on with your life, right?"

I bow my head and knit my eyebrows together with the hopes of seeming studious. "Okay, I'll try to get it done."

Evelyn stands and walks me to the door. "Cham, you're a teacher's nightmare," she says with a smile. "So smart and so unwilling to apply yourself."

"I do apply myself, Evelyn," I say as I grin and step into the hallway. "Just not to anything tangible."

4

Days 'til prom: Still 100

TEXT EXCHANGE WHILE I'M TWEEZING MY ARMPIT HAIRS IN preparation for tonight:

> **A** heyyyy

> **A** Me and Hil are gonna get chasers and stuff but we'll pick you up in a couple hours Cham!

> **C** I thought you guys couldn't hang out after school?

> **H** Abigail's just helping me with history!

> **A** We didn't think you'd want to come

It's sooooo boring

lol asshole I'm a great tutor

See you soon!

"Tell me the plan again," my mom says when I come down-stairs in jeans and a black tank top. My hair is still a little wet down my back. "I want to make sure you'll be safe," she adds, pausing with a book in one hand, the mop in the other. She's going at the kitchen floor mercilessly, no stain left behind.

"Gene's moms are letting him have this party thing," I say carefully. "Actually, it's not even a party—he's just having some friends over, and then I'm sleeping at Abigail's after." She looks at me skeptically, then closes the book and places it on the counter: *Caring for a Sick Spouse*. When she turns toward the mop, I discreetly push the book to the far end of the counter, where pieces of mail collect and swallow each other. "She and Hilary are gonna pick me up any minute," I add. "Besides, I can't miss out on the stuff that senior year's all about, or I'll be put on trial for pathetic teendom. You don't want to feel responsible for murdering my fun, do you?"

"I don't know." My mom frowns, plunging the mop into the bucket and entirely ignoring my joke. "Will there be drinking?"

"Drinking what?" my dad asks, wheeling into the kitchen. Then his head snaps toward the window. "Why is that neighbor up in our tree?" He points to the long barren branches. "Look, Cham."

I look out the window at the beech tree, and then I look at my mom. Before, she used to fly to the window when he said stuff like this. Then she would say, in that tone that crisscrossed scared with exasperated, *There's no one there.* Now she says, not even looking up from the wet marks on the floor, "Huh, that's strange. I hope he doesn't fall."

I'm not at that point yet.

"He really shouldn't be in our yard," my dad continues, shaking his head with disapproval and wheeling toward the table. "If he falls, he might sue us."

"Derek is a good neighbor," my mom says as my phone goes off in my pocket. "He wouldn't do that."

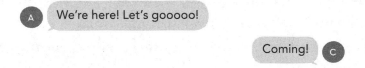

"Please, can I go?" I whine.

"Fine." My mom sighs, then takes her ringing phone out. "It's your sister," she says to my dad.

"You guys are the best!" I call as I head out the door.

When I look back, my mom has the phone to her ear and she's pushing my dad to the dinner table. He's still pointing to the tree, and I feel a pang in my stomach. It's probably just hunger.

I'm halfway out the door when I realize I don't have my good-luck charm. As a kid I had a lucky rabbit's foot. The mature version is the packaged little outfit for the penis, also called a condom.

"Back so soon?" my dad asks as I charge through the kitchen.

"Just need my...toothbrush," I say, bounding up the stairs. All the lights are on in my room because I'm bad at things like the environment. I pull my senior year time capsule out from under my bed and pocket the unopened condom. Yes, it *could* get hot tonight, thanks for asking, condom wrapper. I put the cardboard box back, smoothing one of the corners of its glow-in-the-dark stars. I'm closing the door to my room when I hear my mom doing laundry.

"What do you mean, you signed us up?" she's saying. "Hang on, I'm putting you on speaker. *No*, no one's around." I dart back behind the door and peer toward the bathroom, where her back is to me. She sets her phone down on the washing machine, and it bounces around like it's having a conniption.

The person on the other end is definitely not using "gentle tones" when she says, "It's ridiculous that he hasn't been to a doctor in the four years since he got the diagnosis.

You have to get him some real help, not just the aides who come in and get him washed up. There are things that can be done for this disease if he'd just accept he has it."

"Bridget," my mom says, squirting one of my dad's shirts with bleach where the memory of a spaghetti dinner is hanging on for dear life. "You remember his motorcycle accident.... It's not uncommon to see injuries with cognition later in—"

"He has Parkinson's!" Aunt Bridget shouts. My mom stops moving. The phone rattles against the machine. A diseased lump of *No* and *Please* moves up my throat and stops behind my tonsils, the same place that vibrates when you start to scream. *Help.* "He needs family and community and support, which is why I signed us all up for the Brain Degeneration Walk in April. I know he won't want to go, but since his cognition is impaired, it's up to you—"

"It's not up to me," my mom says stiffly, taking the phone to her ear and sitting cross-legged on the pile of dirty clothes she hasn't dealt with yet. "Nurse's code says respect human dignity, that the primary commitment is to the patient." I can't hear what my aunt is saying anymore. I hear the spin cycle instead. "No, it isn't," my mom argues. "Well, I'm sorry you can't get your donation back, but—"

Now the sound of tears, or a dripping faucet: my mom, the leaky sink, all of us part of a house that needs repairs.

"Fuck!" she suddenly shouts, startling me so thoroughly that I crouch down more. "Fuck!" she yells again.

Then her cell phone hits the tile floor. *Smack*. I don't know what to do. Fortunately, my organs function very well on their own: Throat swallows spit, heart keeps pounding. A few seconds later my phone vibrates, lighting up the darkness in my room.

I make sure my mom's back is turned, and then I sprint on my tiptoes for the stairs. It's not an easy feat, being fast and quiet, but I manage stupendously. I'm just another animal that has to survive somehow.

Dear Universe,

Do you ever feel like you live in two universes? I guess that doesn't really apply to you, but it's okay. I'm talking to me anyway. One universe is the sick stuff, and the other universe is school and parties and boys and best friends. I'm getting whiplash from traveling so quickly between them. Maybe I need a body double. Or something to bring them together, but not worlds colliding. Please, God, not that. It ends up being that I'm one-third in one universe, and one-third in the other, and one-third here with you.

It's just a little unfair, you know? I didn't ask to be part of two universes, but given the options, can you guess which one I'd choose to set up camp in?

"Oh my god, look at Jared's tight little ass," Abigail squeals as we pull up to Gene's house and park behind the cars lined up along the road. To our right, Jared is mooning the basement window, beer in hand and pants down by his knees.

"Looking good," Abigail calls. Then we all sink into the seats and laugh.

"Ready for this?" Hilary asks.

"Really freaking ready," I say.

After we give our car keys to Gene's parents, we head for the basement, "Come on!" Abigail says, linking her arm in mine and leading me down the stairs. There's an energy in the room, where a lot of people are already seeming a little drunk. It's a silly *We're gonna get loose tonight* type of energy that feels contagious, like malaria or insecurity. I can't wait to catch it.

The recently finished basement smells like new wood and a clean carpet. There's a dartboard and a foosball table and a TV in the corner with a wraparound couch. Gene and Doug are dragging a folding table to the center of the room and putting the alcohol underneath it. Gene comes over when he sees me.

"Hey, you," he says, picking me up and spinning me around. I get that lightning storm in my stomach.

"Hi," I breathe, then kiss him. He tastes like beer.

"Let her go, Gene," Hilary says playfully. She's getting cups while Abigail opens a bottle she brought in her tote bag. Hilary takes on her British accent. "We're doing shots!"

"Guess that's my cue," I say, and he sets me down gently.

"Cheers, mates," Gene says as he walks away.

"*Mates* is Australian, not British," Hilary mutters as Abigail hands us each a shot of something that smells like cinnamon, but worse.

"My brother got us Fireball," Abigail announces. "We are officially getting drunk for the first time together tonight."

I sniff the plastic cup, and an anticipatory wave of nausea emerges in my stomach. "I was thinking of something more low-key for the first time I get drunk," I say. My eyes travel over the swarm of people opening cases of beer and stacks of red cups. "Like beer, or a virtual simulation."

"Shut up, Cham." Hilary laughs. "Abigail and I will take good care of you. We remember our first time drinking, don't we, Abigail?"

I see their universe bloom, and I'm just a bee buzzing around it. I laugh. "It was at Abigail's parents' ski condo, right?" I say.

"Yep, spiked hot cocoa," Hilary says, but she's only looking at Abigail. "Vomit."

The harder they laugh, the more I remember that although we came to this party together, for lots of years theirs was just a party of two.

"Come on!" Abigail closes her hand around mine and shouts something about a big booty, because someone just turned the music on and more people have shown up. "We've basically made it," she says, looking me in the eyes with her intense green irises. "It's time to make some stupid decisions and bloom adventures out our assholes."

Hilary wrinkles her face. "Can't we just take a shot and see how we feel?"

"Oh, fine." Abigail puts the plastic cup to her lips, then pushes my hand to my mouth too. I watch us in the mirror behind all the bottles, but then I feel self-conscious.

"PEER PRESSURE!" I shout as she clamps her hand over my mouth. I laugh. "Just kidding. Go ahead, hit me." We put our shots to our lips at the same time, the liquid entering my throat and then my esophagus and then my stomach, all the way into my chest. I swallow my spit, which is slightly on fire, and that fire spreads throughout my whole body. "Wow, I guess that did hit me."

Abigail grins, wiping her mouth and slamming her plastic shot glass next to the still-open bottle. "Let's do it again."

So we do. We drink poison and swallow fire. At first I feel a little wobbly, like I might just puke my brains out, but then I start smiling because I don't want to forget what this feels like, standing in Gene's basement with my lace-up combat boots on and Hilary and Abigail on either side of me and the music is the song that's been playing everywhere we've been for the last few weeks and we've made it. We're here.

"You guys," I yell three shots later. "This is it! We are halfway done with senior year. Prom and graduation and Nicaragua are so close I can practically taste them on my tongue!" I turn toward Gene and give him a big sloppy kiss. "Oh, wait, that's Gene's tongue," I say, and dive-bomb his mouth again.

"Cham is drunk!" Gene shouts to the roomful of people: Marquis with two bottles of beer duct-taped to his hands, Lola doing a body shot off Mara's stomach while she lies on the blue plaid couch, Hilary flirting with Travis against the wall beneath a banner for the Gill School's cross-country team. They follow Gene in raising their bottles in the air and cheer for me and I toss my hair around. I feel like a pop star. I probably look like a golden retriever.

"I'm not drunk," I laugh, letting my watery body sink into Gene's arms. "I'm dreaming in real-life stars."

Gene kisses me sloppily on the lips, and Abigail comes up to us, dancing. "Just a little preview of what's coming at Senior Show," she shouts, then proceeds to break it down, rubbing her butt against the keg like it's the hottest thing in the room.

Gene and I goofily face each other—he's about as

gifted in the shake-your-ass department as I am, and for a few songs we're as free as the musical notes released into the air. My head feels like it's blasted with helium.

"We're doing it," I shout. "And we're doing it together. Just wait until prom—"

The basement door opens, and we all stop rubbing up against each other because one of Gene's moms already came down once and told us to be quiet. "Not gonna go to jail for providing minors a *safe* place to do all the underage drinking they'd be doing anyway," she'd mumbled. But as I squint at the door, I realize the leather-legginged legs are not the legs of fifty-year-old Mrs. Wolf.

"Yay, you're here!" Abigail calls as three girls on the dance team wave to her and descend the stairs. They have everything on that we're not allowed to wear in school, mainly crop tops exposing belly button rings that remind me how much I want a belly button ring. The three of them start dancing, and it gets the whole room dancing harder.

"Hey, we should go upstairs," I whisper in Gene's ear the next time the song changes. I feel fuzzy and warm and a little sick—not necessarily physically sick, but sick with wanting something sick. Suddenly prom does not seem like the night to do it. Tonight does. "Come on."

"We'll have plenty of alone time later," he whispers. "We don't want to miss the party. Besides, I gotta keep an eye on things down here."

"Of course," I say, and pinch his butt before I make my

way over to Abigail, my virginity lodged in place. Likelihood that it will move in this lifetime? You tell me.

"It's really different in Germany," the foreign exchange student from the dance team, Helga, is saying to the circle Abigail's in. "Like last week this guy asked me on a date and we just sat in his car and he was like, *Do you want to touch my thingy*, and I was like, *Um, no.*"

I laugh with everyone else. "What're they talking about?" Gene whispers. I shrug, and he puts his arm around my waist.

"So wait," Abigail says. "In Germany, guys don't just assume it'd be like the greatest honor on earth to touch their dick?"

"No, it's the opposite." Helga takes a sip of her beer and makes a face. "Americans have the worst beer."

"Yeah, yeah, but back to the non-douchey-sounding guys."

Helga shrugs and her short blond bob grazes her chin. She has a heart-shaped face, whereas mine always falls into the category of square. Honestly, I'd be a really hot Lego. "Feminism is sexy there," Helga continues, "and guys who don't know how to treat girls don't get second dates. Like guys hold lessons for each other so they know how to—I don't know how you say it—like sex on a girl?"

Everyone laughs and someone says, "Eat a girl out."

"Yes! Like do any of you even know how to eat a girl out?" Helga looks at Gene's friends from the track team, who are hanging on her every word like she holds the key to their sexual liberation (she probably does).

"Of course I do," Doug says. He thinks that we think he's confident because he always wears mismatched socks with weird things like avocados on them, but socks only tell you one thing about a person: They have feet.

"Come give us a demo," Helga says to Doug, "if you're so certain you know what you're doing."

"I can't just demo on the *air*. That'd look stupid."

"Here," Craig says, opening the snack closet next to the spare fridge and tossing him a pack of hot dog rolls. "Try with this."

The room erupts with laughter as Doug takes one out. "Go on," Helga encourages him. "Let's see how it's done."

"Do it, do it, do it," Abigail chants, and the room follows her lead.

"I obviously know how to eat a girl out," Doug says, his face flushing as he stares down the hot dog roll. It's quite the face-off. Seventeen-year-old boy versus a hunk of white bread.

"Gimme it," Helga says finally, taking the roll out of Doug's hands and sitting cross-legged in the middle of the circle. Everyone leans closer to her; even their cups and beer bottles are drawn toward her. "It goes something like this."

All the breathing in the room stops as Helga holds the hot dog roll up. It's a pretty generic one as far as cookout supplies go—spongy white on the bottom and cooked a little darker on top, where the bread parts and the meat of the situation lies. "Kiss it first," she says, planting her lips on the roll. "Then lick it." Her tongue is a pretty pink as it traces what could be any number of designs on the bread. "If you get confused, go through the alphabet or spell your favorite words. *Like this, right there, keep going.*"

At least two guys in the circle have to fiddle with their jeans. One gives up and puts his beer over his crotch and goes to the bathroom. "Did she seriously just start making out with a piece of food?" Hilary whispers.

"Yep," I breathe, but the thing is, I don't think there's a single person in the room who wouldn't trade places with that hot dog roll.

"Girls, ask for what you want," Helga says, taking a bow and throwing the soggy hot dog roll in the trash. "And, guys, act like you were raised halfway decently and offer, 'cause hookups are for both people, not just little boys in their cars dreaming of some internet porn they don't even pay for."

Everyone laughs, and I'm pretty sure at least all the sex parts in the room are turned on. Why else would we be smiling goofily and semi-clinging to each other? Beer? Hormones? A combination of the two?

Doug passes me a can of Budweiser, and as I hold it in my hands, the red-and-black label takes me out of the stupid fun of this moment. Budweiser was my dad's favorite before he couldn't really drink anymore. After he'd finished his mail route, he would sit in the backyard with a beer and listen to Elvis. I'd bring out letters I'd written to my imaginary friends all over the world, and he'd promise to take them to work the next day and send them off. I can smell the inside of his carrying bag now. It smelled like stamps and letters, and anytime I get a whiff of either, I'm filled with the sense that everything will end up where it belongs.

"I'm gonna get some air, be right back," I say to no one in particular. It takes all my focus to keep my balance as I go up the stairs, but it's a relief when I get outside—no muggy beer, no sweaty beer breath, no Helga needing all kinds of attention.

"Taking a breather?" someone behind me asks. I hear footsteps on the walkway, and I recognize the voice. Turning around while groaning internally, I say, "Oh, hey, Brendan."

"Are you okay?" he asks, opening the fence and letting himself into the yard. Tonight his tutu is yellow. "You're crying."

"I'm not crying, my eyes just water in the cold." I wipe my face and turn toward the house, which is framed by two symmetrical trees, because some people's lives are just tidy like that. *Please let this be a quick and painless exit.*

"Are you sure you're okay?" he calls, walking after me. I do not turn around.

"I'm sure. Just some family stuff, but all good." I lean

down to, what, *befriend* the gnome in Gene's garden? This is not the escape I had in mind.

Brendan shuffles over to me, his sneakers crunching in the cold grass. "You're totally crying," he says, and I eye the shed a few hundred feet away. I'll hide out in there if I have to. "Listen, Cham, I know we don't really know each other, but if you ever want to talk about something—"

He drifts off and I let a few tears fall, but just a few. He pats me on the back awkwardly, like three staccato pats that make me really regret coming outside.

"Well, thanks," I say, "but I gotta get back to the party. Wouldn't want these garden gnomes to hear about my boring family life."

He clears his throat and starts singing. "I only mentioned it becaaaaaauseeee..." He hits a note that reaches the moon.

"Can you please just talk in a normal voice," I say, slurring a little. "If life were a musical, I would have killed myself by now."

"Sometimes I don't have words." He shrugs. "Just songs."

I kick at the grass with my combat boots, feeling like quite the asshole. He hardly seems fazed. "Well, if you change your mind, or if all of this starts to feel empty..." He trails off, looking sideways into the window, where Doug is streaking the basement. *Way* too many things are bouncing around.

"There are too many people down there to feel empty," I joke as I head for the house.

"Loneliness isn't about numbers, it's about worlds," he calls. "And how many people are in yours." I stop and think about turning around, but suddenly it feels more claustrophobic outside than it did in the basement. "Well, have a good night, Cham," he says.

"I am," I say quickly. "I mean, you too."

As I hurry back toward the house, the music gets louder. All I want to do is find Gene and disappear with him. As soon as I get inside, it smells like beer and I begin to feel nauseous. Luckily, I'm a pro at overriding feelings.

Gene is in the corner of his basement, playing beer pong. "Hey, come here," I whisper in his ear as he prepares to throw the ball. "Let's go upstairs."

"Right now?" he asks, surprised, with his arm perched for the throw.

"Get it, you guys," Doug says, stepping toward us and grabbing the ball out of Gene's hand. "Do like bunnies do. I'll take over for you."

"Okay, this just got mortifying," I say, burying my face in Gene's chest. I help myself to his beer, which strongly reminds me of pee. Gene kisses my forehead.

"Thanks for being such a team player, Doug," he says, slipping his fingers through my belt loops as he pulls me toward the stairs. "You're a real pal."

Doug laughs and throws the ball at the pyramid of

cups, where it sinks under a layer of foam. "See you kids soon," Doug calls. Suddenly it feels like the whole basement is looking at us.

"Yeah, girl," Abigail calls as she dances with the empty bottle of Fireball.

"Quick, go go go," I laugh, pushing Gene up the stairs. I'm breathless and thrilled.

"I want you," he whispers as he pulls me through the kitchen, toward his bedroom. My head is spinning and time is speeding up.

"I want you too."

When we close ourselves in his room, he takes his shirt off with one tug over his head. I take a breath and touch the golden cross that hangs on a chain and falls in the center of his chest. I want him. More than the other times. I want to explore that wanting without having to keep stopping. *Too far. Not now.* I want no boundaries. The muscles in his stomach fluctuate as he breathes, and I trace the dark hair that trails down his belly button and disappears beneath the band of his boxers. He tilts my chin up to kiss me. I want to know what it'll feel like. I want to know if we'll say anything while it's happening. I want to know if I'll be different after. I push him toward the bed, and he plays with the strap of my underwear. I lie on top of him, and his hand explores the cheek no one's explored. His hand slips down the front of my underwear and I let him this time. This time is *the* time. *I want to close every space between us until it's nothing but youmeyoume.*

-61-

"Gene," his mom calls, knocking on the door. I jump off him, and the bed creaks almost as loud as my heart is beating.

"Yeah," he says, rushed, fixing his belt and grabbing his shirt off the floor.

"What are you doing up here? It's so late." She yawns. "Tell everyone it's time to wind down. And keep this door *open*. No closed-door sleepovers."

"Sorry, coming." He throws me my shirt.

My stomach somersaults. "I don't feel good," I say, burping a little. When I look down, there's a 76 percent chance I'm vomiting into a shoe. "This isn't exactly how I pictured the night going," I say, and wipe my mouth.

"That's okay," he says, handing me his trash can. "Next time." He pats my back as I produce more orange vomit, and the red condom wilts in my pocket.

"Definitely next time," I add, then retch again so he knows I mean business.

5

Days 'til prom: 89

FACT: EVERY TEACHER AT THE GILL SCHOOL WHO ISN'T EVELYN understands this one very important thing about the second half of senior year: It is a wad of watermelon gum that we are chewing to blow into a glorious pink bubble that will pop on our faces and christen us on the day we graduate. Among other delicious freedoms, we will finally be free to chew gum anywhere we please. Until then, school is a freaking breeze. In science we make ice cream and try to call it chemistry. In Spanish we start a soap opera with English subtitles, with enough seasons to last us well into our twenties. In math we play a computer game we literally played in middle school that involves tiny blue creatures called Zoombinis. When we do get an assignment, it's pretty much an *I*-based answer you can't get wrong.

Then there are the assemblies where they pause normal classes and pile the senior class into the auditorium with its layers of dust and torn maroon seats that expose bits of cushion. Abigail, Hilary, and I scrunch down in our seats and look at possible prom hairstyles while the guidance counselors tell us that the Gill School has a "special schedule for seniors" so that its graduates will do "special things in the world." The point of all the PowerPoints and guest speakers from previous years who've already done special things in the world is to remind us that we're let out of school almost two months before the other schools because we have service work to do. Instead of a weeklong spring break, we get a kind of monthlong "spring break" after graduation that goes from early May to mid-June. Though it's not mandatory, it's kind of a well-known fact that every senior has to pack a suitcase full of ugly hiking socks and partake in Gill's six-week volunteer project abroad. This year we're going to Nicaragua, which I hear has waterfalls. Forty-two days without parents or cell phones or electricity, all while having a "truly formative experience" with my best friends and boyfriend? Yes, please.

"I don't even really get what we're going to be doing," Hilary says to Abigail during lunch on one of those January days that threaten to sacrifice your soul to winter. It's Taco Tuesday, where we're all united after lunch by the orange halo on our mouths.

"Doing some work at the landfill so the kids can go to school? And volunteering in the classrooms, I think," Hilary says.

I sip my lemonade. "Probably just *pretending* to help out in the classrooms while actually volunteering to take our bikinied asses to the beach."

"Cham!" Hilary says. "It's a serious issue! Because kids have to work at the landfill to support their family, they can't go to school and—"

"I know, I know. I'm just kidding." My eyes drift over to Gene, who sits a few tables away from us with Doug and some other guys on the track team. "Whenever we're in the cafeteria, I half expect a flash mob to appear and sing about how Gene wants to take me to prom. Not that I'm obsessed," I add, poking the stringy green-tinted lettuce that's fallen out of my tortilla shell. (Even tacos have a hard time keeping it together.) "Just healthily fixated."

Hilary laugh-chokes as Abigail dons a frown worthy of a large, depressed fish. "Poor Cham," she says, rubbing her tearless eyes theatrically. When she takes a bite of her taco, a glob of ketchup falls to its death on the floor.

"Nice," Hilary says, laughing.

"Karma's a bitch," I say, then look up at Gene just as he happens to be looking up at me. We share a smile no one else can see in a world no one else is part of.

"Heeeeeeeey," someone behind us says, pushing empty chairs into tables to get to our corner. "Gooood afternoon, ladiesss!" The tables closest to us have turned around, and a few people are rolling their eyes. "Sorry to interrupt," Brendan sings, hitting the back of someone's head with his bright red tutu. "Jeez," the girl says, glaring at him like he did it on purpose. "I know it's Taco Tuesday and you're very busy, but Student Council is finalizing plans for Senior Volunteer Day."

Hilary and Abigail look at each other, so I have no choice but to look at Brendan. I don't know how he doesn't mind people staring at him like he's an annoyance from another planet. I guess humans are adaptable creatures. We can get used to almost anything.

"What are they finalizing?" I ask. His face is two inches from the Student Council iPad, and there's a 100 percent chance his fingers are smudging taco prints all over it.

"Well," he says, leaning over us and ignoring our lack of interest, either for the love of Student Council or because of basic male obliviousness. His hair brushes my face. It's a soft perfect curl that's fallen from his bun and smells like peppermint. "We're deciding between the Breast Cancer Polar Plunge and the Brain Degeneration Walk." My eyes widen, and a pogo stick of doom has a field day in my stomach. "Do you guys have a preference?"

"Not the brain thing!" I say quickly, then open my bag of tortilla chips to drown out the sounds of my anxious thinking. His eyebrows shoot up to the lights on the ceiling that somehow get sprayed with condiments sometimes.

"Uh, okay." He sets the iPad down on the table and turns it to me to cast my vote.

"I just feel really strongly about...boobs," I explain through a mouthful of chips.

Abigail throws an anemic tomato at me. "You're being *so* weird."

I eat another three chips. Maybe if my breath smells enough like corn and taco onion, no one will get close enough to talk to me. Ever. "Am I being weird?" I ask innocently. "I mean, I'm *always* weird, so it'd kind of be weird if I *wasn't* being weird, right? Right?"

"Okay, now will you two fill out the survey?" Brendan asks Hilary and Abigail. He points to the remaining tables: two by the snack bar, one by the three bins for trash, recycling, and compost. "I still have a lot of people to ask."

"Sure," Abigail says, leaning over the iPad. "But can't we vote for both? It's not like there's a limit on how much the senior class can volunteer."

"They're on the same day," he says, and I commandeer the iPad.

"God hates suck-ups, Abigail," I say, filling out the survey with a few finger taps. "We're all set, Brendan. Breast Cancer Polar Plunge it is."

He lingers over us and our trays and our pile of napkins. "Uh, okay, well, thanks for supporting Student Council."

"And boobs," I say. "I love me a good pair of boobs!"

Abigail laughs and shakes her head. "Good for you for

embracing your boobs, Cham. Gene can't be the only one giving them some love."

"That's my cue to leave," Brendan says.

Once he's out of earshot, Abigail whispers, "Did you notice Brendan got cute this year? I mean, besides being annoying AF."

Hilary nods. "Puberty did a good job with him."

I look down at my chest. "Now if only puberty would come back for me."

〜

{FEBRUARY}

Days 'til prom: 83

For the last couple of weekends, Gene has had a lot of away track meets, which has reduced our hookups to ten minutes of making out after lunch, with or without leftover food particles in our mouths. Also, because he's been away so much, he hasn't had time to ask me to prom. Not that I need him to ask me to prom to know that we're going to prom together. It's just that the way you get asked to prom says a lot about how much the other person likes you. Does he like me a random-text-with-no-emojis amount or a seven-hundred-balloons-in-the-sky amount?

Dear Universe,

What if my insides have kidnapped a feminist and they're holding her hostage? Not to be paranoid, but sometimes I hear this voice of unknown origin and it's hollering, *Ask Gene to prom yourself, you freaking 1950s idiot!*

Text exchange between me, Hilary, and Abigail when another weekend comes and goes and I still have not been asked:

A: I think you should just ask him.

H: Seriously, what year is it that you're waiting for a guy to ask you?

C: I JUST WANT HIM TO ASK ME

A: Where has he been anyway?

H: Ya. Haven't seen him at school at all

C: Away track meets then visiting college. So lame.

A: How dare he have a future

C: My boobs are too small for dresses. What if I wear cling wrap to prom?

A: No.

A: Speaking of futures how's the college essay Cham?

C: Oops.

A: CHAM!

C: time is infinite

H: You have to take this stuff seriously!

C: You guys have essay brains. I have gaze-at-stars brain

A: *a gaze-at-stars brain

C: See?

A: So you haven't applied to college yet?

C: Define apply

H: It's okay, we'll sneak you in the trunk of my car

C: Well you don't know if you got into State right Hil?

A: She's gonna get in

C: yeah but Abigail you're waiting to hear from other places too right?

A: Ya but probs won't get any money. State's where it's at.

H: don't worry you can go to community college for a year and transfer

I roll off the couch with a heavy sigh. Why does everyone have such a large scrunchie lodged up their butt? This is the time of our lives! We are graduating from *high school*, it is finally happening to *us*, and it is a big freaking deal!

"Answer the question, Cham," my mom says when I join her and my dad at the table. "Have you gotten your applications in?" She's attacking an unidentifiable morsel by the candle with a paper towel, and every so often it squeaks for its life.

"Well," I say, resting my head on the table, "I'm definitely moving in that direction."

"You really should get those in," my dad scolds, arranging and rearranging his silverware. "Your mom and I worked hard so you could go to the Gill School after public school didn't work out." *That's one way to look at it.* "You have to take it seriously," he says. "I would've loved to have had the opportunity. Not everyone gets to go to college."

"I know, Dad," I mumble. "And I'm really grateful, I

promise, but I have so much time. Rolling admission is a real-life example of infinity. It just keeps going and going."

He's looking at me with clear eyes, but his face has the stony quality to it. I really hope it's not one of the lucid, angry days where the cheerful denial and confusion lift and the elephant in the room catches up with him. Selfishly I just want to bring the maple syrup to the table, which I always did when he made pancakes for dinner. I want him and Mom to talk about work and where to plant the tomatoes this year. What I really want is for everything to be boring again.

"Cham, don't joke about this," my mom starts.

"I don't want to think about it yet, okay?" I fold my napkin into a deranged bird that has to sit on my lap because it can't fly away. "There are so many other things to think about, like prom and Senior Volunteer Trip and—"

"Speaking of Senior Volunteer Trip, don't you have papers for us to sign?" my mom asks. "And have you been paying attention during the assemblies? I know you're excited to be in another country with your friends, but there's a lot of preparation involved. You need to contact your host family and—"

"I still think it's too dangerous," my dad says, and I realize I should abort this mission. I pick up my spoon and ignore the chin zit reflected in its imperfect mirror.

"That smells delicious, Mom," I say loudly as she comes over with the pot.

"What is it?" my dad asks, looking down into his bowl as she fills it. His voice has that edge to it, and I know my mom senses it.

"Split pea," she says carefully. "I think you'll like—"

"Mom, can you pass the salad?" I interrupt, pointing to the big glass bowl of spring mix. "And the balsamic?"

My dad looks at the table. "It's right in front of me," he says. "I'll do it."

"That's okay," my mom says quickly, knocking the salt-shaker over. "I've got it." She reaches over my dad. Her sleeve is precariously close to the candle, with its orangey-yellow fire tongue.

"Judy," he says sharply. He turns to her in his wheel-chair, and the napkin tucked into his shirt falls to his lap. "You don't let me do anything." His eyes flash like they used to when he'd catch me sneaking out of bed at night. The anger would pass quickly, and he'd let me watch TV with him, or he'd tuck me back in with his big yellow flashlight. I wish the monsters I have now were more like the ones that dissolved in his light. "You don't let me do anything at all," he repeats.

"What?" My mom pauses with the salad bowl in her hands. "Of course I let you do things."

"Then let me have it."

He reaches his hands out and looks down at them as if he's just noticed how they shake. It's not a caffeine shake or a muscle-exhaustion shake; it's a violent trembling by a brain with no regard for how a hand needs to function. He continues to stare at them, and I wonder what he's telling his brain to get them to steady themselves. I wonder if he sounds angry or sad or patient.

"I'm already holding it," my mom is saying. "I'll just give it to Cham myself, since I'm here."

"No," my dad says firmly.

"You know what," I pipe up, reaching for the bread basket placed neutrally to my left. "I don't really want salad. Spring mix is kind of a hoax. No offense, Mom."

Relief washes over her face, and she sets it down quickly on the tablecloth. A tomato gets jostled around, but otherwise order is restored. She's placing her plaid napkin on her lap when my dad clears his throat.

"Please pass *me* the salad, then." His hands are shaking more the longer he holds them out.

As my mom extends the bowl to him, I keep thinking about that elephant in the room. Either we are hunting it, or it is hunting us, and I don't know how long we can coexist.

"Thank you," he says when the bowl finishes its journey across the table. His knuckles are white and it wobbles a bit. Just when I realize I haven't been breathing, it settles into his palms. "There," he says. "Now, did you want this, Cham?"

"Yeah, sure," I say carefully. "Maybe if I just—"

The bowl slips from his fingers and falls onto the ceramic dish, sending salad and glass and blue pieces over the table and floor.

"Dammit!" he yells, pushing back from the table. "Dammit," he says again, and his voice breaks. I bite my lip until I taste blood, and the iron nauseates me. He throws his napkin at the table and it catches the edge, then falls to the floor.

"Get me out of this chair, get me out of this sweater." He rocks back and forth, but the wheelchair is locked and doesn't budge. "I want to get out of everything. I'm sick of being sick and what it does to you girls, I can't take care of you, I'm useless and a burden and—"

He's crying. I've never seen my dad cry. His face has new formations. It loosens a rock and triggers an avalanche of sadness in me. *Don't cry, don't cry, don't cry.* My mom jumps up to help him with his sweater and knocks her chair over. Her face freezes in a wince.

"Don't help me!" my dad hollers, squirming away from her hands, which are reaching toward his shoulders. "I'm fine, I'm fine. Just let me get to my room."

He struggles to undo the brakes on the wheelchair, then pushes back, but nothing happens. "It's caught on the rug," he says, looking down at the red and navy-blue designs. "Dammit, will you help me with this—"

My mom is already kneeling on the ground as he rocks

back and forth in the chair, never finishing his sentence. Maybe he was going to end it with *rug* or *chair*, or maybe he didn't intend to finish it at all. Maybe the things we need the most help with can't be articulated, because to say them would give them more power than they already have over us.

"Can I do something, Dad?" I push my chair back and walk toward him tentatively as my mom pushes his chair from behind.

He shakes his head and looks down at his shoes. They're brown with Velcro straps because last year was the last year of shoelaces. "I'm fine, I'm sorry to—I mean, I'm sorry, I'm just sorry."

"Don't be sorry. It's okay. Salad is a stupid food anyway." I open the sliding door for them. The hallway is peaceful except for the rubber wheels dragging over the wooden floorboards. My mom pushes the bedroom door open. "Give us a minute," she says.

Back in the dining room with a garbage bag from under the sink, I pick glass and lettuce off the floor. *Just a few more months until I can get out of here.*

The doorbell rings and I walk toward the front door quickly, relieved that one of the health aides is here to get my dad ready for bed. It used to be weird having all these strangers in our house, back when it first became too much for my mom to take care of him and work full-time. Now my dad likes the company, and it's good for all of us to have someone to act like everything is okay, even though it's not actually okay.

I click the latch open, and my heart falls from a very tall building in my body. Brendan's grinning on my doorstep.

Like the doorstep of my *house*.

6

Days 'til prom: Still 83

I SHIFT BACK AND FORTH UNDER THE PORCH LIGHT, WHICH IS threatening to give me second-degree burns. "Uh, what are you doing here?" I ask Brendan.

"Oh, sorry, Cham, I must have the wrong house. I'm a Beth Israel volun-cheer." He sets his container of hot drinks down on the porch and checks his phone.

"Well, good luck finding—"

"Nope, this is the right one." He picks up the drinks with a little tap dance that sloshes cocoa out the holes in the lids.

"You must be the volunteer with the hospital," my mom says, coming up behind me. "I'm sorry, I forgot you were coming today. Come on in. My husband's just getting to his room."

I close the door behind Brendan. My chest is full of horses. They're trampling me in their race to keep these people and places separate. Brendan comes from the world of things happening, and this is the world of things I can't believe are happening. And yet here he is, holding out his hot drinks, and it's their steam that's crossing over first, from that world into this.

Dear Universe,

Wanted: A giant claw to come down and pluck Brendan from my house because he is an intruder from my *other* world, and home is my other *other* world, which is only safe for me, my family, and carpenter ants, which are like family, given that they eat all our food.

As we walk down the hall, my anger toward my mom rises. "I go to school with Brendan," I hiss, as if she hired him specifically to embarrass me. Seeing as you can't hire a volunteer, you probably can't fire one either. She shoots me a death look.

"Remind me about this program, Brendan," my mom calls over her shoulder.

"It's just to follow up with anyone who's had major surgery in the last year," he says, no singing, thank god. "Your husband had his knee done a few months ago?"

"Yeah," my mom says. "He hates hospitals, but we got him there for that."

She continues to lead him down the hallway of my awkward years, and I follow.

"Is that you?" Brendan laughs, pointing to the picture on the wall with my worst orthodontia situation.

"Shut up," I grumble. The closer we get to my dad's door, the more sick to my stomach I feel.

"Mr. Myles?" Brendan says as we step into the warmth of my dad's room. He likes the heat turned up to sauna levels, which makes the pee smell more noticeable, but I guess one polite thing the disease does is dull the sense of smell. "I'm here with Beth Israel Volun-cheers. We tell jokes and deliver beverages." His face brightens. "Oh, hey there. I remember seeing you a few months ago." He looks between me and my dad. "I didn't know this was your dad!"

I cross my arms and nod, my ears feeling very hot, probably because of the thermostat setting and nothing else. I watch Brendan's face and wait for him to laugh or say something or I don't know what exactly.

"How are you feeling?" Brendan looks at my dad earnestly. He makes direct eye contact with him and uses his normal voice, unlike some of the aides who get cheerful and animated in a nauseating way, like Dad's a kid or something.

"I feel fine," my dad says sternly. He rolls up his pant leg and shows Brendan the scar. "I'm recovering pretty well, just surgery on my knee from an old motorcycle accident." The muscles of his face tighten into a smile. "But I could always use something to laugh about."

"Here to serve," Brendan says. My dad presses the button on the bed, and it sits him upright slowly. Brendan hands him one of the cups of cocoa, but then sets it on the table that's attached to the bed as he realizes Dad won't be able to hold it.

"Cham and I go to the same school," Brendan offers. "We have English class together, but it's more of a think-deeply-about-your-life course because our teacher likes philosophy."

"Oh." My dad frowns. "In my riding days, I tried to read *Zen and the Art of Motorcycle Maintenance*, but it put me to sleep."

Brendan smiles. "Yeah, it's not something I'm always in the mood for. We talk a lot about life and death and—"

"Actually, Brendan," I interrupt, "I need to ask you something about the homework. Can you come here for a sec, and then you can get back to your cheering?"

"Er—" he says. I pull him into the hall.

"Look, I don't know what a volun-cheer is, but you need to go."

"Uh, I can't really—" he says tentatively, and I sigh. I didn't really expect him to leave.

"Fine, but please don't mention this at school." I look back at the closed door, then think better of it. "Let's go to the kitchen, okay?"

"I wouldn't bring up your dad's patella at—"

"Not the knee stuff. It's the other stuff," I say as I walk down the hall and close the sliding door behind us.

In the kitchen Brendan leans on the counter. "I'm confused."

"Just don't tell anyone at school he's sick. He was diagnosed a few years ago, but he'd rather think it's brain damage from this motorcycle accident and, yeah, we just go with it."

Brendan looks up at me with wide brown eyes. "Wow, I'm sorry. That must be so awful for him." I feel a jab of guilt. I hardly ever think about what it's like for him.

"Is it Parkinson's?" he asks, and the word hits me with all of its letters. *Parkinson's* is the *Voldemort* of our household. Beyond being the disease-that-must-not-be-named, it is the disease-that-we-shall-not-acknowledge-exists.

I kind of nod and kind of shake my head, hoping he'll get that I mean *yes*. He grimaces. "I'm sorry. If there's anything I can do to help—"

"It's fine, thanks." I jerk my thumb toward the steak knives that are all perky and upright in their wooden holder. "Just like if you tell anyone I'll kill you." It's meant to be a joke but it comes out a little serial-killerish.

"Listen, Cham," he says gently. "My brother was really sick for a while. And it sucked. And I was really lonely 'cause I didn't tell anyone about it. If you want to talk—"

"Thanks," I say, "but I should go." In the quiet kitchen something passes between us. I don't know what it is, but I feel it as it goes. It's as big as a bus and as quiet as the space between songs.

"Well, I should go back in there." Brendan turns, his tutu brushing against the cabinets, then spots a picture on the wall. He laughs. "That can't be you."

"Nope, it's not." I cover the photograph of myself ass-naked at the beach with a diaper on my head. *Baby's first nudie.* "Gotta go, bye."

I head for the front door with my eyes down.

"See you, Cham," Brendan calls, and he disappears down the hall. I don't know if Brendan can cheer up my dad, but maybe he can distract him, which is the next-best thing.

Once I have my sneakers on, I text Gene.

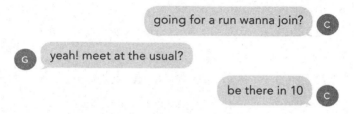

going for a run wanna join?

yeah! meet at the usual?

be there in 10

Outside there are old patches of ice and snow as winter lingers before it goes. With my foot crossed above my knee I bend toward the frozen ground. Space opens in my hip as I stretch one side, then the other, one hamstring, then the other. By the time I take off running, there's enough space in my body to hold me. I pick up the pace. It's as if I'm running out of one world and into another. Soon I'll enter the realm where Gene and I count how many people got mega-wasted at his party, and the only sickness will be the drunk kind that fills bathtubs with throw-up. I will kiss Gene and he will talk about his last track meet that's coming up in a few weeks and maybe I'll hint about things like prom and it'll just be us and our hearts and our lungs.

Dear Universe,
I like cold nights we disappear into.
I like when our shadows touch.
I like the metallic taste in my mouth from his mouth
   from his lungs.
I like Elvis songs playing in my head as I move.
I like what his spandex hints at.
I like everyone tucked in their houses and us escaping
   toward each other.
I like my heart taking up the drums.
I like procrastinating.
Seriously, I like it so much I put off procrastinating.
I like college essays with incomplete endings.
I like imagining us dancing into freedom on prom
   night.
I like you.
Clap once if you like me too.

7

EVERY SO OFTEN I GET A PING OF EXCITEMENT WHEN I LEAVE the house for school in the morning. I walk up the street, avoiding December's ice patches that are continuing their midlife crisis into February, and I'm happy about catching the bus. Obviously, I don't *like* school. I'm not in *second grade*. But as annoying as the rules (and the teachers who just love catching us breaking those rules) are, school is exactly what I need sometimes. There are so many lives going on all around me in the crowded hallways and the deafening cafeteria, and I'm just another girl with a plaid skirt and a backpack on. At home I'm my parents' daughter, and who we are is as much a part of the house as the furniture is.

It gets claustrophobic. My mom decides to embark on

a special cleaning project of the cleaning products. My dad puts the milk back in the oven. At school I'm free of all that as I walk past Mr. Garcia's office, with the countdown to graduation and the vending machine with the condoms that wave as I pass, as if to say, *Look at how intact your virginity is!* At school it's nice to be no one specific, just talking about prom and working on my Spanish so that when I arrive in Nicaragua, I can say a little bit more than *Me llamo Cham.* Unfortunately, the ping of excitement doesn't usually last the whole school day, or even through homeroom. One opening of my in-box, and the ping often turns to a thud of *Oh, shit.*

E-mail received at seven o'clock on Tuesday morning but not read until *this* morning because it's impossible to find a good secretary these days:

Hi, Cham,
Just a reminder that your college essay is due Friday. Looking forward to reading it!
Thanks,
Evelyn

Dear Universe,
In light of this recent e-mail, could you please send me a celestial Uber before last period? Gotta leave

the world real quick. Do me this solid, and I will not make any more desperate requests for Gene to ask me to prom in such a cute way that kittens everywhere shit their pants. I will even write my college essay. Or try to.

—⟶

"How is everyone doing?" Evelyn asks when last period is upon us. (The celestial Uber is decidedly not coming.)

"Good," a few people say throughout the room. It's unnecessarily hot in here. I look over at Abigail, who's fanning her face as she takes notes on her iPad.

"She hasn't even said anything yet," I whisper, and pull my long frizzy hair over my face like a curtain with secrets behind it.

Abigail tucks her short hair behind her ear and rolls her eyes at me. "Doesn't mean I don't have *notes*."

"Thank you for turning your essays and book projects in," Evelyn says, avoiding eye contact with me. *Shit.*

"I'm hoping to have them graded by next week. If you haven't turned yours in, please do ASAP so I don't have to spend the weekend grading. I do have an outside life, you know." She smiles at us. "In the meantime, we're going to focus on philosophy. Let's get into some dialogue and try this again with more energy: How is everyone doing?"

I cough. It's sad when such low enthusiasm is so evenly

distributed throughout a room. I look down at my fingernails and wish they felt more. Evelyn paces in front of her desk. Then her eyes light up as she points to the back of the room. "Yes, Brendan?"

Heads turn. Brendan's tie has a gravy stain on it, proof that the cafeteria wasn't lying about its online menu: It was, in fact, Thanksgiving Thursday. Again. On Friday. "I feel a little blasé about life," Brendan says with his cheek smooshed into his hand. He drags out *blasé* so it's like *blaahhhh-zay*.

"What does that mean?" Doug asks, then looks over at me with an eyebrow raised. I shrug in a cool way because it's very important that Doug likes me, understands how extraordinary I am, tells Gene I deserve a prom ask-cute, etc.

"*Blasé* means 'over it,'" Josie calls out before Abigail can get her hand up. Abigail frowns at the split ends in her hair, which she always does when she's annoyed. There haven't been any updates on valedictorian.

"*Blasé* is 'uninterested because of frequent exposure,'" Abigail clarifies.

Evelyn nods. "Right, girls. And I'm so glad you said that, Brendan." She turns around to scribble on the chalkboard: *blasé*. "Is anyone else feeling some existential despair? Perhaps grappling with the meaning of life in the face of death?"

"Uh, what?" Jared asks, squinting at Evelyn through his clear-framed glasses.

"That wasn't exactly what I meant," Brendan mumbles nearly inaudibly.

From the side of the room by the windows, the heater makes a noise like a mouth breather choking on its own air, and Evelyn pulls a finger puppet out of her pocket. Abigail and I look at each other with wide eyes. The puppet has dark hair and a creepily stitched face with lopsided eyes and an actual Cheerio for a mouth.

"Don't worry, this is why I brought Albert Camus," Evelyn says, holding her pointer up, then turning the puppet to look at her. (She waves to it.) When she turns the puppet to us and waves, I'm the only one who waves back. And then I want to sand my fingers down with a nail file. "Does anyone know who he was?" Evelyn asks.

Predictably, no one does. Not even Josie or Abigail. Over the course of the next twenty-five sweaty minutes, Evelyn tells us all about how her undergraduate thesis was on this French guy who devoted his life to the theory that life is absurd, meaningless, etc. "Camus wasn't a nihilist, though," Evelyn says, scribbling even faster on the board. "No nihilist can say, 'In the depths of winter, I finally learned that within me there lay an invincible summer.'"

"Come again?" Josie says, looking around the room to see if anyone else found that quote a bit startling. No one else is really close to awake.

"Thank you, Josie!" Evelyn says. "It's beautiful, right? But how can someone find beauty in the world if it's meaningless? Aren't the two antithetical? Well, according to Camus—"

Evelyn puts a reading up on the projector about a guy called Sisyphus, who was sentenced to push a rock up a hill but the rock keeps falling back down. (Gravity is the unsung hero of the story.) We take turns reading it out loud, which is probably even more annoying than pushing a rock up a hill.

"This, folks," Evelyn says, speaking as Camus through the side of her mouth as her finger puppet scans the room, "is what I call 'the absurd.'"

She returns to the projector and draws two circles in the margin of the story, one in red and one in yellow, and then a red squiggly line between them. "This is the fundamental conflict between what humans want from the universe—reason, meaning, answers—and what the universe actually is: chaos!" She writes *chaos* in the circle on the right and *meaning* in the circle on the left. Then she writes *the absurd* above a line with arrows pointing to each.

"This class is absurd," one of the hockey guys in the corner says, just loud enough that Evelyn might be able to hear him.

Evelyn continues, "Camus claims that Sisyphus is the ideal absurd hero and that his punishment is representative of the human condition: He must struggle perpetually and without hope of success. So long as he accepts that there is

—90—

nothing more to life than this absurd struggle, then he can find happiness in it."

"Well, that's depressing," Doug pipes up.

"No, it's not," Brendan says. His voice is firm, and I'm not the only one who turns around to look at him. He's not wearing a tutu today, and his hair is all down, and if I saw him on the street and knew nothing about how he sings everywhere, I would think he was cute in a seventies-rock-band-type way.

"This is good," Evelyn says, clapping her hands together. "Yes, let's get into some more dialogue now. Why is it depressing, Doug?"

Doug kind of stutters a bit, and she takes pity on him. "Anyone else want to chime in? No need to raise your hand, just call things out." When no one does, she looks at me. "What do *you* think, Cham?"

I look around the room. "Um, you mean about a guy pushing a rock up a hill?"

"Sure, you can talk about 'The Myth of Sisyphus'...or what about the absurd? Do you agree that there could be an 'absurd' relationship between what humans want and what there actually is?"

"Um..."

She wheels the projector to the side of the room, and Abigail leans over. "Are we really supposed to be enlightened right now? It's freaking *Friday*."

Doug raises his hand, even though Evelyn said we didn't have to. I guess we're just fantastic robots after twelve years of this stuff. "What I think I meant is that it's depressing to keep looking for something that doesn't exist."

Brendan sighs. "It's only depressing if you want it to exist. The actual relationship is kind of hysterical. Like we're all screwing off or trying to do something that matters, but nothing does and we all keep doing it anyway."

Participation is 20 percent of our grade. Given the status of my essay, I take a go at it. "Maybe it's only depressing if you think about it too much. On a day-to-day basis, when you're living life and doing your thing, you don't really have time for, um..."

"Existential quandaries?" Evelyn provides.

"Er, yeah, so I vote that thinking about it too much is the problem. Like, *philosophy* is the problem."

The whole class laughs. Even Evelyn has a smile on her face.

"I like Cham's solution," Doug says.

"But I don't think we can help thinking about it," Brendan says, and we all turn around again. He is relentless. "It might be okay for a little while to do things like homework and college applications and plan prom, but at some point we have to wonder what it's all for. It's gotta be for *something*, right?"

A few people roll their eyes and I'm about to be one of them, but I detect something less than a smile behind his lips.

"Yes, *this* is why philosophy is important," Evelyn says happily. "It's not just an academic subject. It's the consciousness we bring to our lives."

After that, I think we're all pretty tired of so much thinking. Evelyn hands out a book that's actually another thing Camus wrote, a play called *Caligula*, and then she gives us the rest of the period to start reading it. I *want* to want to start reading it, but instead I flip through the pages in my agenda because there are sixty-five days 'til prom. There's only two weeks left to get tickets, which means Gene's going to have to ask me *soon*. Will it be public? Will I be naked, which has only happened 1.5 times altogether, but still?

Opportunities abound: Gene's last track meet; Senior Night, which Abigail is dancing at; prom; graduation; Senior Volunteer Trip. It's just a little hard to think about how despairing the human condition is, when a few weekends ago we danced until we threw up, and in a few more weekends we'll be dancing until we throw up *more*. All the things we've been looking forward to since high school started are finally happening to us. My time capsule is filling up, and it's freaking amazing. *Of course* life is worth living. Maybe it's a sobfest if you're an octogenarian philosopher who devoted his life to that curvy bit of punctuation known as the question mark, but when you're seventeen, the world is just an oyster loving an oyster loving an oyster.

Dear Universe,
Could the half-life of the best time of my life be forever?

~

Days 'til prom: 64

Things aren't going well in the college essay department. No offense to my brain, but holy shit, it is a barren wasteland. I've been able to sweet-talk Evelyn into giving me more time, but I don't know how long my honey-dripped e-mails will work.

Frantic text exchange with Abigail from my bed:

> This college essay is going to be the death of me **C**

> **A** JUST DO IT AND SEND YOUR COLLEGE APPS IN ALREADY

> Last night I dreamt that Gene put on a parade to ask me to prom. I sat upon a float-sized condom. **C**

A: You're obsessed

C: Sorry, rom-coms have set me up for a lifetime of unrealistic expectations

A: Ok bye Cham you're doing your essay now

C: Ugh fine

C: Ok here I go

C: I'm turning my phone off now

C: I'm serious

C: Don't text me 'cause I won't answer

C: 'Cause I'll be working.

C: Hello?

C: DID YOU SERIOUSLY FREAKING LEAVE ME?

Dear Universe,

I just want to know what in the name of kegs and libraries I'm supposed to write a college essay about. *We want to know the real you.* Do you, though, random college admissions person #8099? Do you really want to know that I feel kinda stupid, even though I should feel all liberated, when I take baths and explore those random body parts that *Teen Vogue* says are open for "my pleasure"? Do you really want to know that I cried harder when Jack died in *Titanic* than when my own grandmother died in her bed, because at least she was old, whereas Jack, JACK HAD SO MUCH TO LIVE FOR. And lastly, do you really want to know that I throw pennies away because it seems like more work to actually find my wallet than to pretend one penny could ever make a dollar of difference in a world where everything costs so much more than we know? No, you don't. You don't want to know that I haven't volunteered in some random country and I didn't start a fund so that three-legged lemurs could learn a second language....You don't want to know the real me. *I* don't even want to know the real me. So what do I do? I'm drawing blank after blank here. Send me your rough draft, Universe? I won't show anyone, I promise. As usual, it'll just be between you and me.

After a lot of hours spent making not a lot of progress, I put my sneakers on. If a few days go by and I don't run, my body develops cobwebs. It's not spiders that spin the silk; it's anger and other things that crawl. Running with Gene helps, but I also have to run by myself, preferably at midnight. It feels like a secret that I'm telling and keeping. I'm onto myself.

Outside in the cold, cars whoosh past me. I play this game with my feet where I try to step only on the white line technically made for bicycles. (I force my place in the world when I have to.)

Running didn't always feel this good. Actually, for most of my life, running was truly terrible. I just didn't get it. Like, no, I do not want to play tag with you, random elementary school friend. We will run if a bear starts chasing us, but do you see any bears? Me either. Also, I have short legs and small lungs, which is not a medically sound description of my respiratory system, but I don't know how else to explain why it's so goddamn hard to breathe when I'm power walking to make the bus on time.

Once Gene and I started running together, I was out of that anger management class so fast they doubted I was ever there at all. I ran and I ran and that's how I realized you don't have to be anatomically gifted to move fast. All you have to do is want to get out of someplace bad enough that you don't care about the sweating or the panting or the ferocious cramping of your shins, ribs, and thighs. All you care about is what you need, and what you need is out.

When I get back home, it's dark in the house. I don't want to have to talk to my parents, so I tiptoe toward the stairs in my socks damp with toe sweat. When I reach for the railing, my hand touches something warm and soft, with fingers....

"What the—" I jump back, heart pounding as I scramble for the light switch.

"Sorry, sweetie," my dad says from the foot of the

stairs. He's gripping the railing with his right hand and the doorway to the dining room with the other. His nose is nearly touching the wall, and I feel claustrophobic looking at him.

"Are you okay, Dad?" I ask. I don't want to crowd him more. "What are you doing out here so late?"

"I was just trying to get up the stairs," he says, rocking back and forth a bit, but he's still wedged in the corner, trapped by the railing of the stairs and the doorway to the kitchen, and something we can't see too.

"But how did you get here without your chair?"

"I don't need that thing."

I gulp. I never know what to do in situations like these, and they're happening more and more. If Mom were here, she'd do the right thing because everything she does is right. Everything I do is wrong, which is why it's better if I don't do anything. "Dad, how did you get out here?" I repeat, then loudly, "Hey, Mom?"

"Shh, I don't want to bother your mom. If I could just...Cham, here, grab hold of my arm. I'm exhausted." He moves his hand down the railing, and it shakes so much it rattles the wood.

"Dad," I start, but the porcupine is in my mouth, and if I swallow it, I might cry. I grab his arm like he asked me to, and the shaking subsides. "Why were you out here?"

"I thought I heard something upstairs. I wanted to

make sure it wasn't someone breaking in. You're the only one who sleeps up there."

"But you can't get up the stairs, Dad, remember?" I swallow. It hurts.

"Sure I can. I just need to turn around." He looks at me, then toward the kitchen. There's sweat on his forehead, and his knuckles are white on the wooden doorframe.

"Okay, let's move your leg." He's in the socks with white chicklets on the bottom. I think my mom took them from the hospital the one and only time he was there. "This leg, Dad." I tap it so that he understands. It doesn't move.

"My feet are stuck to the floor," he says quietly. "The floor is just so sticky."

I don't know how to respond. We both know the floor is smooth as a lie. "Let's get your chair, okay?" I spot it by the sliding door, but as soon as I move my hands, he tilts back.

"Oh," he calls out. Fear flashes across his face, and I steady him, but now I feel shaky too. Stuck. "Hold tightly to the railing, okay?" He nods. I get his chair outside the sliding door and push it toward him. Somewhere between this part of the house and that one, he decided he could walk. *What were you thinking? Where do you go when the disease gets in and jumbles everything?*

"Let's get you back to bed, okay?" He nods but doesn't

move from the corner. "You have to let go, Dad, I got you."
I pry his fingers from the rail and drape his arm on my
shoulders. He's so heavy that I stumble back toward his
chair. He falls into it, and I get a shooting pain up my
neck.

"Careful, Cham," he says to me, his face strained.

"I'm okay."

"Don't help me next time. I would've gotten there by
myself. I don't want you to hurt yourself."

I don't know where *there* is. "I'm okay, Dad, really.
Ready?"

Once we've both caught our breath, I push him down
the hall and into his room. I glare at the light coming from
under the door to my mom's room, as if any of this is her
fault.

"I've got it from here," my dad says, wheeling himself
around and reaching for the doorknob. "Thanks."

"Of course, Dad," I say, lingering in the doorway as he's
still reaching. After a few seconds, I grab the knob for him.

"Do you want this closed?" I ask. He nods.

"I love you," we say at the same time, then laugh our
identical laugh, left eye slightly squinted.

"See you in the morning," I say as I close the door.
Before it shuts, I feel a pang of sadness looking inside his
room, where the TV is talking quietly to the furniture, as
if nothing needs my dad around anymore to keep doing

what it does. I lean against his door. *I still need you. We both do.*

―

Dear Universe,

I need to rent a storage space for all my feelings—just a huge, massive building that isn't my body, something with sturdier insides than organs and bones. Feelings like these are just bad furniture: cumbersome, ugly, and I can't contain them by myself.

Days 'til prom: 61

PREDICTION: IT'S GOING TO HAPPEN. SOMETIME BETWEEN NOW and Senior Night, Gene is going to ask me to prom.

Outlook: sunny with a chance of hell yeah.

Text exchange with Hilary and Abigail:

> Wtf do I get Gene for his last track meet C

> A Sex

> A Hil says "A lesson in feminism"

> I'm going with a chocolate cupcake C

> A Boringgggg.

A: K we'll pick you up in 20

C: You guys literally always hang out without me

A: OMG CHAM WE HAVE A HISTORY PROJECT TOGETHER

C: Ew who does homework

A: Exactly. See you soon.

When Gene first invited me to one of his track meets, I felt like I was getting smoothies with the queen. "I have a race," he'd said shyly after one of our runs. "You could come if you want." A boy had never invited me to something that was his. But Gene wanted me to go. I even put on jeans instead of leggings. I've been to almost all of them, and now that it's his last one, I feel like there should be more. He's going to have lots of these in college, but I don't know who he's going to invite to those.

Track isn't a very popular sport at school, which is fine by me. You don't have to pay to get into any of the events, and the good seats are never taken on the bleachers. Me, Abigail, Hilary, and the chocolate cupcake show up at the arena with about two minutes to spare. All the runners are stretching on the sideline, and the air inside is still cool, without a hint of mugginess or sweat.

"Perfect timing," Abigail says as we slide onto the bleachers. She waves behind us to Kelly and Helga from the dance team, and I do this awkward *I-kinda-know-you-from-my-friend-but-mostly-I'm-jealous-of-how-chill-you-are-at-parties* smile. When we sit down I notice how much it smells like rubber and B.O., and I doubt I'll miss it here when Gene's season ends.

I peek under the lid of the box and don't see any signs of frosting. "I think it's safe to say the cupcake has survived," I say, placing it next to me while patting its imaginary head. "Good cupcake. Hang in there just a little longer."

"How about this one?" Hilary asks, reaching across me and passing her phone to Abigail. I glimpse dorm room furniture. Given that the present moment is high school, and we don't even know if Hilary has gotten into college yet, I think this would be very disappointing to the Buddha.

"Welcome runners, students, parents, and teachers," the announcer says. I spot the shiny 42 on Gene's pinny and wave. He smiles in his short shorts and stretches out his hamstrings.

"Wow, Gene has some nicely shaved legs," Abigail says.

I laugh. "He says they make him more aerodynamic."

Helga leans down and whispers, "He should make a rug out of his leg hair and sell his man carpet on Etsy. I just think he has such a bright future, you know?"

"Ha," I say, and Abigail laughs for real. *What* do *you know about his future?*

"Runners for the four hundred, please take your mark,"

the announcer's voice booms. "Runners for the eight hundred on deck."

"Which one is Gene?" Abigail asks, craning her neck.

"Uh, four hundred?"

"Cham, you are the worst girlfriend," Hilary says, suddenly adopting her British accent. "He's the eight hundred, see?"

She points to Gene, who is obviously not taking his mark at the starting line next to Doug. Instead he swings his hairless legs back and forth.

"On your mark," the announcer says, smiling giddily in his glass box at the top of the bleachers. "Get set. Go." There's a popping noise, and Doug and the runners from the other schools we don't care about take off. Their legs chop the air, their hair slicks back, and their faces are strained with exertion, like they're maybe giving birth to a win.

"Is that a dick I see?" Abigail asks. She forms makeshift binoculars with her hands around her eyes and scopes out a dude in purple shorts.

As I'm in the process of determining whether it is or is not a swinging male part, I spot Brendan way at the end of the bleachers. He's alone, as usual, but he doesn't actually *look* lonely. *It must be nice to self-entertain for longer than four seconds.*

"What was the deal with Brendan's brother anyway?" I say casually.

Abigail takes her hands from her face. "It was really sad. He had leukemia and died when we were in fifth grade."

Hilary nods solemnly and lowers her voice. "Really tragic. Remember how awful the funeral was?"

"Terrible," Abigail says. "Brendan was always this quiet, normal kid, and he came back from that summer at the start of middle school just like singing all the time."

"But his brother had just died," I say. Brendan's tutu is lavender today. "He probably didn't know what to do or like how to be."

"I know," Hilary says, "and everyone felt so bad. But then he just got more and more obnoxious, and by high school it was like, okay, dude, I'm sorry your brother died, but you're annoying AF."

I don't know what's going on with my face, but Abigail and Hilary look at each other, then look at me. "I know it sounds bad when we talk about it now, but when it was happening it was just, I don't know," Abigail says. "It's hard to explain. I guess you had to be there."

"Yeah, I guess so." We're silent for a minute as conversations continue around us. The runners on the side of the track are doing warm-up stretches, their butts in their tiny shorts pointed toward us.

"Oh my god, did we not tell you?" Abigail asks me suddenly.

"Tell me what?"

She and Hilary grin and look at each other. "We decided to go to prom together!"

"Wow," I say, moving the chocolate cupcake box closer to me.

"Yeah, don't wanna go through the hassle of finding a date when you're the person I like most in this school anyway," Abigail says, looking at Hilary. "Except for you, Cham." She adds the last part quickly and rests her head on my shoulder.

I smile. "That's great, you guys." Sometimes I forget there were years before these that I wasn't part of. Everywhere Hilary and Abigail went, they showed up on a bicycle built for two. Since I transferred, they cart me along in one of those sidecars most likely to get hit by a bus. Or an overeager cyclist. It's like I'm constantly trying to get on their level and see over their handlebars.

"Is that seriously it?" Abigail asks as we watch the runners cross the finish line within a few seconds of each other. There's scattered applause around us.

"That was fast," I say.

The next thing we know, the boys are walking back toward the bleachers, faces beet red beneath their sweat crowns.

"Damn, that was kind of anticlimactic." Hilary cranes her neck to see if anyone else is coming, or if they're going to do another lap, but nope.

"Congratulations to all runners," the announcer says

with very little congratulation-ness in his voice. "Now for the eight hundred."

"Did you get your Nicaragua forms in yet?" Hilary asks suddenly. I shake my head, watching Gene approach the starting line with his eyebrows fiercely furrowed.

"Ugh, they're a bitch," Abigail says. "They're taking my parents forever." She turns to me. "Cham, do you need us to remind you to get yours in? You've been known to forget important shit."

"Nope," I say cheerfully. "I'll remember because I *want* to go to Nicaragua. Nothing I forget is ever worth remembering."

"On your mark," the announcer says. "Get set!"

"Go, Gene!" Hilary calls, and as soon as the gun pops, Gene takes off with the six other guys next to him. I love how funny his face is when he runs: It's strained and intense, and one of his eyes gets bigger than the other. The guys pass us in a flash of shiny material: red, purple, mustard yellow, white, and black. Within a couple of minutes of the muscles in their legs flexing past us, they cross the finish line, the guy in red followed by Gene followed by everyone else we don't care about.

"There you go, Gene!" a woman calls from the other side of the bleachers. I look over and wave to Gene's moms, who are sitting next to each other in the new sweatshirts they got to alert the media about Gene's college acceptance. I look around to see if my dad would be able to get into this place. Judging by the cement stairs coming out of every exit door, it seems the building was built before society grew a conscience.

"Coming in second at two minutes and forty-five seconds, Eugene Wolf," the announcer says. Gene jogs back toward the starting line, then faces the bleachers, looking directly at me with the tiniest smile playing on his lips.

"Is he confused?" Abigail asks, and there are murmurs of the same question around us too. Suddenly he pulls his pinny over his head, exposing the sparse but determined happy trail beneath his belly button.

"Ow owww!" someone on the bleachers calls.

"Oh my god," Hilary squeals. There's a black question mark painted between the indents of his stomach, the shiny paint starting on his chest and ending by the waistband of his shorts. He tucks his wet hair behind his ear and my stomach drops. Sweat has smudged the paint a little, but it's unmistakable. This boy is asking a question.

"I'm gonna cry," Abigail whispers. "Are you?"

"I'm a little frozen," I say with a grin. "And also like really overheating." Gene hasn't taken his eyes off mine, and my face is burning up in an exquisite fire.

Doug jogs over and stands to Gene's right. He takes his shirt off, revealing a painted *M*.

"Is this what I think it is?" Abigail says. I'm grinning

stupidly, and there's a tingling in my body that goes all the way from my butt on these hard bleachers to my toes nestled in their knee-high combat boots.

"This is the cutest thing ever," Hilary says as Smith takes his shirt off, then Dan, and JJ, so that they're standing there shirtless and smiling before the bleachers, spelling out *PROM?*

A loud "Awwwwww" sounds from the bleachers all around us.

"Um, wow, there's a lot of you here," Gene calls into the crowd, looking around, then laughs. "Will you go with me, Cham?" he asks, a pearl of sweat running down his stomach.

"Yes," I say, a frog in my throat as I'm smiling like a goof. The bleachers are all croons. Even the metal stairs are wetting their pants over how adorable this is.

"Okay, cool!" He comes running up the bleachers toward me, the muscles in his stomach flexing as he breathes.

"Stand up," Hilary hisses, pushing me from behind. With Abigail's help I stand on my legs, now 98 percent water, thanks for asking.

I walk down the stairs right into his eyes.

"That was the sweetest thing I've ever seen in real life," I say. His body pressing against mine smells like the armpit of an onion, but I like how raw he is. I even like the damp question mark he leaves on my coat when he pulls away.

"Good thing you said yes," he says, giving me a rather sweaty kiss on my lips. "That would've been awkward."

I laugh and catch Hilary and Abigail staring at us. Hilary's phone is pointed at us, which I pretend to roll my eyes at, but really, thank god for iPhones and friends willing to capture moments like this. "I have something for you," I say. I grab the cupcake off the bench and hold it out to him.

"What's this?" he asks.

"Open it."

He undoes the tape and lifts the top off. I got my ask-cute. It's now or never. *I love you! I LOVE you! I loooooove you! I love . . .* "I love chocolate cupcakes," I blurt out.

"Me too!"

I take the cupcake from him and swipe my finger over the frosting and lick it. I think I drool a little bit.

He laughs. "You're so hot," he says, and then he rubs some of the paint off his stomach. "Did I do okay? I wanted you to like it, and I wanted to do it here because I just love that you get running, you know?" He stuffs the cupcake in his mouth. "Damn, this is good."

"I loved it, thank you." *Okay, let's try this again.* "Really loved it, just like I love chocolate cupcakes."

He kisses me, the chocolate on his lip meeting the chocolate on my lip.

"I love chocolate cupcakes too," he says, then looks up at me shyly. "And you. I love you."

I triple in size to accommodate my heart. It's big and beating so fast. "That's what I meant," I say, looking at his lips because I can't quite look into his eyes. "I love you too."

Dear Gene,

I want to break the world record for longest kiss while running. I want to shower with you. I want you on top of me when your parents aren't home and whoever we really are comes through in the dark. I want to wear all your T-shirts. I want to redefine happiness using your name. I want to dance with you in the middle of the room on the best night of our lives. And then I want to be naked side by side until we fall asleep, curled together like we're meant to be, sharing the same dream.

Days 'til prom: 57

After something like that happens, things change weather-wise. There's more sunshine, regardless of the cloud cover. And every dormant plant in my mom's garden wakes up feeling alive. I've placed my ticket from the track meet into my senior year time capsule, on top of the unopened condom. I don't think it'll be unopened much longer now that I know Gene likes me enough to risk public nudity and public humiliation, all for his public declaration of love.

Text exchange with Gene after I drop some heavy hints that things should get heavy soon:

G My parents are gonna be gone Senior Night

G Like overnight

G Idk how much you were looking forward to sleeping on the floor of the gym with 100 other people…

C Would anyone notice if we left at like 11?

G Doubt it.

C Should we?

G Do you want to?

C Do you?

G lol obviously

C lol same

C lezzzzdoit

G wish it were tonight

C one more week ;)

9

{MARCH}

Days 'til prom: 51

WHY IS IT THAT WHEN YOU HAVE SOMETHING TO LOOK forward to, time passes even more slowly? In the days leading up to the day that I am probably going to finally do it, every single clock limps toward the end of the day and gets more crippled with every hour. It gets to the point where I start avoiding any and all time-telling devices because no matter what the numbers say, I'm always disappointed. When we did some more dress shopping after school the other day, Abigail said that in preparation for Friday night I should watch some stuff online and then do some practicing. Hilary said that was TMI, and then Abigail yelled at her for stigmatizing female masturbation when boys "like win a Pulitzer when they wax poetic on their dick sessions." My theory on the whole thing is that practice makes perfect, and that's all I'm going to say about that.

"You're awfully smiley," my mom says when I come downstairs on Friday with a bag packed and new underwear on. "What's so great about Senior Night?"

"It's just one of those *things*. Dance team puts on a show, Student Council has a raffle with stuff you'd actually want, we get to make sundaes and take pictures and do karaoke and yeah. Plus, Gene asked me to prom," I blurt out. Then I hear something. "Is that Elvis?" I look around for the source of the music and catch a glimpse of myself in the window. It's true, I am awfully smiley. I just can't help it.

"Dad, is that you?" I call through the sliding door. "Turn it up!"

My dad wheels in with his speaker, and I grin. It's been so long since he's played music after dinner.

"Cham got asked to prom!" my mom tells him in a voice second graders use to convey crushes to one another while furiously nose-picking.

"Oh?" my dad says, turning Elvis down.

"Gene painted his chest after his track meet and it spelled out *PROM*?"

"Romantic," my dad says, with just as little eagerness

to stay on this topic as I'm feeling. "But I doubt this guy is as smooth as I used to be. Have I ever shown you the go-my-man, Cham? Mom and I used to do it. Show her."

My mom dances toward my dad, moving like a train, chugging her arms back and forth. He does the same thing with his arms, and then she kisses him loudly.

"Ew, you guys!" I say, but honestly I'd like to put this moment in a snow globe because a time is gonna come when I'm gonna need to hold something and remember.

As Elvis plays and my parents move around each other, there's a wheelchair between them, and it is just a chair with wheels, with none of the other things attached.

"Dance with us, Cham," my dad says.

"You know I hate dancing, Dad. And Gene's gonna be here any minute to pick me up. We can't be late, 'cause Abigail's dancing first."

My dad sticks his lip out, which he used to do when I pouted as a kid. Now I complain instead of pout. "Please? Make your old man's night!"

"Fine, one move." I crouch down like a frog, then spring up with my arms spread wide. "Ta-da! Amphibian-themed shooting star! Okay, now I leave you to have a romantic Elvis Christmas in the beginning of March."

"We want to meet this boyfriend sometime," my mom calls after me. My dad is fiddling with the speakers, and the result is an eardrum-crushing static avalanche. "You said it wasn't serious, but it's starting to seem a little serious.

You've been dating for what? Five months now? I think we deserve an introduction."

I scoot toward the stairs. "Ummmm—Anywho, Abigail's gonna drop me off in the morning."

"Have fun, love you," my dad says, waving me off. "And wish your mom luck at the dentist."

"I have work tonight, not the dentist," my mom says gently. *Just when I thought everything was back to normal...*

"We love you, Cham," my dad says, and I turn around to kiss him before I open the door.

"I know," I say, because I do. "I love you too."

QUESTIONS FOR THE UNIVERSE

1. How long would it take to shave my whole body?

2. Is there one right way to do it for the first time? Should I aim for glorious? Awkward? Mind-blowing?

3. On average, how many bubbles are in a liter of Coke?

4. If the world were ending, how long would you stay?

5. When I was doing sit-ups in gym class, something started to feel really good so I kept going, and then it felt really good and I kind of peed a little, and I just want to know IS THAT NORMAL?

6. Does rolling admission extend into my twenties?

7. I know it's not Father's Day anytime soon, but what would mean the most to him?

8. What gift can I give Abigail after Senior Night to prove that I'm a much better friend than Hilary while acknowledging that Abigail is an underappreciated genius who better win valedictorian?

9. Is a tomato a fruit or a vegetable?

10. Does anyone else spend as much time thinking about me as I do?

11. I can answer that last one for myself: no.

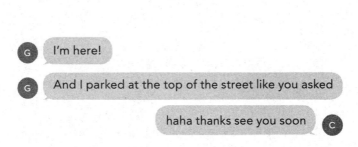

G I'm here!

G And I parked at the top of the street like you asked

haha thanks see you soon C

As soon as I'm out of the house, I sprout lovely invisible wings. I fly across the muddy lawn that's starting to grow new versions of itself. When I open the door to Gene's car, I close myself into its box of Bob Dylan music.

He kisses me. One hand is resting on the steering wheel, and the other finds my leg. I settle into the seat and rest my feet on his spare sneakers and extra sweatshirt and half-empty Nalgenes. His hand travels toward the pocket of my jeans. Then my zipper. But before he crosses those several inches where the material is stretched between good and really good, my breath catches in my throat.

"Come on, we can't miss Abigail," I say.

"I know." He brushes a hair out of my face, then tilts his head toward me and kisses me harder, his tongue swirling in my mouth, and my tongue swirling back in his. He moves the seat belt across my arm and unbuttons my shirt. His fingers are warm on the skin beneath my collarbone. "You're so beautiful," he says. It ignites the pilot light in my deepest furnace.

"We should go," I murmur, biting his lip. He makes a noise from somewhere in his throat that I've only heard a few other times, but I want to hear more of it. Much more of it.

"Okay, okay, later," he says.

"Are you sure your parents are gonna be gone all night?" I ask as he drives up my street toward school.

"I'm sex positive," he says, then salutes the windshield.

"Wow," I laugh. "That was so bad."

"You liked it," he says, grinning.

I grin back. "Only because I like you."

School is so weird at night. Lights you never knew existed get turned on, and custodians you've never seen before open closets you thought were pretend. Inside the front entrance, balloons frame a banner that reads WELCOME TO YOUR NIGHT, SENIORS! Our whole class is trickling in loudly, and a little way down the hall, Evelyn is handing out itineraries. There's the dance performance, the debate performance, and the make-your-own-pizza thing, which is not a performance but could become one. Gene and I hold hands as we walk toward the auditorium, passing a poster for the Breast Cancer Polar Plunge.

"Aw, man," he says, "I was hoping everyone would vote for the Brain Degeneration Walk. I do *not* want to freeze my balls off."

"Damn," I say, but a chorus of angels is singing a cappella in my head. My mom still hasn't broken the news to my dad and me about the walk, but I doubt she's changed her mind. I don't know how I would have dealt with both school and parents in the same venue. The same zip code is bad enough.

"Wow, I would not like to dance in front of all these people," Gene yells over the music blasting in the auditorium. We take a seat next to Hilary, and he and I play elbow-footsies on the armrest. The whole senior class is plopping down in the maroon-felt seats, and there's something exciting and loud and warm about that, especially when someone turns around and looks at me and Gene together. I exist, he exists, we *do* exist together.

Brendan walks to the middle of the stage and says, "Welcome to Senior Night!" He's holding a microphone and wearing another tutu over his jeans.

"That dude never turns down an opportunity for

attention," Gene whispers, and by the sounds of the whispers around us, I assume other people are saying something similar.

"Maybe he's really lonely," I whisper back, and then I lean over Gene. "Hey, Hil, does Brendan have friends? I only ever see him with Student Council people, and I figure since you're an officer—"

"Sure, he does. Student Council people," Hilary says. She's sitting next to a beautiful arrangement of yellow tulips and blue bulbous flowers that travel up a thick stem and come to a point. The tissue they're wrapped in is sparkling and GODDAMMIT I FORGOT TO GET ABIGAIL A BOUQUET BECAUSE I WAS SO BUSY WITH MY FREAKING ARMPITS.

Gene leans over and examines my face. "Hey, don't worry, he's so cheerful all the time."

I fiddle with the shoelace of my combat boot. "Yeah, but everyone puts on an act when people are around."

"I don't!" Gene has a funny smile on his face, like we're telling jokes around a campfire together. "Do you?"

"Of course not," I say.

"Sorry for the technical difficulties," Brendan says. He's tapping the microphone, and it's piercing my eardrum with its thumping. "Please welcome your dance team, led by senior captains Abigail Castillo and Rose Williams."

They shimmy onto the stage as everyone claps. They

have big fake eyelashes on and baggy pants and tight shirts and special sneakers that moonwalk or something. "I'll let their dance moves speak for themselves, or *move* for themselves." Brendan laughs and the auditorium becomes more silent than it's been all night. "Let's do it!" Brendan yells, and a cross between a hip-hop and an electronic song blasts through the speakers in every corner of the auditorium.

The lights fade to black except for two white spotlights that are following Abigail and Rose as they body roll toward the audience. The music begins to rise, their bodies shaking faster as the beat quickens. Just before the beat drops, they freeze, Abigail with her butt an inch from the floor and Rose balancing nearly on her head.

The crowd gets very, very silent—and then my phone rings.

"Seriously?" someone yells into the darkness. The beat drops and Abigail and Rose keep going, but they stumble a little.

"Shit." I reach into my pocket, which is screaming like a newborn baby, but I can't get the phone out of my jeans without standing up.

Mom is on the screen. I turn it to silent and hit ignore. A second later it's vibrating in my pocket again. I ignore it until I get the fourth call.

"I hate when Ma just keeps calling like that," Gene whispers.

It's not really like that. Mom doesn't call four times in a row unless—

"Um, actually I should get this. Be right back." I hop up and stumble in the dark over people's feet and legs. "Sorry, excuse me," I mutter as I step on something squishy enough to be a leg but small enough to be a foot. I hurry up the dark aisle and burst into the hallway by the fire extinguisher. Ahead is a bright pink poster with a smiley face that says SAFE SPACE. *Liar.*

My phone vibrates as it rings a fifth time, and I pull it out of my pocket.

"Mom," I hiss in lieu of a hello. My hands are sweaty and the phone is hot on my cheek, causing a bit of my shimmery lotion to melt onto the screen. "You called right in the middle of Abigail's performance, and you just gave me a heart attack because you know I only keep this on for emergencies—"

"Oh, honey, I'm sorry. I hate to do this, but I have to pick you up." There's a car horn in the background and some static.

"What, why?"

"The aide just called out, and we're already short-staffed at work, so I can't leave. Meet me in front of school. I'll explain in the car."

"But, Mom—"

"I said I'll explain in the car."

She hangs up. I clench my right fist, which is the stronger of the two, to keep from putting it through the fire extinguisher's case. *It's not worth getting suspended, or whatever they do to people who play with fire.* As I walk toward the entrance of the building, the sounds of the auditorium get farther and farther away. I text Gene.

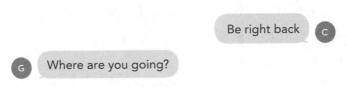

Be right back

Where are you going?

I pause. I don't want to sound like a weenie who promptly answers every one of her mom's calls. I need an excuse that makes me seem a little mysterious as opposed to a little breastfed.

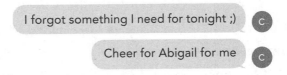

I forgot something I need for tonight ;)

Cheer for Abigail for me

I cross the metal detectors and hold opposite wrists, starting to dig my fingernails in, when I see my mom's headlights. I immediately shove my hands in my pockets as she stops outside the sign that declares the Gill School a place of ECSTATIC LEARNING. *Gag me with a compostable spork.*

I step out the main entrance of the building and into the chilly parking lot, avoiding my mom's eyes as I slide into the warmth of the car.

"Thanks, Cham, sorry about this," she says. Before I close the door, I hear a cheer from inside the school, just audible enough to remind me I'm missing something.

As we drive, I scowl out the window and track the moon as it moves imperceptibly slowly through the trees. "I know your night's just starting, but it shouldn't be more than an hour before they get a replacement over to the house." She speeds through an intersection where a yellow light is flashing and I grip my seat belt.

"Senior Night is a once in a lifetime thing, though."

"I know it is, Cham, but you know what happened last time your dad was home alone at night."

"But now that he uses his wheelchair all the time, he's much safer." My voice breaks as she takes a corner too quickly and my body presses against the hard, indifferent door. "He wouldn't be able to get into the car now. Besides, he hasn't driven in a year. There's no way he'd try to do that again."

She takes a sharp inhale of breath and raises her voice. The sound seems to hit the windshield of the car and shatter it. "Please don't give me this shit right now, Cham. He gets confused. I understand you have a very important schedule, but it's an *hour* and then you can get back to your night."

I look out the window while trying to keep the hot tears out of my eyes.

Begrudging text to Gene sent upon coming to terms with the new reality of my night:

Just had this family thing come up ugh C

G oh noooo

can you tell Abigail I'm sorry I missed her C

G Wait aren't you coming back?

Yeah, but I gotta go home real quick.
I'll be back in an hour C

G Is everything okay?

It will be. C

G You're still coming over tonight right?

Ya :) C

By the time we pull into our driveway, the anger has turned to dread. "What if he has to go to the bathroom?" I ask. "I don't know how to use the plastic thing, and it's so awkward both of us pretending like this is not what's happening. Or what if—"

"Relax, Cham, it'll only be an hour, max." She unlocks the car doors, but I don't undo my seat belt. "Come on, I'm going to be late."

I open the door without looking back at her. I already know what her face is doing—that grimace thing that makes her mouth look small because the world isn't what she wants it to be. Or I'm not what she wants me to be.

I slam the door harder than necessary, and it echoes off the garage door, along with the sounds of her tires leaving the driveway. When I can't hear her car anymore, I kick the stone wall in her garden. Then I kick it again. The hurt feels good, but I have to be careful about doing things like that. I don't want it to get like it got in middle school. The thought of going back to anger management almost sends me back to anger management.

"I'm home," I yell as I open the front door. The lights are on in the kitchen, but it's as quiet inside as if no one were home. "Dad?" I call, quickly taking my shoes off and hurrying toward the living room.

"Hey, sweetie." He wheels into the kitchen just as I'm getting there.

"Hi," I say, still feeling a bit pouty until I register the look of pain on his face. "Are you okay?"

"I was just looking for some aspirin," he says, with one hand on his temple. "I have a headache all of a sudden."

"Oh no. Let's get you some water." We both make our way over to the cabinet next to the fridge. His wheels sound like they're dragging something unidentified behind them across the tile. (Who isn't dragging something unidentified along behind them?) The chair hits my leg and I stiffen. *Relax, Hell Queen, he's your dad.*

"I'm sorry Mom bothered you," he says as I hand him an aspirin.

"You're not bothering me."

"Well, I'm sorry."

"Come on. You know I don't mind." I get him a glass of water for the aspirin.

"Thanks." He swallows. "But you don't have to stay here, Cham. I'm not a *baby*."

He takes one more sip, and I put the glass down on the counter more loudly than I mean to. "Dad, you know you can't stay here by yourself."

"Mom said to think of it as father-daughter time."

"It'll be nice," I agree, but I'm thinking about Gene and Abigail and Hilary and how this is one of those nights that's ours, that freshmen and sophomores and juniors know about and wait for, and now it's happening to me and I'm not there. The refrigerator makes some exasperated throat-clearing noise and I lean against it, looking at my dad. His attention has flickered toward the window again. Whatever universe he's glimpsing when he slips through that pane of glass, no one else is privy to it.

"So what should we do?" I ask, breaking the silence and looking around the house. There's a big bookshelf next to the TV, and in the corner of the living room the wooden chessboard is collecting dust mites. The game got too complicated for him around this time last year, but we could try checkers.

"Let's just relax." My dad wheels over to the light switch and flicks it a couple of times. Nervous fiddling with things is the most annoying part of this disease; just ask any bad daughter anywhere. "You can heat up some of the soup on the stove, and we'll eat together and talk. Mom and I just used the restroom, so you won't have to do that."

Thank god.

He wheels toward the dining room table and calls over his shoulder, "Afterward I can drive you to your friend's house."

I don't bother reminding him that he doesn't drive anymore. I take out my phone to text Abigail, but what am I supposed to say? My dad's situation hasn't exactly come up since we've been friends—not the wheelchair, not the sickness, nothing—and I'm not about to try explaining it with a bunch of emojis. What excuse is good enough that I missed her in Senior Show? The reddish-orange walls are coming for me, and the chandelier and the small circular bulbs embedded in the ceiling. I've never been in such a closed space.

Second set of begrudging texts sent to Gene:

Taking longer than expected but be there ASAP

I don't wait for Gene to respond. I'd rather not know what's going on at school. As long as I don't see my phone, there's no proof I'm missing something.

"I'm sorry you had to come home," Dad says quietly. "I'm so useless with this knee."

"You're not useless." On the top of the bookshelf, there's a picture of him on his motorcycle. I take in this younger version of him: tight jeans (yikes), no helmet, same smile. *You're still that person*, I realize, looking over at him, the age showing by his eyes and the disease showing, well, everywhere.

"Get me that blanket, will you?" He points to the woolen plaid shawl on the sofa, and I drape it around him. His shoulders feel smaller than they used to. "Thank you."

"I'm gonna heat up this soup Mom left, okay?"

He nods and I pretend to have at least a modicum of kitchen skills. The stove clicks on way too eagerly, and I watch for little bubbles to appear in the green split pea soup, like a potion or a swamp with a bunch of dying fish. Every so often I look over at him next to the fake fireplace, where we turn the illusion of coziness on and off with a clicker. His head is drooping. He's falling asleep.

"Dinner's ready, Dad," I call into the silence so silent it hurts my ear canal.

He jolts awake and wheels himself to the table, rubbing his eyes. "I must have dozed off," he says, gripping the table as soon as he can reach it, and pulling himself forward. I take two ceramic bowls from the cabinet, then think better of it and grab two plastic ones instead.

"It's um, oh, whaddayacall it?" he mumbles as I set everything down on the table. *Word retrieval. Another thing to go.*

"Split pea." I pour some into his bowl. "Have a taste."

He takes the spoon from me. "I got it," he says, and immediately spills some on his shirt. This is the sort of thing I'm always trying to avoid, but why? The worst that happens is there's a mess to clean up, and aren't we always cleaning something all the time? I jump up and get a wet paper towel.

"There's someone outside," my dad says, suddenly wheeling to the window and peering through the curtain. At first I think he's in that other universe again, but then I hear tires in the driveway.

"Must be the aide!" I do an about-face and charge for the door. *Sweet, sweet freedom.*

I turn the outside light on and peek through the window by the door. With my hand to it, I can feel the chill of the night and its freedoms. I squint at the walkway, where a pair of sneakers is visible. They are not the white marshmallowish clogs the aides wear. They are boy sneakers. The figure comes into view, and that's when I realize it's not the aide. It's Gene.

10

Days 'til prom: Still 51

IN FIGHT-OR-FLIGHT SITUATIONS, I'M THE SORT OF ANIMAL THAT neither fights nor flights. Instead I shut down and sweat enough to solve the global water crisis, if only I could figure out how to harness my potential.

"Be right back," I call to my dad, throwing his blue puffy mail carrier jacket on. By the time I crack open the door, Gene is already up the stairs and on the porch, his face holding a smile for me.

"Hey," he starts tentatively, but I dart behind the door and slam it shut. *Uh-oh.* "Cham?"

"Hey," I say, opening the door just a crack.

"What's up?" His eyebrows are raised, and there's an army of question marks in his voice.

"Nothing."

He peers around me curiously. "Can I come in?" He steps forward into the doorway, and I draw the door closed on his foot. "Ow!"

"Sorry, let's just stay out here." I squeeze through the door and lurch forward into his arms, more or less plowing into him so that he'll back up a bit. "Hi." I tuck my chin inside the coat's collar. It smells faintly of my dad's cologne and that stale, moldy smell of closets holding things that haven't been used. I'm like a turtle, but sadder and not as cute. "Sorry to disappear like that. I'm having, uh, a family thing."

"Yeah, I got your texts. What's going on?" he asks, pulling away from me to peer nosily into the house. "Cham?"

"Sorry, um, I can't really explain right now."

"Are you okay? You're acting really weird." The question gets picked up by the wind and rustles through my hair. "We could go inside and—"

"No," I say quickly, and back up to the door. "You can't come in."

"Is something going on in there?" he asks suspiciously. He steps around me and peers into the glass on the side of the door with his hand shielding his eyes and leaving a smudge on the pane.

"No, just fucking stop." I grab his arm and yank him a little harder than I mean to.

"Whoa," he says, backing away from me with his hands up. "I can't tell if you're kidding or not."

"It's just—"

"Okay, I guess you're not kidding."

"I'm not trying to be mean." I sigh. "It's just—" But there are too many things in this world merging into that other world. If they collided fully, they'd crush me between them. "I'm sorry, just, I really need you to go."

"Fine, Cham," he says exasperatedly. He starts to leave, then turns back halfway down the porch stairs. "You're not like in trouble, are you?"

"No, no," I say quickly. I see movement in my peripheral vision—my dad has wheeled himself over to the door and he's looking out the window. *Shit.* I wish I could kiss the concern off Gene's face, but I can't function in two worlds at the same time.

"I feel like I can't trust you right now." He grimaces. "You're obviously hiding something from me, but I'm not gonna beg you to tell me."

"I know. I promise it'll all make sense, but you gotta go. I'll text you." I turn back to the house and wait to hear his footsteps disappear, then his car door slam. A moment later he's backing out of the driveway. Another second and he's out of sight.

When it's just me in my dad's mail carrier coat facing the house, where only one light is on, I let myself get pulled into myself entirely. I want to close up inside my room with the lights off and the projector on until everything is better. Until *he* is better, but I guess that'd require a cure for the incurable.

—

Dear Universe,

I'm sorry I can't tell you the truth.

I'm sorry for littering even though there was a
    trash can.

I'm sorry it rained on Saturday.

I'm sorry for not telling you what's wrong with him.

I'm sorry I'd like myself more if I were different.

I'm sorry about this disease that isn't hideable.

I'm sorry clothes aren't optional.

I'm sorry the earth has only one follower, and the
    earth never follows the moon back.

I'm sorry this is a bad apology.

Mostly I'm sorry I don't know the instruction manual
    about me.

I don't know how long I stand outside, but when I get back in, the tips of my ears are numb. It's warm in the mudroom, and immediately the smell hits me. "Dad?" It's vomit and it's everywhere, but I don't know where exactly. I rush into the kitchen and find the sliding door open. I almost gag in the back of my throat. My dad's wheelchair is parked outside the bathroom door.

"Judy, I need a little help," he says from behind the cracked-open door.

I breathe through my mouth and falter outside. "It's me, Dad. Mom won't be back for a bit."

I move his chair out of the way and keep my eyes on everything else in the bathroom that's above where he's slumped over the toilet: the smudge-free mirror, the rack with the bright white hand towel.

"I felt nauseous . . . dizzy," he says, leaning his elbows on the toilet and wiping his mouth. "I got sick—" He seems to lose his train of thought.

"Dad?"

"Sorry," he mumbles into the toilet. "I—I couldn't make it fast enough."

"It's okay. You're okay." I crouch down next to him.

He looks at me for a second. Then something disappears from his eyes and his whole body seizes up. His legs become rigid. Some instinct takes over, and my brain processes the chaos, one detail after another: him in his pajamas on all fours with his legs stiff and shaking, the toilet with the mess around the sides of it, the wheelchair in the doorway watching everything. I try to touch him, but fear is the funniest thing. It's completely invisible and totally physical, and I'm no match for it at all.

"Dad," I say, shaking his shoulder a little. "Dad, are you okay?" He's stopped seizing, but his eyes are only half-open.

"Dad," I say, trying to pull him up to more of an upright position, but I can't lift him. A panicky feeling starts to take over, but then his eyes open a little more.

"Judy, I got so dizzy."

"Dad, it's me, Cham." My eyes burn like all the onions in the world are being cut open at once.

"I can't get my balance." He continues as if he didn't hear me, swaying on his knees as he lifts one and then another. His voice is hoarse, but maybe he'll tell me what to do. If he just tells me what to do, I can do it.

"I'm gonna call Mom," I say, taking my phone out of my back pocket.

"Don't call my mom."

"No, I'm gonna call *my* mom."

I hold the phone to my ear and open the bathroom cabinet for a paper towel or a new roll of toilet paper, but as the phone rings, I realize I have no idea how to start cleaning this up.

"What's up, Cham?" my mom answers briskly. "How's Dad feeling?"

"Not good, he threw up and kind of collapsed in the bathroom, I don't know what happened, he just—" I bite the inside of my cheek until I can picture my teeth coming out the other side.

Then he starts to shake again, not like he usually does, but more violently throughout his whole body.

"Mom, his eyes are like rolling back in his head and he's shaking a lot and—"

"Cham, listen, you should call 9-1-1," she says calmly. The bones in my hands are rigid, and my muscles are petrified, and words are having a hard time unfreezing themselves from my mouth or my throat or wherever words are formed. "Cham, call 9-1-1," she repeats. I try to command myself to move, but I'm paralyzed and it's terrifying. My body is a prison that I am trapped inside. I watch him struggle to get up, his hands shaking and his legs too. *Is this what he feels like?*

I reach out my hand to hold his, then I steady my voice. "I'm calling right now."

Dear Universe,
I will miss the whole show. I will miss the whole night.
I will miss whatever I have to for him to be okay.

Time and sound and space somersault around one another in many minutes of confusion: sirens, firefighters, the ambulance with the white stretcher. They drop my dad off in the emergency room, and one of the EMTs walks me to the waiting room. My body is here, but that's just my body.

Texts sent to Gene while I am someplace unknown entirely:

Situation got worse C

Gonna be a bit more than an hour C

G Is everything okay?

G I'm kinda pissed

G and freaked out

G You really didn't want me in your house

I'll be at school as soon as I can C

I'm sorry C

G Can I do something?

Tell Abigail I'm sorry and I'll call her ASAP C

G If you tell me what's going on maybe I can help

The text I do not send: I don't think anything can help.

Every second waiting outside the ER while my dad is inside with my mom and the doctors is agonizing. Part of me is bummed about tonight, but the other part of me can't even believe there's a part of me that's bummed, as if there's another world that could even be slightly as important as this one. At first I try to keep on top of what's going on at Senior Night. People are posting pictures and videos and stories of themselves making their own pizza, bouncing in the inflatable castle, competing in a Ping-Pong tournament.

Eventually it makes me feel worse, so I play a game in my head where I create stories for people waiting outside the ER with me: *The guy with the oxygen tank is Jimmy. He's made a crash landing from Mars and hasn't adjusted properly. That other guy with the bloody hand had a fight with a mirror. The mirror won.*

Eventually, around ten, after three hours that felt like three days, my mom comes into the waiting room.

I jump up and she gives me a hug. "Is he okay? What happened?"

"He's okay. Come on." She pushes the doors to the ER open. As soon as we step in, we're submerged in the chaos of other people's emergencies. I block out the sounds of computers and monitors and people in pain and doctors with instructions.

"What happened?" I repeat, hurrying to keep up with her.

"They don't know what happened exactly. It was some sort of neurological episode. He lost consciousness at a bad time and was lucky not to really have hurt himself."

"I don't get it, though."

"It's like a stroke, but not exactly."

"What do you mean, *not exactly?*" We stop in front of a wing with ten beds, all with their curtains drawn around them.

"That's part of what's so frustrating about his sickness, Cham. They don't fully understand it. It's related to his brain degenerating, but they don't know exactly *how.*"

"Well, that's stupid." I glare at a nurse wheeling a cart of some unidentifiable red liquid, as if it's her fault that science doesn't have all the answers.

My mom kisses my forehead. "He's not himself, okay? It was traumatic getting him here. He's very confused about where he is, and they've given him meds, so just..." She trails off.

When she opens the curtain, the rings scrape the metal rod.

"Hi, Daddy," I say. He looks very small under the blankets with his salt-and-pepper hair staticky against the pillow. Either these hospital beds are ginormous or I never realized this particular quality about humans: how utterly tiny we are in the face of everything that happens to us.

I approach his bed and touch the cool metal railing. "Hi, Dad," I say again. My voice is too loud or too perky or too high-pitched. Everything is wrong. He turns his head and jolts his arm toward me.

"They're keeping me locked up here. I'm a prisoner. You gotta get me out of here, Cham."

My eyes widen and nearly fall out of my head. I look at my mom, wishing that she'd warned me better or that she'd fixed this already. She takes his hand in hers.

"It's okay, Scott, they're just doing some tests on you. They're here to help you."

"No, they're out to get me. Look at them in their

uniforms," he says as a nurse walks by, fumbling with her stethoscope. "I'm gonna sue them. I'm gonna sue them all."

A bit of spit flies from his mouth and hits me like acid rain. This isn't my dad. This isn't the person who held my hand in the car after I lost the spelling bee because it's impossible to spell tomato with an *E*.

"You're okay, Dad," I say in a wobbly voice that couldn't possibly be convincing.

"I'm not okay," he scoffs. "Look at me." He holds up his arm with the clothespin tracking his blood oxygen. It's attached to a machine by the wall. "They're keeping me tied to this bed without food or water."

I don't realize I've been backing away from the bed until I hit the boundary of the curtain. "He's confused," my mom repeats. "The delirium will wear off soon, I hope. We should let him sleep, but I thought it might help—"

"You girls want to keep me here, don't you?" He points his finger at us, and it's steadier than usual. "Cham, help me get out of here."

"I'm sorry, I can't. You have to stay."

The flap of his gown slips down his shoulder, where a bruise is growing down his arm. He shakes his head and makes a *tsk* sound. When he looks at me again, his face is like a stone sculpture of his face, but the features are slightly off.

"You're a disappointment, Cham," he says, and turns onto his side, the sheets making a terrible starchy noise, his breath getting heavier. "You are such a disappointing daughter."

Dear Universe,

My bones come apart like tectonic plates. What was normal shifts and falls. Everything is moving and changing position and getting kicked out of where it was. How do you survive an earthquake? How do you stay steady when everything everywhere is breaking down? And afterward who comes in to sort through the wreckage?

11

Days 'til prom: 50

A SPLATTERING OF TEXTS RECEIVED LAST NIGHT AND OPENED this morning:

7:37 PM

G I hope things are okay

8:02 PM

G I know you said it's a family thing but you were acting so weird at your house

8:02 PM

G Like you were lying to me about something

9:42 PM

G Do you know when you'll be back? We should talk in person.

10:09 PM

G I guess you're not gonna make it back to school tonight?

9:11 PM

A WHERE ARE YOU?

9:37 PM

H Gene's been wandering around like a lost puppy

11:10 PM

G I'm worried

11:12 PM

G Can you please answer?

11:48 PM

G Guess not.

7:12 AM

Gene I'm sorry I never texted C

7:12 AM

I know I ruined our special night C

7:12 AM

I'll explain later C

7:17 AM

Ugh Abigail C

7:18 AM

This family stuff is complicated C

7:18 AM

I'll explain as soon as I can but right now
we're still in the hospital

9:12 AM

Just got your texts / talked to Gene

9:12 AM

He said you kicked him out of your house?

9:12 AM

Is your family okay?

9:12 AM

So sad you couldn't come to Senior Night :(

10:12 AM

I don't really wanna talk right now

10:12 AM

hope everything's okay with your family

10:36 AM

I'm sorry about everything

10:36 AM

Phone's gonna die

10:36 AM

Ttys

Sometime in the middle of the night, they moved my dad to a new room, where they gave him more pills. Here, in between bouts of kind of sleeping and checking texts, I look at people's feeds for updates from Senior Night: Gene and Doug stuffing pizza in each other's mouth, Abigail dancing with Helga in the moon bounce, Josie winning the superlative Most Likely to Succeed. In one picture of Hilary's, I see Gene talking closely with Helga at the drinks table, and it makes me want to throw my phone down. I know it's stupid to be jealous, but sometimes I'm stupid. Eventually I turn my phone off. Maybe if I don't see any more pictures or texts or calls, I won't have missed anything at all.

"You're awake," my mom whispers as she comes into the room holding a disposable cup of sludge. "The doctor will be in soon."

"Dad's been asleep a long time," I say, looking over at him in the bed.

"It was the medicine," my mom says for like the eighth or eighteenth time. I help myself to some of her coffee.

"He was really agitated. He was saying all these things, that I disappointed him." I puncture the rim of the cup with my nails, carving out little moons in the material.

"He didn't mean it. Just remember, it's not him, it's—"

"I know. The disease." I try to see my reflection in the dark liquid surface of the coffee, but you know that feeling of looking and looking and still not seeing?

"Why don't you go home and get some sleep," my mom offers, straightening her back to meet the doctor who's talking to a nurse outside the doorway. "Or maybe text

Abigail or go for a run. It'd be good to get out of here for a bit."

I shake my head. My bones feel too heavy to run. "I'll stay. I'm just gonna get some breakfast."

"Okay. Give yourself a break, Cham. This stuff always takes a while."

I stand and nod. When I'm in the hallway I look back. My mom's in the seat by my dad's bed, and he's sleeping so deeply he's not even snoring.

That's when I realize that this could be it. *It* it. Up until now I hadn't thought about there being a real ending to this. Sure, I'd thought about an ending, but *an* ending is different from *the* ending. *An* end is prom and graduation and Nicaragua. But *the* end, the Real End, is a lot more final than that. It's completely and totally irreversible, and it could be anytime, from now to years from now. I walk toward the stairs. The only real deadline is the final one. It's not up to any of us and we can't push it back.

The cafeteria is lively—not the food, the food is soggy—but there aren't sick people who get breakfast in bed as the one perk of dying. There are other people between these potato-colored, windowless walls, and I couldn't be more psyched to see them. "The hash browns are worth waiting for," the woman in bright yellow scrubs says to me as I get in line. *I highly doubt that.* As I browse the cooler for a drink, I hear my name from somewhere in the corner of the cafeteria.

"Cham?" My body freezes. *I'm not "Cham" here.* "Cham?"

I turn from the cartons of lemonade and orange juice and spot Brendan, of all people, eating by himself in the corner of the cafeteria.

"What are you doing here?" he hollers. Approximately everyone in the cafeteria turns in their blue plastic chairs. "Are you okay?"

I glare at him and select an orange juice. *I'm fine,* I mouth, then hurry toward the register. When it's my turn, I hand the woman my mom's debit card.

"Sorry, we only take hospital bucks here." She points to the sign by the computer. It says SORRY WE ONLY TAKE HOSPITAL BUCKS HERE.

"Oh, um, I don't have hospital bucks." I consider putting my food back, but I'm starving. "Are you sure you can't take a card?"

She pats down her thinning, orangish-dyed hair and eyes what I imagine is a growing line behind me. "I've worked here ten years. I'm sure."

I look down at my scrambled eggs, wondering how I'm supposed to divorce them so soon, before we even got married.

"Hi, Jackie," Brendan says, appearing beside me. "I can get her." He's wearing a maroon vest and a sticker that says

I'M SO HAPPY TO VOLUN-CHEER! He holds his hospital ID out, and she takes it with a smile. "You got it, Brendan."

Once she swipes his card, we walk toward the dispensers for napkins and plastic ware. I wonder if I should say *Thank you* or *Thank you so much*. "Thanks," I finally say.

"Don't worry about it."

We hover by the recycling bins as I wolf down my breakfast. The eggs taste like packing peanuts.

"So is it your dad?" he asks.

I start to shake my head, but then my lip trembles. "Yeah."

"What happened?"

I look out at the gloomy cafeteria and lean against the three bins behind me: compost, recycling, trash. I feel comforted knowing there's a proper receptacle for everything. "I found him in the bathroom after he had some sort of episode thing and yeah..." Remembering it is like remembering a TV show, a dark one with very good acting, an Emmy-quality nightmare.

"Wow, that must have been awful," he says.

"And now he's all confused and thinks the doctors are holding him here against his will, and when I said I couldn't get him out, he told me I was a disappointment." My cheeks are hot and my armpits are sweating. "It's just that this sort of thing happened last year and I completely froze and didn't call the ambulance and he could've died and now this time even though I did—"

These tears in my eyes are giving me salt goggles.

Everything is blurry, including signs that hang from the ceiling and the shape of Brendan as he comes closer to me.

"Do you want a hug?" he asks. "Laughter and hugs. Best medicine."

I hesitate, then nod, even though it's so cheesy. At this point I'd let an ax murderer hug me, just as long as some 98.6-degree something will grab hold of me and keep me from falling.

"That blows," he says, and puts his arms around me and gives me a squeeze. He's a lot taller than I am, which puts my nose a bit beneath his armpit. It smells like he just showered. "Really blows."

He pulls away from me, and I remind gravity to work its magic on me. *Keep my feet on the ground and the hair on my head. Feel free to ignore any remaining tears, though. You can give those the middle finger, and they can fall right back up into my head.*

"I'm sleep deprived—I don't know what I'm saying." I pull back and make stern eye contact with him. "Tell no one about this."

Brendan laughs. "If you haven't noticed, people don't exactly gather round when I open my mouth." His smile flickers.

"That must be lonely."

He nods and clears his throat. "Well, I have to do volun-cheer rounds. Maybe I could stop in and talk to your dad later if—"

"Hell no. I mean, thanks, but hell no."

"Well, I don't know if you're doing anything, but if you're looking for some time to kill, you could come with me on a round." He starts to walk away. I pause for a moment, deciding what to do. Finally I run after him.

"Hey, wait! What's a round?"

In the children's ward there are large posters covered in brightly colored handprints and trees and suns. Friendly forest creatures wave at me. I don't wave back. Brendan walks in wheeling a suitcase he grabbed from one of the volunteer lockers, and I trail behind him.

"Are you moving into the children's wing?" I ask, pressing the button so that the doors open automatically.

"Are you moving toward permanent sarcasm?"

"I thought laughter healed the world," I grumble to myself, stepping out of the way of anyone in scrubs. We turn into a hallway with a large bin full of toys at the end of it. Midway down the hall, Brendan stops abruptly and knocks on a door. It has a paper plate on it that reads *Sal* in puffy paint.

"Come in," says a man's voice.

Brendan opens the door and I see a middle-aged man holding up a book to a hospital bed full of stuffed animals. He looks a bit old for the children's ward, in my opinion.

"Sorry to interrupt," Brendan says. "Should I come back?"

I look back and forth between the two of them.

"Hi, Brendan!" The pile of stuffed animals erupts, and a little girl launches out of bed wearing bright green pajamas. She goes right for his legs and gives them a hug. "Is that the magic suitcase?"

"Shh—not so loud!" Brendan says with mock alarm, "You don't wanna wake the stuffies!"

Sal looks around with wide eyes. Chuckling, the man gets up from his bedside chair. It's the hospital kind that is just comfortable enough to coax you into the worst night's sleep of your life. "How are you today, Brendan?" he asks.

Brendan reaches into his pocket and smooths a fake mustache onto his lip.

"Brendan is good," Brendan says, putting his suitcase on the bed and opening it up. *Now I remember why he's so annoying.* "This is my friend Cham. She's hanging out today if that's okay with you."

The man smiles at me, but Sal frowns skeptically. "Okay, but I can still pick first?"

"I'm gonna grab some coffee," the man says, heading for the door. Brendan gives him a thumbs-up sign.

"Bye, Daddy," Sal calls.

I look at Brendan, waiting for him to fill me in. "Uh..."

"Cham doesn't know how to play, so we have to show her." Brendan puts the suitcase on the bed and Sal jumps on it. "Go ahead," he says. "You can pick first."

She rummages through the items, spilling them onto the

bed. There are all kinds of things inside the suitcase, from masks to polka-dot gloves to glasses with big noses attached.

"Sal will take the dragon head." Sal puts the mask covered in dark green sequins on, and her eyes are visible through the mouth. "What will you pick?" she asks, turning to look at me.

"Um." Again I look at Brendan for some sort of explanation. When it's apparent there won't be one, I walk hesitantly toward the suitcase, then take the first thing I see. The shiny plastic crown is a little small on my head.

"I'll pick this."

"*Cham* will pick the crown," she corrects me. I look up at Brendan like *Are you poisoning the youth of America with third-person speak?*

"Cham's never done this before," Brendan reminds Sal, stroking his fake mustache. The brown hairs catch the dismal hospital light. "Can you explain it to her?"

Sal giggles and pulls the sequined dragon head up so it doesn't fall over her eyes. "Sal doesn't know how to explain it. It's just fun."

"Then let's show her an example."

Brendan takes a seat on the edge of the bed. Sal and I watch as he makes a pillow with his hands and pretends to sleep on it. When he "wakes up," he's looking at me. "Brendan is tired today. He had bad dreams that it rained coconuts."

Sal laughs and sits up straighter. "Sal is mad today." She

runs her fingers over the green sequins covering her head. "Sal wants to go home and see her kitty, but she can't leave yet because the rash is still there and no one knows why."

"That's poopy," Brendan says, and Sal giggles. He looks at me. "Your turn, Cham."

I adjust the crown on my head and try not to feel awkward. "So I just tell you about my day?"

"*Cham* tells us," Sal corrects me.

"Uh, okay, well . . ." I glimpse my reflection in the window. My hair is a frizzy mess, and my eyes are practically swollen shut. Add the crown and I look like I hunt baby animals for fun. "Cham is tired today too," I say, recalling the restless sleep in the chair by my dad's bed. "Just like so, so, *so* tired." *She had a nightmare that turned out to be true.* "And Cham is scared," I hear myself say. I take the plastic crown off, and some of my hair catches in it. "Cham is really, really scared." Sal looks up at me with a little frown. I get up quickly and wipe my eyes. *Why did I have to turn something silly into something depressing as hell?* "I should go."

Sal picks at one of the dark green sequins. "Sal is scared too." Her voice wavers some but holds. For a moment I'm afraid she's going to cry, and then I'll really have done it. Instead she sits up straighter and pulls off one of the dark green sequins. It flutters to the bed. "You know, it's okay to be scared," she says with authority.

I turn back toward her and then look at Brendan. He

nods. "Brendan's scared most minutes of most days. That's why he carries a spare pair of underwear."

"Ew!" Sal hoots. "Maybe Brendan needs a diaper!"

I laugh with them and place the crown back in the suitcase, feeling lighter somehow, but also heavier. Like I've sunk into a deep part of myself that I've been fighting against. After an eternal heartbeat, Brendan says to Sal, "I think it's time for Sal and Cham and Brendan to rest. How about some checkers?"

"I get red!" Sal is back to the elation that greeted us.

"You guys rest while playing checkers?" I ask, a smile returning despite myself. "How does that work?"

"Well, sometimes it's a lot to be a Brendan—"

"And a Sal," she pipes up. "So we give that Brendan and that Sal a break, and this Sal and this Brendan take over for a while. Don't worry, she'll come back," Sal says quickly as I try to keep a nonjudgmental look on my face.

"Brendan's going to be himself his whole life," Brendan says to me. "Sometimes I relieve him of that." They start playing checkers and I think about that. *I'm going to be myself for my whole life too.*

Brendan beats Sal in about five minutes. "No sick-kid privileges," he says, hopping over her last piece.

"Aw, man."

Brendan folds the board up and opens the suitcase. "Brendan and Cham gotta go now," he says. "Is Sal ready to come back?"

She scrunches her eyes closed and takes the dragon head off. "I'm back," she says. Brendan pockets his mustache and gives her a high five.

"I'm back too. See you later, Sal," Brendan says, then to me with a smile, "It's time for Cham to come back too. Come on." He holds out his hand to me. Before I know what I'm doing, my hand is in his.

"I don't think Cham is ready to come back." Sal giggles, shattering my inner silence.

"Cham?" Brendan squeezes my hand.

"Oh!" I pull my hand back, mortified. I guess that *was* a strange time for holding hands. I step into the hallway as Sal is following Brendan toward the door. She waves, and he puts his suitcase down to give her a good-bye hug. Strangely enough, I'm actually *glad* I opened my big fat mouth full of feelings. It seemed to help all of us.

"See Sal soon?" Brendan asks. She nods, then waves again as he and I walk down the hall in silence. The wheels of the suitcase slide against the floor. We're quiet until we reach the elevator.

"Well, I should go," I say, pressing the button. "But what was up with that?"

He laughs and plays with the fabric of his tutu. "Wasn't it obvious?"

I shake my head.

"When my brother was dying, he started putting on this costume every day and telling stories about himself, you know, narrating his life. He put on a mustache and a tutu and he'd say things like 'Looks like Adam won't be dying today!' or, on bad days, 'Everyone say farewell to Adam! This could be it!' The therapists thought he wasn't facing reality, but I think sometimes the only way to know the truth about ourselves is to *not* be ourselves for a little while. Like, trick ourselves through our suffering."

He looks at me without blinking or turning away. I study the features of his face and try to piece that together. "Heal with laughter?" I ask.

"That's the goal." A curl has fallen out of the little bun on top of his head, and he tucks it behind his ear. "Well, I should snag this," he says as the elevator doors open.

"Yeah, I should go too."

"What's your number?" he asks, holding the doors open with his foot as he takes his phone out.

"Uh, mine?" For some reason it makes me nervous. Not that I think he's asking for my number *like that*.

"Just in case you need a distraction," he adds, looking up at me with thick, dark eyelashes that I've somehow only noticed now. "Or want to talk about being scared."

I swallow a tangled lump of feelings. "Right, uh, here, I'll put it in."

When I'm done, he presses the button and removes his foot. "Nice to see you get the feels, Cham," he teases.

"I love getting the feels," I call through the crack

between the doors that's getting smaller and smaller as they inevitably move toward each other. *I love them so much that I lock them in the basement of my heart like a hostage.*

The doors fully close. It's just me staring at my warped reflection in the metal panels. I snort, then snort again, realizing I needed to take the elevator too.

Dear Universe,
Have you ever been wrong about a person? When you go to school with someone day after day and year after year, it becomes impossible to really know them beyond how you think you know them. Being in high school is essentially being stuck in how everyone sees you and knows you and has seen you and has known you. If there were a way around that, do you think it'd be possible to fall for someone you never even expected to stumble over?

Later that afternoon, the door to my dad's hospital room is open. He's looking out the window with a stony expression on his face while my mom and I wait to go in. It's the calmest I've seen him since we got here, but he looks so *sick* with all the machines keeping track of him. *Aren't you scared?* I wonder.

"Oh, he's awake—let's go in, Cham," my mom says,

putting away her phone. "I know Dad would like to see you."

"Would he?" I mumble. "He said—"

My mom has duffel bags under her eyes. "He was confused, Cham. I know it hurt, but he didn't mean it. You are not a disappointing daughter, so let it go, okay?"

She takes her glasses off, cleans them even though they're not dirty, then leads me through the door. "Are those fingernail marks on your wrist?" she asks suddenly, taking my arm and pulling my sleeve up.

"No." I yank my hand back.

She pauses for a minute, the decision playing out on her face, whether or not she'll believe me. "I know it's a stressful time, but if you're not managing your anger okay, I need to know about it." She lowers her voice so that none of the nurses or patients around us can hear. "Are you scratching yourself? Because if you're starting to hurt yourself—"

"Mom, I was never *hurting* myself. Digging my nails into my skin like three times in eighth grade isn't *hurting* myself."

She glares at me. "Don't downplay self-harm, Cham. Three fingernail marks is still three fingernail marks. If you feel like you might be going down a slippery slope—"

"Mom," I say too loudly, "I know how to ask for help if I need it."

"Good." She sighs, then knocks lightly on my dad's door,

even though it's open. "Scott?" she says as we walk in. "How are you, honey?"

My dad turns to look at us, his face unsmiling. "I feel lousy. Look at me."

"Are you in pain anywhere?" my mom asks, touching his forehead gently.

"Everything hurts."

"Can I get you something, Daddy?" I ask, my voice kind of squeaking. His hospital gown is fresh and it fits him properly now, but the more he looks like he belongs here, the more disconcerting it is.

"I just want to go home," he says.

"I know, honey." My mom kisses him on the cheek. "Soon."

There's a knock on the door and we all look up. "Hey, Mr. Myles," a doctor with short hair and a big smile says. "I'm Dr. Bhatti, part of the neurology team here at Beth Israel."

My dad extends an unusually steady hand to shake hers.

"It's not really shaking, Dad!" I accidentally shout. I look up at him, expecting his face to register a miracle. It doesn't.

"See?" the doctor says, smiling. "Didn't I tell you the medicine would help?"

"It makes me nauseous," he says flatly.

"Here," my mom says, offering him a white paper cup

from the bedside table. "The nurse said you could take this anti-nausea tablet."

"I don't want all these pills," my dad says, and struggles to get up in bed.

"Mr. Myles." The doctor looks back and forth between me and my parents. "You have a quickly progressing state of Parkinson's disease, especially rare for your age. Treating with a high dose of L-dopa could greatly increase your quality of life. You've already started seeing the benefits."

My dad looks out the window and says nothing. The rain is saying plenty.

"I had a motorcycle accident years ago," he finally says, turning to look the doctor straight in the eye. "Concussion, brain damage, stitches, everything. The doctor I saw then said there might be repercussions later in life, and here we are."

"I understand that," Dr. Bhatti says gently. "But your chart shows that you already received a diagnosis a couple of years ago. It never hurts to get a second opinion, but my opinion is also that you have Parkinson's."

"No one knows anything," my dad says angrily. "You people can't help me. There isn't even a clear set of symptoms, let alone a cure." He shakes his head. "Don't get my hopes up that you can help me with your medicine. I won't buy it."

Suddenly I understand. Denial is much more than a fear of facing the truth. It's a fear of facing hope, of *allowing* light into a dark place, only to find out later that the flash-light's out of batteries, the fire's gone out, the sun is dead. Now the hole you made just lets the rain in. And you're standing in a dark room that's filling with water.

I climb over the bedrail and squeeze myself into the space between it and my dad. He puts his arm around me, but his voice is still angry. "When I was young and on a big adventure, I had a motorcycle accident and I got hurt and I'm paying for it now. I took a risk and now I have to live with the consequences, but I wouldn't take it back. None of it."

The doctor grimaces and tucks her iPad under her arm. "I don't know what else to say," she says. She turns to my mom and hands her a packet of papers and a few bottles. "You have my suggested treatment plan."

"So I give these to him three times a day?" my mom asks, one hand on her hip, one hand holding the pill bot-tles. "And those for the nausea and that for the panic?" She keeps talking about my dad like he's not even there. "What if he has an episode again? Should he be taking anything for the agitation?"

"No, try this for a few months," the doctor urges, nearly turning her back to the bed. It's like my dad has been dis-missed to his own universe now, the Universe for People Who Can't. It's a million degrees, but I snuggle closer to the warmth of his body.

"I really wish you'd brought him in sooner," Dr. Bhatti

says to my mom in a hushed voice. "We could have been treating him properly, and this whole incident might not have happened. It's really dangerous not to undergo proper treatment when—"

"I was complying with his wishes." My mom's face stiffens. "Besides, was it really so crazy then to think—I mean, *couldn't* it be the accident?"

Dr. Bhatti touches my mom's arm. "Mrs. Myles. Scott has Parkinson's. I know you want to protect your husband, but the best way you can protect him is by giving him the proper care."

My mom walks the doctor out and they talk in lower voices than before. *Progressive . . . confusion . . . stiffened gait . . . hallucinations . . . trouble swallowing . . .* I stuff my fingers in my ears so I don't have to hear about the inevitable: how the disease will progress, which symptoms are likely to get worse, what will inevitably happen when it wins.

"Bye again," the doctor calls before she leaves. "I hope to run into you at the Brain Degeneration Walk later this month!"

"Yes, you too," my mom grumbles.

My dad opens his eyes and puts his hand up, then pushes the button to sit up in his bed.

"What walk?" I ask my mom when the door closes, pretending this is the first I've heard of it. She doesn't seem to hear me.

"Let's get out of here," my dad says to my mom. "Please."

"I know this was a lot," my mom says, getting my dad's shoes and clothes off the spare chair. "But we're going home now, honey. Things are going to get better."

"Much better," I echo, but my mouth tastes like aspartame as soon as I say it.

"It's not going to get better," he says, ignoring the sweater my mom is holding out to him. "And neither am I."

Dear Universe,

I would guesstimate that if the average human spirit weighs 13.8 pounds, mine is coming in around an ounce. There comes a point when you can't operate from two separate worlds anymore. They have to line up, otherwise it's impossible to function in either. Science dubs it an eclipse when the earth, moon, and sun form a line, casting shadows and obscuring each other, but there's no specially named event for their collision. In other words, eclipses are cute. You can get special glasses for them. A collision, on the other hand, would be gruesome: no catchy phrase, no witnesses. You know the dinosaurs? No, you don't. You know their fossils.

12

Days 'til prom: 49

"Oh my god, is everything all right?" Abigail answers when I call her on Sunday after a long sleep. "I was so worried."

"Yeah, everything's okay." Except that my dad hasn't left his room, and anytime my mom or I bring him food, he says, "Get me out of this place. I want to go home." His face is even angry when he sleeps. "I'm sorry I missed your show."

"Aw, thanks. Don't even worry about missing it. Just like, what happened? I know it couldn't be good if you missed the whole night."

I look up at the ceiling. When my projector isn't on it's just an expanse of black. "Um, my dad had this whole episode thing and we thought he was having a heart attack and yeah."

"Oh, Cham, I'm so sorry. That must've been terrible."

"It was a lot," I say, recalling how steely his eyes were when he said I was a disappointment. "But how was Friday night? What did I miss? Was it fun?"

"So fun! I mean not *so* fun," she adds quickly. "It's not like you missed anything *big*, and there'll be plenty of other fun nights, like prom and stuff, so don't worry about it, but, yeah, it was good."

"I saw the video. You broke it down as usual."

She laughs. "Thanks."

I open up my senior year time capsule and move the items around. "Did anyone even sleep? I saw the mats getting set up in the gym and people getting sleeping bags but—"

"Hardly. I mean, it was probably four AM when that started."

"And how did superlatives go?"

She pauses. For a second I wonder if we have a bad connection. "Hilary and I won Class Friendship," she says finally.

"Oh," I stammer. "Congratulations."

"It's just 'cause we've been friends so long, you know? It's not that we're *closer* than anyone else."

"Yeah, totally, one sec." I stuff the time capsule box back under my bed and cough a little, not knowing what to say.

After a few seconds she says, "So have you talked to Gene? It must kinda suck that you didn't get to your special night?"

"Not yet. I feel really awkward about kicking him out of my house and kind of disappearing on the night we were supposed to do it."

"It was a family emergency, though." *Not when I kicked him out.* "True. Hey, I saw like eight pictures with him and Helga together. It's stupid to be jealous, right?"

"Yeah...they were having some long talk 'cause they're in this group project and—"

She goes on and on about how security has to come from "inside oneself." Then she catches me up on everything I missed. *Doug hooked up with Jared. Danika snuck booze in and almost got caught 'cause she was too drunk again.*

It's too much. I need a shuttle back to that world to comprehend that it exists. I just don't know if there's a vehicle that can move fast through dark space.

After Abigail and I hang up, I torture myself by looking through more pictures of the night. I know I have an e-mail from Evelyn about my essay, but I just don't see how I can focus on that when there's this picture of Abigail and Hilary receiving their big BFF hearts. Oh, and Gene with Helga *again.* Speaking of, why the hell is Gene being so distant? I know it wasn't cool to keep him out of my house, but Abigail's right. Family emergencies should be a free pass to be an impolite hostess, secretive girlfriend, and whatever else I need to be to keep my worlds separate.

Nervous text exchange with Gene that I just want to get over with:

I'm so sorry about Friday night. I know I owe you an explanation. Can we talk? G

G I need a little space, Cham.

Well wanna go for a run? C

Sorry, I guess that's not really space. C

Ok, guess I'll just see you in school tomorrow. C

We're okay right? C

Days 'til prom: 48

Selfie in the girls' bathroom, where a certain girlfriend attempts to explain her rudeness with the help of her friends who are better friends with each other than they are with her (not an opinion, but a fact the whole school voted on): high ponytail, freshly brushed teeth, honest eyes.

"I'm sure you'll be fine after you talk in person," Hilary says, handing me a bag from inside her backpack. "Do you want to borrow some of my makeup?"

"Yeah, Cham, you just need some color," Abigail chimes in, pinching my cheeks in front of the mirror.

I splash water on my face. Once Abigail's passed me a paper towel, I burrow my face in its starchy brown ill-absorbent material.

"Seriously, you're welcome to any of my makeup," Hilary says.

"Is that a hint?" I ask.

Hilary shakes her head innocently, then unzips the makeup bag. "Well, okay, maybe a small one."

Abigail frowns and tilts my face toward hers. "It looks like you haven't slept since you hit puberty."

Hilary swipes blush on me and takes out some tinted lip balm. When she opens it I say, "Ew, what is that?"

It smells like vanilla got it on with cinnamon and had a baby called strawberry fields. You know when too much of a good thing becomes an awful thing?

"I hate makeup," I say, fanning my now-stinging cheeks.

"Well, sometimes it's good to expose yourself to the things you hate," Abigail says. "You know, for personal-growth reasons."

Hilary attacks my lip with the balm and dons her British accent. "You're gonna love it, darling, just love it." She pockets it again and heads out of the bathroom. "Good luck, Cham darling."

"You got this," Abigail says knowingly, and slaps my butt as she follows Hilary out.

"Okay, thanks, bye."

I wait until she's closed the door to turn to my reflection. After a few seconds of licking my sticky lips, I nod and say, "Okay, time to find Gene." A girl flushes the toilet and comes out of the last stall with a creeped-out look on her face. Like she's never talked to the mirror before? Please. I have my best conversations with things that don't answer.

The lunch line is short, and I order two chicken sandwiches just so I can have two sides of Tater Tots. When I catch sight of Gene at the other end of the cafeteria, and he catches sight of me, it's not the war-separated lovers' look I had hoped for. It's confusion. Distance. He says something to Doug, who turns around to look at me, and then Gene walks the perimeter of the cafeteria toward me. I do the same, past tables of people separated by grade and interest, even though we're probably separated by much less than we think.

"Hey," I say to Gene when I reach the table where he always sits.

"Hi," he says, hands in his pockets.

"How are you?"

"Um, you know, okay." He sits down and I pull a chair toward his. We're on the outskirts of the cafeteria, but I feel like we're on the outskirts of two separate universes.

"So what happened?" he asks. "You kicked me out of your house and pretty much disappeared all weekend. I had no idea—"

"I know, I'm sorry."

"Like that was really shitty."

"I know, but please, just listen." I reach for his hand, but he pulls away. The lines on my palm don't get a chance to cross the lines on his. "I promise it wasn't just me screwing with you. My dad has this health issue that's really hard to talk about, so I had to go home and be with him, but then we ended up having to go to the hospital and—"

"I don't get it, though," he says. "You still could have told me something instead of pushing me out."

"No, I really couldn't, at least not then, but everything's okay now, well not *okay*, but—"

I drift off, he picks at some foreign object on the table between us. "Well, I'm glad things are better, but I have to tell you something too," he says apologetically.

"What?"

He looks down at his hands. "There was this thing with Helga at Senior Night." I see her across the cafeteria with Rose and a few other girls from the dance team. *No no no no no.* "And, um, well, it's just that I kind of think—" He finally looks up from his hands, and his voice goes up like it's a question I'm supposed to answer. "I kind of think that maybe we should break up, 'cause Helga and I kind of kissed?"

"What?" I jerk away from him and my elbow ends up in the ketchup on my tray. It's a minefield, sitting this close in the cafeteria, but we are soldiers of love. Or so I *thought*.

"I'm sorry, Cham, but I was upset Friday night and I started talking to Helga—"

I back my chair up into the chaos of the cafeteria. "*Helga* Helga?" As in the German exchange student who tongued a hot dog roll in front of the whole senior class? Yes, it was hot, but c'mon. *Anyone* can tongue a hot dog roll.

"She opened up to me about how hard it is being so far away from home, and I was really comfortable talking to her about stuff too, and we ended up talking for like hours—"

"So while I was at the hospital with my parents, you were with another girl?"

He blushes. "Well, yeah, but you pushed me away—"

"BECAUSE MY DAD WAS SICK." I clench my fist and stare at my chicken patty. If it weren't dead already, I'd murder it.

"Cham, I didn't mean for it to be like that."

"We were going to *do it* this weekend. And now, two days later, we're breaking up?"

"I'm sorry," he says. "I'm really sorry."

"I can't believe you."

"You're the one who was acting so sketchy," he says exasperatedly. "You never let me come in when I pick you up, even when it takes you forever to get in the car because those boots lace up all the way to your knee. I mean, you literally pushed me out of your house the other day, and I don't know, I have this feeling you're not letting me in."

"Not letting you in?" But what if it's a mess inside? What if keeping you out is the neighborly thing to do?

"And that's fine, 'cause like this is just a fun high school thing, but then we should have *fun*. We're graduating soon and going to college. It's not like—" He loosens his tie and doesn't look at me as he says, "What I mean is, high school is almost over. I realized when I was talking to Helga that I want to have fun for the rest of it, not be tied to one person, you know?"

I peel the bun from the chicken patty, feeling its meatiness between my fingers. Then I wind up and slap him across the face with it. The grease coating my fingers feels damn good.

"What the hell!" he cries, jumping back out of his chair. He's touching his face like he's a burn victim, but the patty was lukewarm. "Are you kidding me?"

A few people nearby gasp/laugh, which is a combination of *Oh shit!* and *LOL*. They point their phones at me, but I can't stop my hands. I pick up a handful of Tater Tots and whip them at him one by one: assault by tiny compact potatoes. I keep firing my deep-fried ammunition, but the laughter does something to me. Suddenly my eyes are burning.

"Come on, Cham. Those are too good to waste on him," Abigail says, coming up behind me and gently pulling me away. "Get back to your lunches," she directs the gawkers, shooing their stares with her hand. "Mind your goddamn business, okay?"

"Psycho," some guy behind me says.

"Fuck off," I say to no one and everyone. One of the lunch aides is headed toward me, shaking her head. I turn around and weave through tables, thinking that the faster I run, the faster I'll disappear. And it's true to an extent. The sooner my feet hit the floor, the sooner I'll get to the place where no one can see me. And if no one was there to see me, did my heart really break at all?

13

Days 'til prom: Still 48

IT'S CHILLY AND GRAY WHEN I BURST OUT OF THE BUILDING. Even in my skirt and combat boots, running feels as good as hell, just me and my feet coming down on the ground, getting far, far away from Gene and school and everything else in that world.

"God fucking dammit," I yell, then run faster, past the fire station and the sub shop and the dog-grooming place. The air smells like mud and new things being born in mud. Instead of feeling refreshed, I feel like I'm under mud too. Mr. Garcia gave me five days of detention. Five! The world just has no sympathy sometimes. Gene kissed someone else. My worlds finally got in the way of each other. Everything's coming apart. *Where am I going? Where do people* go?

I keep going past the center of town, toward the office buildings, the strip malls, the dump. The muscles in my legs burn as I run up a sand hill in the back of a parking lot. The hill is high enough that I can maybe figure out where to go from here. When I get to the top and the only view is more parking lots and sand and office buildings, Evelyn's voice rings in my head, pouring her heart out about philosophy: *It's not just an academic subject. It's the consciousness we bring to our lives.* I laugh out loud in between gasps of catching my breath.

Suddenly I get it. People don't ask questions because they want to give another generation of kids too much homework to do. People ask questions because they're scared and confused and lonely and exhausted and tiny and outraged and at one point really, really unsure of everything they never thought to question. The universe is wild and chaotic and untrustworthy and for some reason we're here in the middle of it ordering lattes.

Dear Universe,
AM I THE ONLY ONE WHO JUST REALIZED THIS IS FUCKING ABSURD?

⟿

"Cham?" my mom says when I get home. My feet are more blister than skin, and I leave my combat boots at the door. "Would you like to tell me why I got a call from school?" she asks, leaning against the doorway of the mud-room.

I sigh. "It was just a week of detention from stupid Mr. Garcia."

"Detention?" my mom says incredulously. She grabs the bottle of Pledge off the floor and sprays the area by our feet. "What detention?"

"Um, just a small five-day penalty in the grand scheme of things. I didn't even hear Mr. Garcia give it to me; school just sent an e-mail. Like how *impersonal* do you get?"

She makes a *tsk*ing noise and continues spraying the floor as she makes her way into the living room. I figure I'd better follow her. "It was your English teacher who called, and it wasn't about detention. She says you haven't turned in your college essay, and she's very worried about you." I sink into the couch and she sits next to me. "I know I haven't been focused enough on your schoolwork, but I thought you had it under control." She looks at me with her asymmetrical eyebrows, which is exactly where I got them from. "I'm guessing that if you haven't finished your essay, you haven't finished college applications."

I shake my head and she sighs. "You said you were going to do them a month ago. I need you to tell me what's going on in your little world over there." *Which one?* "What was this detention about?"

I dig my knuckles into the balls of my feet, then dab at

the blisters lining my achilles. "Gene kissed someone else," I say, my face quivering. "And I got a little mad and—"

I hiccup/cry/snort, which is an amazing throat-and-nostril feat.

"Oh, sweetie." My mom sets the Pledge on the coffee table and hugs me. My heart rate aligns itself with the clock's loud ticking on the wall behind us.

"It's turning up all this old stuff," I mumble. "Like being mad and having nowhere to hold it all. Next thing I knew I was throwing Tater Tots at him. I think it was mortifying, but I was too mad to care."

My mom grimaces as she strokes my hair. "What else?"

"I said some stuff. I don't know. It was ugly and the whole school saw and it was kind of the end of Cham's dignity as we know it."

My mom kisses my forehead. "Do you think you maybe need to go back to anger management?" she asks gently.

Those are the cursed words. Forget *damn* and *hell*. Anger. Management. Is. My. Condemnation.

"I do *not*—" I start loudly, then clear my throat and take a more pleasant tone, 'cause like case in point. "Need anger management," I finish sweetly. "I just need the world to piss me off less."

She stares off into the place where the ceiling meets the wall. "We need a solid plan to finish senior year on a strong note and get your college applications in. When I was talking to your English teacher, we agreed you should try tutoring for the essay. She's going to give you more time, but only if you get help."

I scowl and push the fluid around under my blister.

"Evelyn said this boy named Brendan and your friend Abigail are the only seniors still tutoring." I put my head between my knees. *Why, Universe, are you doing this to me? Between you, me, and my patellas, this is bullshit.* "Do you want me to set something up for you?"

I glare at her. "You can't be MIA from my life for the last year and then suddenly step in."

"What the hell does that mean?" my mom asks sharply. I wince and her face softens. "I'm sorry, I didn't mean to snap. I'm just...go on."

"Well, you're so busy with Dad and everything, and I know you have to be, but—" Angry mom hasn't been around for a while, not since my dad got sick and she became the self-help guru. *Tidy your house! Tidy your emotions! Tidy your life!* A part of me wants to keep it that way, but another part of me wants to say what I haven't said, not even to myself. "I just don't think it's fair for you to get mad when I'm fending for myself here."

My mom stands and takes a duster to the pictures lined up on the mantel. "I'm sorry, Cham," she says, slowly moving down each frame. "I know it's hard, but I can't double-check every single thing you do, although I guess now I'm going to have to. Otherwise your college applications—"

"Mom," I say quietly. "How am I supposed to leave?" She turns around with the duster suspended in the air. "Like how am I supposed to just go to college? I overheard the doctor telling you Dad has, what, a year, maybe two, of semi-decent brain functioning before it's all taken from him—his movement, his speech, everything. I'm not gonna start a new chapter in a new place and be all rah-rah about my future when he's *dying* here."

As soon as the words float out of my mouth and into the living room, I realize how true they are.

"You can't sabotage your whole future before it even has a chance to start," my mom says, dusting a family picture so hard it goes flying to the ground. "Are you just gonna put your life on hold?"

"It already *is* on hold! Don't you feel this weird limbo we've been bobbing along in for the last few years?"

"Well—"

"We never talk about it! Dad doesn't even acknowledge that he's sick *when he's in the hospital*, and you just go around scrubbing things like if only we were a little more sanitary, everything would be okay." I try to stand up, but the skin on my feet is too raw. "College is just this stupid thing people get fixated on because it makes them think they have some control over their future. It's such a load of bullshit, and I'm so tired of mucking around in it. *Nothing* is okay. And it's nothing college can fix." I get up and the stinging in my feet gets more pronounced.

"It's like the human condition or something, to be fucking fucked."

My mom puts the duster down. "What is it, Cham?" she asks, running over to me. "Is it starting to happen? Your face is getting really red. It's happening, isn't it?"

"No, it's not," I lie. "Nothing is happening."

"Sit down," my mom urges. "You need to stay calm."

"I'm fine."

"Head between your legs. Close your eyes."

"I am not having an outburst!" I limp back and forth, tapping my fingers together, just hoping I don't lose total control, burst into flame, and start a fire on the floor.

"Picture the waterfall," my mom is saying.

"Mom, just stop."

I clutch opposite wrists under my sweater and dig my fingernails into my skin until the red in my vision is replaced by the red of my blood rushing to the surface of my skin.

"Mom, I'm fine," I say as she tries to put her hands on my neck. I run my fingers over the marks my nails made. "I just, I have to go, okay?"

"Where are you going?" she asks.

"To my room."

"To do what?"

"Homework? Hide? I don't know. I literally have no idea what to do right now."

She grimaces. "Maybe we should meet with your guidance counselor or your old therapist."

I shake my head. "I just need a little time alone, okay?"

She nods. "Everything's gonna be okay, Cham. Take an hour or so to get yourself sorted out." She pauses, and I can see her fighting with herself to say more. "I know you think I clean too much, but you'd really feel better with a tidier room. Do you want me to do some vacuuming?"

"Ugh, Mom," I say as I go upstairs, fighting an eye roll. "Definitely don't come up here with that thing." *I'm too afraid I'll get sucked in.*

Selfie from the safety of my bed: mascara running down my cheeks, zoom shot on a fat tear, ketchup stain on blouse. Meant to look emo-punk, actually looks clown-hired-to-murder.

Pictures to be deleted:
- Gene's big toe next to my big toe, appendages in like/love
- Gene shirtless and his hair wet after a ten-mile run
- Selfie of Gene and me kissing (before I knew his mouth was full of lies)

Pictures to unlike:
- Helga
- Helga and her insufferable blond hair

- Helga kissing the American flag like the United States isn't the bully of the goddamn world
- Helga and Danika trying on identical prom dresses
- Helga dancing at Senior Show with her leg up by her eyebrow like a monster without bones who's still more lovable than me

Picture to send the universe: middle finger up, eyes looking directly into the camera, spinach between my teeth.

A: Holy shit are you okay

A: Where the hell did you go?

C: Not okay.

C: But going to be okay.

C: I think

C: Idk. Wtf am I supposed to do

A: honestly I say screw him

A: and don't listen to everyone at school who now thinks you're crazy

A: It's bullshit that girls aren't allowed to get angry

If Gene threw things at you they definitely wouldn't call him crazy

Anyway, like I say screw him

It'll be so much more fun not to be tied down. Prom, graduation, Nicaragua. Life is happening baby we gotta soak it up.

I throw my phone across my room. Suddenly none of those things seem appealing at all. I gotta go fix this. I gotta fix it ASAP.

Text exchange with Gene:

Can we talk?

Are you sure you want to "talk"?

You threw your lunch at me.

I'm really sorry about that

Can I come over?

No.

I already have my sneakers on

Cham don't

Already left

Gene is watching from his window when I get to his house, breathless from the several-mile run through the woods. My mom hates me running there at night because she thinks there's something out there that can hurt me. She's wrong. Most things that can hurt a person are inside them already.

Gene comes out looking very displeased as he walks across the lifeless brown lawn. Approaching him, I feel light-headed, agonized. I can hardly catch my breath, and it wasn't *that* long a run.

"I'm so sorry about today," I start.

"I'm sorry too," he sighs. "About Helga and stuff. I know it's a douche thing to do."

I wave my hand dismissively. "Come on, run with me," I say, touching his elbow gently. "It'll be easier to talk about it if we're running."

He shakes his head, his shadow stretching up the dark lawn toward the house, where the lights are on but in none of the rooms I recognize.

"I'm sorry I couldn't tell you or let you in my house or anything," I say. "I know it seems like a weird thing not to tell you about, but it's so hard to explain feeling like I live in two worlds and I'm just kind of stuck in both of them because for some reason I just can't—"

I look away as my tongue goes numb, then my lips, then my whole face. There's nothing wrong with numb, though. Just ask the gods of Novocain.

"I'm sorry, Cham," he says softly. "I had no idea. That's

literally the most you've told me about yourself since we started dating." He looks down at his feet, and the silence is tense where I wish it were soft. He shifts awkwardly. "It's just too late, you know?"

"Come on, Gene. We can move past it."

"Cham." He shakes his head slowly at me. "We're graduating. It just doesn't make sense—"

"Yes, it does. What about prom? And Nicaragua?" I imagine growing roots right here in his lawn. "You can't just get feelings for someone else because I couldn't come over and have sex with you."

"It was *not* like that," he says, sounding offended, even though I'm the one who should be offended.

"Okay, well, I'm here now, and what we had is still here. We'll go to prom like we planned and—"

"I think we should just go with our friends as a group. One big good-bye to high school. It'll be fun not being tied down to one person."

"So now I tie you down?" The words jostle around my mouth, like cats trying to get out of a bag.

"I'm really sorry, Cham."

"You can't do this to me, not now." An angry ball of energy is launched inside me. It's a game of Ping-Pong and I don't know how to play. "It hasn't even been a day," I say lamely, looking down at my shadow touching Gene's shadow and thinking how sad it is that this is what touching each other has come down to.

"I know, but a lot changes in a day."

I'm about to disagree, but then I have a vision of my dad in the hospital bed. It's a quick vision, but it lasts long enough to chill me. A lot *can* change in a day.

"What can I do?" I ask, my lower lip starting to shake. I look up to keep the tears from responding to gravity, and a moth flies toward the streetlight.

"It's not you, it's—" Gene starts.

I roll my eyes. "Yeah, Helga, I get it."

Just saying her name turns my spit to acid. My face flushes. I look up and see Helga in the window, peering out and quickly putting the curtain back as she sees me looking at her.

Fuck you, Helga. Fuck the fiery blister of your pie hole where you once made out with a hot dog roll.

"You're such a dick," I say to Gene, turning from him and his house toward the road and the dark woods. "I hope you have a really great ten minutes with Helga before she flies back to Germany." As I cross the street, I leap over a fire hydrant on the other side and call over my shoulder, "I'd say go to hell, but I never want to see you again."

Dear Gene,
I want to hurl my heart at you. I want to drown you in my blood. I want to run through your window and shatter in your eyes. My chest is nauseous. My heart

is full of vomit. I hate you. I hate how you walk with her. I hate feeling you not wanting me. I hate the lack of explanation about the lack of me. There's a scream in my throat about to get out. I'm screaming now. I can't stop. Listen. This is the sound I make.

14

Days 'til prom:
Seems irrelevant now

NOTICE FROM THE GUIDANCE DEPARTMENT RECEIVED WITH thirty-two days until graduation, because that's what I *should* be keeping track of:

Dear Chamomile,

We hope this notice finds you well. Unfortunately, it has come to our attention that you are missing a significant assignment in English class, which is threatening your ability to pass the class, in addition to your eligibility to attend Senior Volunteer Trip. Failure to complete this overdue assignment in two weeks will put you on academic probation, which could result in making up the course over the summer. We have these measures in place to ensure academic excellence. We want

you to succeed and are here to provide support so you may do
so. Let us know if you have any questions.

    Best,

    Mr. Garcia

∽

Dear Universe,

I'm sorry for interrupting you with my presence, but
WTF? You absolutely bitch-slapped me these last couple of weeks, and my ears are ringing because of it. I
should feel scared about maybe not being able to go
to Nicaragua, right? I should get some essay tutoring,
right? And if Brendan and Abigail are the only people
tutoring, I should choose Abigail, right? The easy and
obvious answers don't feel easy or obvious. Honestly,
they don't really feel like answers. Could I please have
a sign about what the hell to do next? And not like
KICK ME, but a sign. Try not to be subtle about it. I lean
toward oblivious even on good days.

∽

"Oh god," Abigail says, startling me with her minty breath
in my face as she plops down next to me in English a couple weeks after Gene dropped my heart like a hot potato.
"You look awful, Cham."

I rest my head on my desk and talk into my arm. "I saw
them at lunch today, and he was just hovering around her

like a fruit fly on a banana, and not just any banana—a smart, highly cultured blond one."

"What a dick," Abigail says, unzipping her bag and taking out her class "necessities": highlighter, notebook, Post-it Notes in two different colors. "You should've thrown the kickball at his balls in gym."

"I'd rather not think about the things inside his pants. It's too depressing."

I squint at what Evelyn's written on the board:

EXISTENCE AS IT IS, IS UNBEARABLE.
I MUST HAVE THE MOON OR HAPPINESS OR SOMETHING.

"Caligula said that. Or something like it," Evelyn rambles. "Okay, get out last night's homework, please."

I point to Abigail's book. "When's that due, anyway?" I ask her.

"Uh, today."

I rub my temples. If it were any hotter in this classroom, it could be the post-gym-class sauna. "Fuck."

Abigail laughs. "How do you never know what the homework is? She says it like eight times in class, *and* we get e-mail reminders."

I lower my voice to a whisper. "This is confidential, but I can't remember things I don't care about."

Just then Doug walks in. He's very deliberate about not looking at me, which just seems unfair. Shouldn't *I* be the one ignoring him? It was *his* best friend who left me for someone who doesn't even go here. Or did I lose the right to properly grieve this breakup when I launched potato morsels at Gene's head?

"Here, I'm about to save your ass." Abigail slides her copy of *Caligula* toward me and starts talking very quickly, breathing apparently optional. "So this emperor's lover who is also his sister dies, and he realizes the world is a steaming pile of shitty nothingness." She points to the chalkboard and the yellow crescent Evelyn is drawing. "So then he becomes freaking obsessed with the moon because he wants something out of this world, something that—"

"Why the moon?" I ask. "Seems kinda random."

She shrugs. "Well, *technically*, the moon is outside this world, and let's be honest, people throughout time have had a major boner for the moon." She twists a piece of her hair, and I get a whiff of her flowery shampoo. "It's kinda fascinating up there in the sky, just so big and sad and with us all the time like—"

"Maybe you should take the moon to prom instead of Hilary."

"*Anyway*, so he's all boohooing about the moon because even though he's so powerful, he can't have it. Then he kills everybody. Then they kill him. The end."

I blink at Abigail. "No wonder you got accepted to State in December," I tell her.

She manages a small curtsy by pulling her plaid skirt

away from her chair and bowing her head. "Yeah, I'm an under-the-radar genius."

"Okay," Evelyn says loudly. "Everyone, get out of *Caligula*." She glowers at the clock. "We have lots to do before the volunteer-trip assembly this afternoon."

While everyone rustles through their bags for their books, I scan the pages of Abigail's copy, paying special attention to the pages that have sticky notes on them. The door opens quickly, then slams shut, and Brendan comes in, humming loudly.

"Hey, Cham," he says, and his purple tutu grazes my desk as he passes.

"Hey," I squeak, not because I'm nervous, but just because I sometimes keep a mouse in my throat.

Abigail looks behind her as he passes. "That was random," she says.

"Uh-huh." My stomach is doing this weird thing. *I'm probably just hungry.*

Evelyn puts her piece of chalk down and turns to face us. "Okay, before we dive into *Caligula*, I want to discuss your final project," she begins, twirling *Caligula* in her hand. "All I want is one speech to the class in which you formulate your beliefs into a coherent philosophy that answers this question."

She turns to the board.

WHAT MAKES LIFE WORTH LIVING?

She smiles at us. "Back up your answer with examples from your life. This is a chance for you to connect experience with theory. *Plus*," she says, like we've truly won the jackpot, "you get to talk about yourself!" She smiles, and the bright lights in the room illuminate the stubble growing past her buzz cut. "Any questions?"

Josie raises her hand and everyone turns to look at her. "I don't get it."

"Me either," one of the hockey guys in the corner says. Evelyn sighs and pulls the Smart Board out. When she turns it on, a more cohesive project description pops up. There are phrases like *Explore what makes us most human!*, *Determine your convictions!*, and *Present your theories to the class!*

I glance behind me at Brendan, and he widens his eyes at me. I hide a smile and look back at Evelyn. "We've been reading all these different philosophers in class over the last few weeks," she says, leaning on her desk. "Now I want to hear from you. What do you think about this life situation?" She waves her arms over her head, I guess to denote life. "No need to write a play or a book or a hypothetical situation; just examine your own life. It's important that we start to bridge the gap between what we study and what we live," Evelyn continues. "Especially before you go off to college."

I look over at Abigail and she blinks dramatically. *Cremate me now*, I communicate to her.

"Now, let's talk *Caligula*!" Evelyn turns the Smart Board off and holds her book up with both hands like a judge giving a score. "Let's start with personal reactions. Go ahead, Josie," Evelyn says, nodding to Josie's incredibly straight arm, which shot up before Evelyn really started her sentence.

"I found it uninspiring," Josie says. "Caligula thinks he's had this big *aha!* moment when his sister dies and he realizes"—she flips to a page in her book—"'men die and they are not happy,' but that's not really groundbreaking. He just sounds mega-depressed."

"Yeah," Jared says. "Maybe if he got some therapy, he wouldn't kill everyone just because life is 'meaningless.'"

Abigail puts her hand up as soon as Jared finishes talking. "Caligula was whiny. I liked the guy Sisyphus who just kept pushing that boulder up that hill. He accepted the absurdity of his situation, whereas Caligula destroyed everything to try to reach something beyond this world...." She flips to a page in her book with a large green sticky note. "Symbolized by the moon, I guess?"

In my head, I replace the words on the chalkboard with our current situation: *High school as it is, is unbearable. I must have the moon or happiness or something....*

The discussion keeps going and going. Meanwhile, real life is going on out there in the *real* world, beyond our theories. My dad is at home, probably with an aide right now, finishing lunch or watching the afternoon news, while his brain gets destroyed in ways even science doesn't understand.

"Cham?" Evelyn says. I look up abruptly.

"Good day," I say. A few people laugh.

"What are your thoughts on *Caligula?*"

I stare at the board and the notes Evelyn has put up there. There's enough stuff for me to put an answer together, but I just don't have it in me.

"I'm sorry, but this all just seems so pointless to me," I say, tracing the initials carved into my desk. "Caligula would probably agree that high school is meaningless and we all graduate and we are not happy." I clear my throat. "I mean, we might be happy for like a *day*, but then everyone's running around doing stuff for college and hauling ass over grades and scholarships. We're all looking for a...moon," I go on, which is quite genius, if I do say so myself. "We want something out of this world—but the closest star we land on is college...and I think that sounds really expensive."

Somebody stifles a laugh. It's important not to look up at a time like this. "Like my old friend Caligula, I just want something outside all of this." *Yup*, I realize as I catch the horrified look Abigail is giving me. *I want the fucking moon.*

"Interesting point, Cham," Evelyn says. "Have you given any thought to what there is outside the world of high school and college? And if so, what are you going to do there?"

"What do you mean?"

"Well, there actually *is* a world outside high school. You potentially have a moon," she says. "So what are you going to do about it?"

"Um..." The only sound is the rain hitting the window. "Become an astronaut?"

The whole class laughs, and Evelyn shakes her head, but even she is smiling.

"Since you're stuck here for the next month, you might want to think about what would make the rest of your high school experience meaningful." The intercom rings and Evelyn frowns up at it.

"Will all seniors please report to the auditorium, all seniors to the auditorium," the secretary drawls.

"All right, tomorrow we'll pick up where we left off," Evelyn says amid the noise of everyone getting out of their seats. "That's something you can all be thinking about," she adds. "A meaningful rest of high school!"

I take my sweet time putting my two school supplies into my backpack just in case the timing would work out for Brendan and me to walk out the door together. It doesn't.

"If I don't get valedictorian, none of this shit will be meaningful," Abigail says, linking her arm in mine as we walk out.

It's a prime opportunity to ask her for help with my essay, but instead what comes out is, "Honestly, I think I'll be happy with my high school experience as long as I don't have to take a feral cat to prom."

~

"'ello, love," Hilary says, British accent in full swing when Abigail and I take the two seats next to her in the auditorium. The room is dark, but not dark enough to hide Gene and Helga canoodling in the back row. A few rows over from us, Brendan's taking a seat, and for some reason I remember how he laughed in the hospital and his fake mustache went askew. *Don't worry, that's natural after a breakup. The heart goes haywire.*

"The time has come, seniors," Mr. Garcia says, sitting on the edge of the stage with his legs dangling off, "to finalize groups and trip plans for Nicaragua. As you know, this is a rare opportunity that the Gill School provides to build homes in devastated areas, work with local children—"

I smooth one of my unruly frizzies down and look back at Gene involuntarily.

"You okay, Cham?" Abigail asks, peering around me to look at him. "Want me to mince and sauté his balls?"

"Ew." I slink down in the felt chairs. "I'm hunky-dory, just want high school to be over."

Abigail and Hilary share a glance that I pretend not to notice. "Come on, Cham, you can't only be excited about prom and graduation and stuff when you have a *boy*," Hilary says.

Easy for her to say. For everyone else, life going on means life getting closer to Big Things, and none of those involve more aides, more medication—or in the worst scenario, none of those things at all.

"In leaving cell phones behind and immersing ourselves in the work at hand, we're giving our full presence and attention to helping," Mr. Garcia says, then signals to someone at the back of the room to turn the lights off and start the PowerPoint. The first slide tells us that the following presentation will cover everything from how to drink water in other countries to which types of mosquitoes ruin your chances of reproduction tenfold.

I take my phone out, hiding it under the zipper of my backpack.

Text sent from one world to the other:

How's Dad?

Hilary elbows me and I jump. "Hey," she hisses. "So I was waiting for the right time to tell you this, but I have some news." She strokes her cool blue hair.

"When it comes to tap water," Mr. Garcia is saying, "don't drink it. Don't even look at it."

"Yeah?"

"I got into State, too!" Hilary whispers, kind of bouncing in her seat. Abigail looks over and grins, and they're both staring at me, and it takes me a second to register the significance of this.

"Wow," I say, sitting up straighter and summoning all the positivity I can muster. "Congrats! Are you gonna like room together and stuff?"

"We're gonna try," Abigail says.

"But ya never know, do you?" Hilary says in her stupid British accent. I want to pull her cool blue hair out.

"Well, I'm really excited for you," I say, leaning down to see if my mom has responded.

Abigail squeezes my arm. "And you can room with us second semester if you get your applications in!"

"My grades probably aren't—"

"Well, then you can go to community college and transfer after." She says it with such genuine enthusiasm for my future that I wish she'd lend me some.

"I mean I haven't looked into community college at all, but, yeah, totally." I feel my phone vibrate, and I stick my head in my backpack to read it. It's very crowded in this room. It's like being inside a throat that's closing.

> M — No texting in class. Focus on school.

Yeah, because school is so important right about now.

"So there you have it," Mr. Garcia says as the Power-Point clicks off and the lights come up. "We'll finish checking in with teachers today about progress reports just to make sure all students are cleared academically."

"You're okay, right?" Abigail asks. "You haven't gotten any warning e-mails?"

Not if you ignore the one in my in-box this morning. "Uh, yeah, I think I'm good. Just gotta finish my essay this weekend."

"Do you want help?" she asks. I find myself shaking my head. Her eyes are full of concern for all the things in this world that I haven't done yet, but essay deadlines aren't real deadlines. Real deadlines are the ones you can't push back.

"So now for your groups. Group one." Mr. Garcia scrolls down the iPad. "Danika Sandhu, Doug Freeman, Cham Myles, and Helga Huber."

"You gotta be kidding me," I breathe. "You gotta be fucking kidding me."

"I'm not going, remember, Mr. G?" Helga calls out. "Gotta get back to Germany."

Damn right you do.

"Oh, that's right, okay then, let's put Brendan Gordon there."

"Not going either," he sings from the way back of the auditorium.

"Why wouldn't you want to go to this?" Hilary whispers.

"Yeah. It's *freeeedom*," Abigail says. "Our parents can't even bother us once. We can make calls with the community phone, but they can't reach us. Ever."

I look down at my combat boots. "What if there's an emergency, though?"

Hilary laughs. "Whatever it is, it can wait a few days."

"Yeah," I say, remembering how my dad was slouched on the bathroom floor. He could have been there for hours if I hadn't been home. "Totally."

"All right, seniors!" Mr. Garcia says, raising his voice to be heard over the chatter that's started, people standing up and collecting their things, eager to get out of school even thirty-nine seconds early. "Our next big class activity is the Breast Cancer Polar Plunge this weekend. In the meantime, have a good week!"

"Shit, that's this weekend?" I groan.

"You were the one who practically tackled me at lunch to vote for it." Abigail laughs. I grunt in response.

"Should we all wear bikinis?" Hilary asks as we file out.

"Ass-naked is the call," I say, decidedly not mentioning that I'll be at the Brain Degeneration Walk, hiding out in a porta-potty. I'm sure Bad Daughters burn in hell, but I'll be all right. Any burn I get turns into a tan eventually.

Dear Universe,

I want all of this to be over.

I want Gene and Helga to elope someplace special,
  like hell.

I want a root beer float.

I want new soles for my combat boots.

I want an umbrella instead of a trash bag.

I want directions to my life.

I want Band-Aids.

I want six ways to be a better daughter.

I want someone to name a constellation after me and
  take me there to flourish amongst my stars.

We're almost out of the auditorium when I hear my name. "Hey, Cham," Brendan calls from a few rows over. He waves to me, and I override my feelings of self-consciousness. Kind of.

"Don't know what this is about, but see you guys later," I say to Abigail and Hilary, then cut across the line of people milling out the door.

"Uh, okay, bye," Abigail says.

I step out of the auditorium and into the bright hallway, waiting for Brendan by the windows to the courtyard.

"What's up?" I ask when he approaches me.

"Just wanted to see how you're holding up." Someone passes and I think I hear them say *Tater Tots*. My ears get red hot. "That's why I ignore them," Brendan says, smiling a little with his dark brown eyes. "People suck."

"They really do." A few girls Abigail is friends with on the dance team walk out of the auditorium. They're talking about prom and how far the beach is from the town we're staying in in Nicaragua.

"It should just be called Senior Vacation," Brendan mutters. I nod.

"Mr. Garcia just told me I can't go if I don't pass in my English essay," I blurt out.

"That sucks," he says. "I mean, if you were looking forward to spending even more time with the senior class."

"Ugh," I say, and forehead-plant the rain-streaked window.

Brendan puts his hands in his pockets. "Anyway, just wanted to see how your dad is and how you are."

"He's, um—" He hasn't spoken or left his room, really. If I thought things were bad before this, well, let's say the dominoes in my life haven't just fallen; they've thrown themselves on the ground and now they're playing dead. I look up into his face, and something about his nose and his eyebrows—the whole arrangement of his features—makes me feel safe. "I don't think he's doing okay."

I'm about to say more, but down the hall Gene is coming toward us. I don't know how to be in the presence of both of them. Maybe I'll burst into a couple of pieces: only some of them Gene will recognize. Most of them Brendan will.

"Are you gonna be okay not to throw things at him?" Brendan whispers.

I burst out laughing, even though nothing else in me feels capable of it. "No promises."

"Well, catch ya later, Cham. Hey, Gene," Brendan says, walking away.

"'Sup, dude," Gene says with a head nod. Brendan's tutu brushes Gene's khakis as he heads down the hall. I watch him go, avoiding Gene's face as long as possible. His tie is loose, and his blue-gray eyes don't show how everything has changed between us. All those butterflies that used to fill my stomach when I saw him? They die. I'm a receptacle for a bunch of dead things that once knew how to fly.

"Hey, so this is kinda awkward, but"—Gene reaches into his pocket and pulls out my prom ticket—"I figured I should give this to you so you can get into prom and every-thing. No need to pay me back," he says quickly.

"Okay." I take the ticket from him. Our fingers do not brush during this exchange. We are bits of space debris on a parallel course, and even though I never pay attention in science, I know their solitary fate.

"I miss you," I accidentally whisper, then stare out the window into the courtyard so I don't have to look at him.

"It sucks—" he starts to say, and for a second, I think that maybe it isn't over. For a second, I am wrong. The bell rings.

"I'm sorry it has to be like this," he adds.

"Didn't I mean anything to you?" I blurt out.

"Of course you did, but—"

"I just didn't mean *enough* to you."

There are fewer and fewer people in the hallway. I don't know if they're looking at us. For once I don't think I care.

"You did, but I have to get to going, Cham, I'm sorry."

He starts to walk away, and the veins in my fist bulge. I'm speechless, dumb.

"So that's it?" I call after him. *But you made me feel special*. And isn't that what it comes down to? We all have this tiny secret belief that we're a freaking treasure, and even though we shave our legs and leave patches on our knees and sometimes fall asleep without brushing our teeth, we still think we're special, maybe even magnetic. Not so mag-netic that when we walk by the kitchen, pots and pans fly out of the cabinets and attach themselves to us, but strong enough not to be replaced by someone else in thirty-five minutes.

"Cham," he says, brushing his hair out of his eyes. "This year was really great, but we're about to go to college. Did you really think—"

If one more person says the C-word, I swear I'm going to drop out. Become a monk. Start an ant farm. "Never mind, Gene," I say, turning my back on him. "Just never mind. That's all the closure I need."

I walk away, getting faster and faster. I want to run, but the blisters on my feet are raw and oozing still. I want to move until I feel something besides this angry ball of energy shooting around my body like I'm a pinball machine. But no matter how quickly I hobble, it's not fast enough. I look down at my combat boots and realize I am in a flesh prison. That's all skin is: entrapment.

And then it dawns on me that this is just a small version of what my dad might feel like. *Oh my god, how is he not screaming every minute of every day?*

The angry ball of energy gets more and more frenzied. I pass the last stragglers hurrying to catch the bus, then duck into the nearest bathroom.

I think I might actually explode, but there I am in one piece in front of the mirror. I want to punch it. I want to feel glass shatter in my hands because that's part of what I liked about punching the bus window a little too close to

Ava's face. It hurt me. It seemed better to hurt in my hand than in my heart, or whatever it is that breaks when I look at my dad and he's looking at the neighbor in the tree. *How do you do this?* I close my eyes. My forehead rests on the dirty mirror, with its smudges and streaks, as if every time someone looked in it, a little piece of them stayed. I wind my hand back and then make eye contact with myself.

"Please, Universe," I say aloud, my fist still by my ear as I clench and unclench it.

"Not that. I do not want to dip into the dark shit of hurting myself. Please. Not. That. However my dad does it, help me do it too." I pause. It's a little creepy whispering to myself in the girls' bathroom. My hand twitches and I keep going because I don't really have energy to be self-conscious right now. "I know these are just stupid blisters and he's been stuck in a body that's been getting worse and worse, and I know it sucks to be one of those people who only relate to something when they personally experience it, but as you know I kind of suck, so please help me." I sigh. I keep clenching and unclenching. "I'm truly sorry for interrupting you with my presence when I'm sure you're very busy with other, more worldly affairs, but show me how he does it so I can do it too. Help me do it and help him do it and help all of us do it."

I clamp my eyes shut and clench and release my hands until eventually the pinball gets smaller. It's the size of a punctuation mark when I can open my eyes and look at myself: frizzy hair, two asymmetrical eyebrows, a nose that's never been pierced. I take a deep breath and fill my lungs with air the quality of the bathroom. Somehow the anger has passed, as if the universe is holding it for me.

I sink against the wall and slide to the floor. This is the exhaustion that always sets in after the anger. Everything has been sucked out of me to feed the fury. I'm just so tired. Like so so so so so tired. How is everyone else not fucking exhausted? How are we not all exploding all the time, Mentos-in-Pepsi style? How does everyone just walk around being a person, while I'm so confused?

A girl comes into the bathroom and takes a pair of scissors out of her bag. She starts trimming her bangs. I watch from the floor, liking the sound hair makes when it's cut and how the clumps of hair scatter and fall at their own pace. Maybe all I need is a good haircut. A haircut that means business, one that says I am a boss child who will pass English class. "Can you do that to me too?" I ask. "Not bangs, just like all of it."

"Um, you should go to a hairdresser for that. Besides, like head lice."

Asshole, I mumble to myself, but I walk out of the bathroom secretly relieved that I didn't accidentally end up with a mullet. Of all the things I need right now, a popular haircut for guys in the seventies isn't one of them.

Dear Universe,

Wanted: A fuck

Just kidding. Keep your fucks. I have too many: how Hilary and Abigail are gonna forget about me, what people think about my dad, whether or not my boobs really exist at all, what I could've done differently to keep Gene from falling for someone else. Could all the fucks get lost, please? Like take a sick day, a holiday, a vacation. Just once I'd like to get through school not feeling like a chicken in the world where the egg came first. The good thing is, I'm getting so strong hauling around all these fucks every day. The bad thing is, I feel weaker.

15

WEEKEND SCHEDULE OF A HIGH SCHOOL SOCIALITE:

1. Start English essay.

2. Finish English essay.

3. Find a brilliant excuse to get out of the Brain Degeneration Walk without also going to the Breast Cancer Polar Plunge.

4. Procrastinate doing all these things by doing something of greater importance, i.e., spending time with my ailing father before he kicks the bucket and I forever regret being the worst daughter ever.

5. Yeah. Let's start there.

"Hi, Dad, coming in!" I call, rapping on his door and uncapping the protein shake. I'm not a doctor, but since my dad is having a hard time eating, maybe we should be giving him real milkshakes, not these impostor shakes that come in plastic bottles stamped with *FortifY-um!*

"Come in," he says wearily.

"How are you?" I say, putting the tray on his table and sniffing the bright pink drink before I hold it out to him.

"I hate that stuff," he says, not looking at me. He's eaten maybe twenty total bites since he's come home from the hospital, and his face is sunken in.

"I know, I'm sorry. Can I get you something else?"

"Just sit with me," he says, turning his head toward the window. "You and your mom and the aides always get me things, but you never just sit with me."

This sort of guilt feels like being stabbed to death with a take-out knife. I pull a chair up to his bed and look around the room. I don't know what to say, so I put a straw in the drink and hold it out to him. "How about just one sip?" He shakes his head and I set the drink down. There are flowers on the table and get-well cards, and sunlight is coming through the window for the first time this spring, but it feels like it should be raining.

"There's a book somewhere on the shelf down there," my dad says, pointing behind me. "It's an old paperback with a bright purple spine. If you can find it, will you read it to me?"

"Yeah, of course," I say, getting up. "I thought you hated reading."

He smiles. It's the first smile I've seen since before the hospital. "I do. That's why I want you to read it."

I get down on the floor to look. After a few seconds I pull out a softcover book with its purple hues slightly faded.

"*Zen and the Art of Motorcycle Maintenance?*" I read.

"I was on a trip up the West Coast, trying to find myself, and I got this book, but then I was too busy riding and messing around to read it."

I laugh and read the back cover. "'An inquiry into values'?" I flip through the pages.

"Let's see if we can get into it," he says. "Put that light on."

I do as I'm told and start reading. Every so often my dad twitches and readjusts himself in bed. The shaking in his hands has lessened, but it's been replaced by these fast, jerking motions. I want to know if he's comfortable, but I don't know what to do if he isn't. There's only so many times you can fluff up a pillow. And what if he's bored? I can't juggle, and I don't know any dad-appropriate jokes. I guess reading is fine, but if this isn't the most slumber-inducing book to ever make it to a printing press...

"Wow," I say after a few minutes have passed and all the spit in my mouth has gone on hiatus. "This guy really has a lot to say about motorcycles. And parts of motorcycles. And how different kinds of weather affect different parts of motorcycles." I read the back cover again. There's no way the book could go on like this for three hundred pages. There must be *something* else here. "So he takes this trip and tries to work out like his life philosophy?"

"Kind of." He takes the book from me, and his hands are almost steady as he turns it over a few times. "Nope, still doesn't interest me," my dad says abruptly, handing the book back to me.

"What?" I laugh.

"Inquiries into life. Philosophy. I'm just not interested in thinking about living. I'd rather just live." He sighs. "Get my keys, will you?"

"What keys?"

"For my bike. It's been a long trip, and I want to go home now."

I swallow, trying to process how we went from there to here. How do you know you were in the same world with someone? When it ends. "We *are* home, Dad," I say.

"Come on, Cham, I'm not stupid."

"Dad, we're home. I promise." He glares at me, and his distrust settles into my stomach like cement. I look around the room for proof. "See? There's you and mom at your wedding." I point to the framed photo on the wall. "And your service award when you retired from the post office back when snail mail was still called *mail*. And look at the flowers from Aunt Bridget. It's all right here." I give his hand a squeeze. "I'm here."

He closes his eyes. "I'm glad you're here," he says quietly.

I rest my forehead on his arm. "Me too."

Sitting there in the warm, quiet room while my mom is finishing a shift at work, I want the days before the hospital back, when he was happier and moving around and eating. I know it's a trap to think like that, though. During *those* days I wanted the days before the *diagnosis* back. With a sickness that gets sicker, it's just another type of sickness to keep wishing for what came before.

I feel myself drifting off. My head droops toward my chest, then snaps up at the sound of my phone ringing. Abigail is talking before I've even said hello.

"Come get your nails done with me and Hilary!" she shouts over some pop music. It sounds like they're driving, or having a dance party in the middle of the road. "We're getting acrylics now so we get used to them before prom."

"Always good to plan ahead," I say.

"What?" my dad asks, opening his eyes and looking disoriented. I mute the phone to keep Abigail and Hilary out of our world.

"One sec," I tell him. I step into the hallway, where it's cooler and doesn't smell like artificial strawberry. Hilary is singing in the background of the phone, but they sound farther away than the distance two phones can cross. I don't know that they'll be able to properly hear me, even when I press unmute.

"Cham?"

"Hey, sorry about that, I can't today, gotta work on my...essay and stuff." *Why would you bring that up?*

"Aw, do you want help?" Abigail asks.

"No, thanks. This is between Cham and her MacBook. Text you later," I say, and hang up quickly, pushing the door to my dad's room back open. "Sorry, Dad, I—"

He's asleep. The sun is casting a shadow from the window frame on his salt-and-pepper hair. If I were to write an essay about this minute, I'd say it feels the way coffee tastes, a little bitter in my heart and acidic, but also like honey: sweet, raw, unfiltered.

Dear Universe,

What if one of the most beautiful things we can do isn't Instagram-worthy? What if it means forgoing adventure and bikinis just to keep someone we love company? What if the places we really need to go don't have gate numbers or foreign languages or program titles with the word *service*? This whole year

I've kept a senior year time capsule under my bed because I want memorable, life-changing, yearbook-quality Stuff. But what if I had it wrong? What if the Real Stuff is just a quiet accumulation of moments like these?

I close the door to my dad's room with a soft click. I take my phone out and scroll through my contacts until my finger lingers over a certain name. Before I think not to, I hit the call button.

"Hey," I say when he answers. I know I'm about to talk way too fast. "I don't know if this is weird, but do you wanna maybe come over? I heard you're still doing some tutoring for essays and if it's not too late—"

"Okay, yeah," he says.

"Okay, cool. Thanks."

"Sure."

"So like when?" I ask with all the nonchalance of a mammal giving birth.

He pauses. "How about now?"

～

In the mirror by the front door I smooth down my hair. The results are impeccable because my hands are sweating. Who knew it was this nerve-racking to write a college essay?

"Hey," Brendan says when I open the door. He's wearing

a black tutu over his jeans, his hair still a little wet in the bun on his neck.

"Hey," I say, then suddenly, stupidly, I start smiling.

"What?" he laughs, jamming his hands in his pockets.

"Nothing!" I hover in the doorway. It feels like spring outside, like cool, new things. "Just like thanks for your help and coming over and stuff. I'm pretty screwed with this essay."

"It's all good. Ready to Susan Sontag this shit?" I squint at him. "She was an essayist," he explains.

I sigh. "Poor Susan." I pull the door open and step aside for him to enter. "You can leave your shoes on, my mom's at work," I call behind me.

He takes them off anyway. "So how's your dad?"

I pause in the kitchen making sure I closed the sliding door. "Good? Sick? A little of both?"

"And how are you?"

"Mentally, spiritually, and emotionally curb-stomped," I say cheerfully, leading him up the stairs to my room. Pushing the door open reveals how unprepared I am for company.

"What's that?" Brendan asks, pointing to the upside-down cardboard box on my bed. One of the glow-in-the-dark stars has fallen onto my comforter.

"Oh, that's embarrassing." I quickly collect the contents of my senior year time capsule. "Close your eyes!" I shout, and snatch the never-been-opened condom off the bed. I suspect my ears are turning as red as the package: *In case things get hot.* Brendan sits on the floor and shuts his eyes as I put the notes back into the box, plus the corsage Gene got me for homecoming. I'd wanted to take him out of the box completely, but you can't replace your history.

After pushing the box under my bed, I sit down on the floor across from Brendan and pull my knees to my chest. He peeks an eye open, then closes it again. I face-palm his forehead.

"Ow," he laughs, jerking back. "Why are your hands wet?"

My face heats up and I wipe them on my jeans. "I keep an aquifer in my palms for rare and endangered life-forms." He cocks his head at me.

"Okay, I'm getting my essay stuff out now so you don't hit me with your flippers again." Brendan takes his laptop and a folder full of school supplies out of his bag.

"I do not have flippers!" I laugh, hiding my face in my hands, face positively burning. "Dear College Admissions Person," I say through my fingers. "I hope you appreciate this essay, because it has been so freaking embarrassing to write."

"Great topic sentence," he says. I look up to find him spreading the contents of his backpack on the floor around us: laptop, pens, sticky notes. This is not how I pictured a boy being in my room for the first time. He has *flash cards*. But then again, that boy wasn't supposed to be Brendan.

"What are those for?" I ask, pointing to the stack in his hand and feeling slightly out of place between my own four walls.

"Your essay," he says, clearing his throat in mock formality. I've never seen his face up close for this long before. Abigail is right: Brendan got cute. "Let's start by exploring feelings."

Now, in addition to sweaty palms, I have kiddie pools under my armpits. "I'm not very good at feelings."

"Cham—" He puts his hand on my shoulder, and I'm surprised by how deep his voice is, not even a hint of a musical note in it. "We're going to write this essay and you're going to pass English and things aren't always going to be shitty."

I look away from him, wriggling my shoulder out from under his hand. He turns the laptop so we can both see the essay prompts. *Describe a challenge you've overcome. Discuss an event that's sparked personal growth. Provide the measurements of your asshole.*

"Ugh, those all sound terrible."

"So what do you want to write about, then?" he asks.

"I don't want to write anything." I roll over onto my stomach, accidentally inhaling a bit of rug lint. "I'm from middle-class suburbia, never had a life-threatening disease or an essay-worthy mental illness or any sort of compulsion to clean bathrooms." I drone on, voice deliberately Great Plains–like in flatness. "The extent of my hardship was going to anger management after getting kicked out of public school a few years ago, all relating to my dad's being diagnosed with a disease that basically turns your life into a saga of suck. The end."

"Tell me about this saga of suck," he says.

I close my eyes. "You've seen my dad. You know the symptoms: rigid gait, tremors, loss of speech."

"But symptoms aren't even half of what something feels like," he says, stretching out on my floor, his tutu sticking straight up toward the ceiling. "What's it like for you?"

I smooth a frizzy curl between my fingers. "It's like being a bee stuck in amber. I can't move and I can't think so I just stay frozen there in a world that is not my usual world of flowers and rainstorms and I don't know—" I laugh, feeling suddenly self-conscious. I wish I could turn the lights off and the projector on so that we could see my fake stars, but you can't just turn the lights off when a boy's in your room. He might think you like him.

"Wait, say all of that again," he says, tapping his keyboard.

"What? No."

"Come on! Let's just take some notes."

I glare at him. "As much as I'd like to milk my dad getting sick for all I can, I don't see getting an essay out of it."

"Why not?"

"Because I don't want to go there."

"Go where?"

I roll my eyes at him. "What are you, a freaking therapist?"

He gives me a look. "Do you want to write this essay or do you want to maybe fail English and be kept from Senior Volunteer Trip?" I glare at him. "It doesn't have to be about your dad. We can switch topics," he offers. "What do you do that you really love?"

Besides making out and dreaming about getting the hell out of here? "Running, I guess."

"Okay," he says, fingers poised on the keys. "What do you love about it?"

"Um, one sec." I slide the box out from under my bed and unfold something I wrote on a Gatorade wrapper after a run a few months ago. I read out loud: "When I run, sometimes it's like the world opens up. I lose touch with my feet and my legs and I notice other stuff besides my boring old body. There's more sky and more horizon and everything is closer but also more infinite. It's freaking amazing, like the world is unfastening. Gene says that's just endorphins and that's why he runs too, but it's not just endorphins, I promise. It's not chemical or hormonal or whatever it is that our bodies give off and make. It's wading through unsolved stars in my heart."

When I look up, Brendan's looking at me, and he could be *looking* at me. His eyes are all *You're a person with a heart and I have a heart too.* I become very interested in my computer. Maybe he's not feeling any of those things. I'm just saying he *could* be. Hypothetically.

"Keep going," he says. "What are the 'unsolved stars' in your heart?"

"I think of them as alien familiars," I say, blushing.

He pretends to type vigorously. "That clears everything up."

I laugh and feel myself retreating into myself. "Never mind, okay? I don't know what it means. It's just what came out after a run one day, so I wrote it down. It doesn't like mean anything."

"What if it does? No one uses a term like *alien familiars* randomly."

I put my head between my knees, and my hair falls around me like an unruly curtain. "They're things we like rampage the universe to find, only to realize we've known them all along."

"That's beautiful," he says softly.

"It's a hypothesis entirely backed up without facts."

"What does—"

I clear my throat loudly. "Nope, enough about me. What'd *you* write about?"

Brendan laughs, and I pull my head up only so I can

shake it vigorously as he talks. "Wait, don't change the subject, there's something there."

I sigh. "Writing about running isn't even half as good as running. And anything I say about my dad getting sick isn't half as bad as him being sick, so really I don't see the point in trying to write an essay after all."

He cocks his head. "You just shut down sometimes."

"Surprise, I'm a robot! So what did you write about?" I ask again. "Enlighten me with your college essay. It must have been pretty good if you get to tutor people now."

He looks down at his computer and laughs. "Oh, just wrote about how all my friends are dead people. You know, the usual."

"You're joking right?"

"Nope."

"What does that mean?"

He smiles and shrugs. "I read a lot. Actually, I read a lot of quotes because I hate reading books, but the quotes I like are usually by people who died a long time ago, and I know it's kinda cheap just to collect the good stuff, but I guess that's where I am right now."

I let go of the strand of hair I've been stroking for the last ten minutes. "I don't really get what you mean."

"I have favorite writers and stuff," he says, drawing the computer into his lap, "but I've never read their books. I've just read quotes from their books online. And it feels like these people are keeping me company."

He becomes fascinated by a speck of dirt on his screen. I think he's embarrassed, which makes me want to scoot closer to him. "What's one of the quotes?" I ask.

He taps the keyboard, then reads aloud. " 'Do not feel lonely. The entire universe is inside you.' "

"Wow," I say, feeling something stir inside me. It could be the universe or it could be the breakfast I forgot to eat. "Who said that?"

"Dead poet friend named Rumi."

"Rumi, huh?" We share a brief look punctuated by a tiny smile.

"Okay, back to your essay," he says. I groan.

"High school is a torture chamber. It's unbearable! I must have the moon or something."

He laughs. "Okay, Caligula. Keep talking. What have the last four years been like?" he asks, fingers poised over the keys. Now that he's told me the status of his BFFs, I can't just blow his question off. I try not to think too much and let the truth come out.

"The last four years have been hard," I say slowly. "Really hard."

I close my eyes, and my mouth takes on a mind of its own. "It's been sad and awkward, like *really* awkward sometimes, and annoying, which I know is bad to say, but in a way I feel like I've been asleep for most of it, like I kind of shut down because it was too much or something." I keep going, feeling safe behind my closed eyelids. "And other days it's totally fine and I think we all kind of forget that no one can predict this disease. He could live with it for years or he could deteriorate and die in the next couple of months and, I don't know, everything is so up in the air."

I wipe my eyes. The more things I say, the more things I have to say, as if all the words have been strung together like pearls and I am throwing them up one bead at a time. "Sometimes I just want to be the one being taken care of because it's stressful. And I know that's selfish, but like I never know what I'm doing, and I just want a normal relationship with my parents where I can hate them sometimes without worrying that they're gonna croak the next minute."

I trail off and open my eyes. He's typing furiously. When I clear my throat, it makes no sound, given that it's rivaling the Kalahari in humidity. "I need a break," I decide. When I go to stand, my feet are pins and needles. I plop back down and fall against my bed.

"Do you need help?" he asks gently.

"Sure."

"There's so much stuff here, Cham," he says, closing his laptop, then standing in front of me. He holds his hands out awkwardly and I reach for him. Our fingers touch the way toes touch the water when it's freezing—that is, like trying not to touch at all.

"Um, here," he says, holding his arm out to me instead.

I grab it quickly and stand, launching forward, and he has to grab onto me.

"You okay?" he asks.

"Yeah, good, thanks." His hands are big around my shoulders, and I become most parts electricity. It's not a personal reaction, it's a *dermatological* reaction. "You can let go," I say, and I'm a little disappointed when he does.

As we come down the stairs, I hear a voice that doesn't belong to my mom or my dad or any of the aides. An elevator drops into my pelvis. By the last step I can see the kitchen, and everyone in the kitchen can see me.

"Hey, Abigail," I say as nonchalantly as I can muster. She's sitting across from my mom at the table, and my mom has the sanitary wipes out. God help us.

"Hey, Cham—and...Brendan?" Abigail says.

"Hey." The four of us orbit each other's awkwardness until finally Abigail takes over the situation, which is what Abigail is best at. She stands up and clacks her fingernails together. The acrylics sound like music, but less melodious and more anxiety-inducing.

"I was just gonna see if I could help with anything on your essay." She watches my mom take another wipe from the container. "You sounded weird on the phone, and I just wanted to make sure you were okay."

"Oh, right, sorry."

"How sweet," my mom says, covering every surface of

the table and leaving behind a sluglike trail of *Kills 99.9 Percent of Bacteria!* "Maybe the three of you could work together? You tutor as well, right, Brendan?"

"Yeah, we've actually made some good progress with Cham's essay," he says, before I can stop him. I'd like to belong to the freezer now.

"Wait, *Brendan* is helping you?" Abigail glares at him. "I offered so many times," she says in the voice of a soldier suffering wounds from the war of senior year. *I'm supposed to be your best friend,* her eyes say. I stare back. *But you and Hilary won that award.*

Abigail's face is reddening. My mom is biting her lip as she holds the wipe up, as if she could disinfect the air between us.

"We could all work on it," Brendan offers, echoing my mom in sentiment but not in hopefulness. Abigail looks at me and I look at the lamp. "Uh, or we could take a break, since we were gonna do that anyway, and then work on it tonight in Google Docs? When's it due?"

"Midnight," I mumble. I look back and forth between Brendan and the door, hoping he'll catch on. "I'll text you. Thanks for the help."

"Sounds good. Thanks, Mrs. Myles," he calls, not bothering to untie his sneakers before he stuffs them back on his feet and opens the door. "See you guys later."

Once he slams the door, it's just me, Abigail, and my mom waiting to see who'll talk first.

"I'll let you two girls hang out," my mom says quickly. She heads toward the sliding door and closes it behind her, taking one last swipe of the handle as she goes.

"What was up with that?" Abigail asks, looking behind her as if Brendan might be coming back. "Cham, what the hell is happening?"

A tear wiggles out of my emotional grasp, but how am I supposed to say anything? I cross my arms and shake my head.

"Fine," she says. "I'm not going to beg you to let me in. I get why Gene got fed up with you being so secretive."

She stands up and goes to the front door, but an aide comes through at the same time Abigail's trying to get out. The aide is pushing my dad, who still looks gaunt and exhausted, but his eyes are clear and his hair is neatly combed.

"Hi, Cham," he says, locking his wheelchair and sounding surprisingly lucid. "Who's your friend?"

Abigail steps toward him quickly. "I'm Abigail," she says, smiling as she extends her hand. "Are you Cham's grandfather?"

My dad cracks a smile. "No, just her old man."

"I'm so sorry, I didn't mean to—" Abigail stutters.

"I've been gray since my twenties," my dad says, his smile widening. "I'm used to it."

The aide laughs and pushes him forward. "You've been a little over twenty for thirty years, Scott."

Dad chuckles at that, and the laughter breaks the tension. It's the happiest I've seen him since the hospital. He pats his hair down in the mirror by the door, his hand jerking in the new way that's replaced the near-constant trembling.

"Well, I'm going to walk my friend out," I say, heading for the door and hoping Abigail follows. "Be right back."

I lean down and kiss my dad on the cheek. The aide missed a spot while shaving him, and the overlooked bit of stubble scrapes me, like it used to when I was a kid and I jumped into my parents' bed in the morning.

"Nice to meet you," my dad says to Abigail as I open the door.

"You too!" she says, then follows me onto the porch. The door closes behind us and we're silent as we look out at the yard.

The sunlight isn't strong enough to be classified as warm, but green things are coming up in my mom's garden. I picture them under the soil just struggling to break through the newly-thawed surface, and what it must feel like to be in so much darkness, then suddenly light.

"What does he have?" Abigail asks, quietly breaking the silence as we head for her car. I shake my head and stuff my hands into the pockets of my jeans.

"What is it, Cham?" Abigail puts her arms around me. I like her hugs more than anyone else's. She always smells like baby powder, and it's not creepy because I know she wasn't rubbing up on any babies.

"It wasn't a heart attack or heart stuff," I say into her soft hair. "He has Parkinson's." The word bounces off the car and then the nearest tree and punctures my eardrum as slowly as the disease ruins a body. "He has Parkinson's," I repeat, and look up at the sky only to discover that the world has not ended. "He's had it for a few years."

Abigail takes a deep breath, her green eyes so green they need a new word for *green*. "I'm sorry, Cham. I'm so sorry."

"We thought something was wrong for a while, but then when I was in eighth grade, he was chaperoning our field trip to the aquarium, and this little smarty-pants bitch was like, *My nana had Parkinson's, blah blah blah, I think he has that.*"

Abigail's face crumples into a weird smile. "Oof, and then you punched the bus window at her?"

I grimace. "Yeah."

She laughs. "You're a badass."

"Something like that."

I pick up a fat green caterpillar on some soul-searching journey from one end of the driveway to the other. Now that I've started talking, it's easier to keep going. And you know what? It feels better. "We obviously would've had to face things eventually, but she said it in front of the whole class and…yeah." Abigail hugs me again, then bends down to tie my combat boot. I guess it came undone with all this fighting my heart's been doing. "I'm sorry I didn't tell you. It's just not something my family talks about." I place the caterpillar down, feeling I've imposed on its destiny long enough. "You know when someone is embarrassed about something and you feel embarrassed for them because *they're* embarrassed? Not because the thing is actually embarrassing, but because it's so goddamn hard to watch someone try to hide something they can't hide…."

Abigail nods. "I get it. You just wanted to keep him safe."

I nod as I realize *Yeah, that's exactly what I wanted to do.*

Her eyes are marbles of concern, which is another reason why I don't tell anyone anything. Pity is the lowliest of human emotions. "It makes sense to try to hide what he wants to hide, but…that's not your job, Cham, okay? You have to tell this to Gene," she urges. "If you explain everything to him, he'll understand why you wouldn't let him into your house, and he'll realize what a star you are and what a not-star Helga is."

I shake my head. "It's too late. I think launching potatoes at his face sorta sealed the deal."

"I'm sorry." She hugs me so hard she squeezes a tear out. "That really sucks. All of it."

"Maybe I'll get a college essay out of it! Title: 'Girl's Dad Gets Sick and Then She Learns Things.'"

"Um, yes, can we talk about that, please?" She pokes me with a bright pink egg-shaped fingernail. "You asked *Brendan*, which at first I was like mega-bitch-mode about, but then I saw how you were looking at him in the kitchen—" She clasps her hands together and bats her eyelashes.

"Oh my god, I was *not*." I laugh—a combination of nervous laughter and happy laughter and relieved laughter and *Wow, I'm experiencing a lot of emotions.*

"Come on, Cham, high school is almost over," she says, pulling at one of my frizzy curls. "Maybe besides graduating twelfth grade, we could graduate from our own shitty self-consciousness."

"You're never self-conscious."

"I know." She does this ass-shaking move as she walks toward her car and opens the driver's-side door. A mischievous smile creeps across her face. "But you are."

"Dick!"

"Hey, with graduation comes big things."

"Or just *things*."

"Big things," she says, nodding knowingly and turning her car on. The music blasting from her speakers fills me with the urge to dance. I squash it 'cause like we're in public. "See you at the Breast Cancer Polar Plunge tomorrow?"

"Yes," I lie, because I can't think of something better to say.

"Repeat after me, Cham," Abigail says, lowering her window as she backs out of my driveway. "Big fucking serendipitous things."

16

Days 'til graduation: 30

Dear Universe,

I know you're having a ball up there at my expense, but cut it out, okay? The deadline for Nicaragua is coming up and I have to *do* something, decide things, determine which course of action to take, which I guess is going to lay the foundation for my summer and also my whole life. How can I possibly choose which world to stay in while the other world moves forward without me? *No pressure, though! Definitely don't panic!*

What better way to spend a Sunday morning than picking up neon-orange T-shirts with my mom so we can walk in circles around each other in the name of brain degeneration?

"I am not going to this," my dad says as I'm doodling on the refrigerator whiteboard. (A lopsided heart with squiggly arms dons a pair of swimmies as a big wave comes.) He has one arm through his shirt and the other defiantly at his side. "You are not going to push me around a track with a bunch of sick people while other people watch."

"Scott, your sister got us the tickets, and the doctor highly recommended we connect with people who understand. We've been doing this alone for four years. It's time we start taking suggestions." My mom yanks his arm through his jacket sleeve while going on and on about the importance of community. "I got the ladies at work involved, because what we're doing hasn't been working. The sickness, whatever you want to call it, is progressing. We can't just *not* go. "

"Oh, yes, we can." My dad whips his head around and squints out the window. I hold my breath. He doesn't say anything about the tree, which makes me hopeful that today is a good day. Or would be, if mom weren't a dictator.

"We are doing this as a family," she says, and shuttles us into the car as quickly as she can. It's one of those days in spring when all the birds come out of the cracks of winter and suddenly there's hope again that we're not going to have to wear long johns forever.

For the whole ride, my dad sits in stony silence. I never

used to be afraid of him, but sometimes the disease replaces his gentleness with harshness. It's freaking scary. Unlike the monsters under my bed that he used to shoo away, this is petrifying because it's real.

By the time we get to the track at school, my level of dread is up over my ponytail. The chorus of cheerful voices belonging to the women my mom works with threatens to smother me—death by upbeat pillow. Why do we have to be amped about something so terrible? It's disingenuous, and I look hideous in this shade of orange.

We pass streamers and posters and clusters of people in matching T-shirts with corny things on the front. The turf is saturated with water; mud is threatening to do a global takeover.

"Hey!" one of the women calls to my mom, and before I know it, we are jammed under a tent with this woman my mom works with and eight other ladies who probably all go by Donna.

"Over here," one of the Donnas says, setting my dad up next to a woman in a wheelchair.

"THIS...IS...MY...MOTHER...VIVIAN," Donna says to my dad. "She has Alzheimer's," Donna whispers to my mom.

"Nice to meet you," my dad says, and it is obviously not very nice at all.

"Cake?" another Donna asks, coming around with a slice that says *Fight* in pink icing.

"Why do I have to keep this old lady company?" my dad whispers to my mom. Vivian is putting a bright T-shirt on and trying to hand me another one too. She also keeps calling me her "sweet Carla," which, honestly, is kind of nice.

"Because we are being proactive," my mom says.

"Judy, is this your husband and your daughter?" yet another Donna asks. "So nice to meet you both. Cham, I hear you're about to graduate from high school. Where are you going next year?"

"No idea," I say, wishing I could wrap this T-shirt around my head and shrink to a size that requires a microscope to find. "I might take a year off or something."

"That's the first I've heard of this," my mom says with an eyebrow raised.

Donna laughs and slaps Mom on the shoulder. "I think that's a great idea. More and more kids are doing it. Gap years are fantastic. They have so many programs out there now. You have your whoooooooole life ahead of you." The way she extends the word, it sounds less like an opportunity and more like a life sentence.

"Come on, Cham, Scott," my mom says. "It's time to do a lap. When Aunt Bridget gets here, I want her to see us involved."

Right, because this is a performance. The important thing is that people see us as involved. My mom pushes my dad over the turf of the football field, and I follow. We shuffle along into the music and the bright colors and the smell of hot dogs. There's a table with raffle tickets and people playing Frisbee and tents scattered all over the turf. I guess this sort of thing makes people feel happy. *Some* people, I mean.

Dear Universe,

Pump the brakes on your enthusiasm. I want to be tolerant and stuff, but I can't stand people rallying behind the cure for a disease as if the disease is a dragon and we are mighty princesses, deserving of everything in the mighty freaking kingdom.
Fight Alzheimer's! Fight Parkinson's! Yeah, let me go sharpen my knife. Everything is just something surviving because something else is dying. It's not like our side is "right." We're not the freaking royalty or the chosen ones. We're just people, and we're here because a bunch of horny DNA succeeded in getting it on. My dad isn't "brave," and we aren't "good people" (but maybe you knew that already). He's stuck in his bodily situation like we all are, except his is worse, more confining, inevitable. I know I need to do something, but this is not it. If I must wear this color orange, at least let me stand in traffic.

"That girl looks like you," my dad says. He waves at some girl who does not look like me, and she smiles and waves back. I think she feels bad about his wheelchair, which makes me hate her, and then myself for assuming that.

"Isn't that your friend?" my dad says suddenly, looking toward the entrance to the track. "What's his name? Victor?"

"I don't have a friend named Victor," I say, but then I look around and realize who my dad's talking about. My heart involuntarily flings itself against my chest. Brendan is pitching a tent with Gill School colors and setting up lawn chairs under it. He looks up and waves at me uncertainly.

For a second I am frozen. Though I'd quite like to hop aboard a spaceship and ditch both worlds entirely, it's been exhausting keeping the two separate. Something about this collision feels inevitable, maybe even destined to be by the powers of the universe. I'm a strong girl and all, but I'm no match for the sun, moon, stars, and space debris.

"Uh, I'll be right back," I tell my parents. I head to the Gill School tent quickly, feeling nervous and exposed, like I don't have anything on, not even this stupid orange T-shirt. Speakers are blasting pop music. Josie and Danika brought face paint, and it's pretty much a party, the iPad in Brendan's hand working like a bouncer to check everyone in.

"Hey, Cham," Brendan says curiously. "I didn't think you were coming to this."

"Uh, yeah, my mom didn't give me much of a choice."

Helga and Gene come through the gate by the concession

stand. Behind them a pack of seniors march in. Jared and Marquis are wearing gratuitously large backpacks and holding big shopping bags full of snacks. "Why are there so many people from school here?"

He cocks his head. "Didn't you get the e-mail? We changed our volunteer event to this one."

Between my mom looking back over her shoulder at me, and Helga and Gene looking into each other's eyes with no regard for me, I can't really process what Brendan's saying to me. "Wait, why did it get moved?"

"Someone suggested it'd be more...*supportive*...so we changed it," Brendan says. "I mean, Student Council did." He avoids my eyes by bringing his face very close to the iPad in his hand. I feel like I'm on a carnival ride with none of the fun and all of the nausea.

"What? Why?"

"Well," he starts, "someone came forward and asked—"

"Was it you?" I ask, shielding my eyes to look at him. Ahead of me Danika is painting a butterfly on Josie's cheek; behind me, my parents are talking to one of the Donnas. The world just isn't big enough for all these worlds.

"No, it wasn't me," he says. "And if I knew you were going to be here, I would have told you. I swear," he adds quickly, and his voice sounds nervous, as if he's lying.

"This doesn't mean anything to them." My voice quavers. "It's just something to check off to soothe their guilt and graduate and move on."

"I know, Cham, I'm sorry—"

"So it *was* you?" There's a fire building in my throat. "After all the things I told you about wanting to keep this stuff private, why would you do this? And not like *warn* me?" My spit tastes like acid and the putrid stuff left over after vomiting. "I put so much trust in you. How could you just go against me like that and get the school to change the event?"

"Cham, I didn't—" His voice is strained. I back up, wishing I could draw a heavy cloak around myself to keep everything out.

"I thought you understood. I thought of all the people in their own worlds, you understood *my* world." My mom and dad pass again, and I wipe my eyes quickly, as if jamming my fingers in there can keep the tears back. "I don't think you know me at all, and it's better that way. I just wish I never told you anything—"

"Cham." Abigail's voice is behind me, and the next thing I know, she's standing beside us. "What's going on?" Her face is a contorted tissue.

"Hey," I say. "Nothing. It's just that Brendan changed the event and—"

"What? I'm the one who asked school to change it," Abigail says, looking between the two of us. "In your driveway yesterday, you said it felt better talking about your dad's Parkinson's and like airing all that shit out, so I thought—"

"So you thought, *Hey, let's get the whole school here?*"
She winces at the sarcasm in my voice, but I don't care.
"How could you think this is something I'd *want*?" I ask
incredulously. "It just blows my mind."

"Cham, you'll feel better if you face things," she says,
shifting back and forth, nervously adjusting her ponytail.
"When I was talking to your mom, she said you guys wanted
to be more proactive as a family, and, I don't know, I wanted
a grand gesture to prove to you that we're here for you. I feel
like a terrible friend for not knowing what was going on. I
just want you to be okay, and I thought that if—"

"That if you forced everyone from school to come here
without telling me that I'd somehow be grateful for all
the 'support'?" I put air quotes around the last word, my
mouth tasting more and more like bile.

"I'm sorry that you're pissed, but isn't it better not to
hide anything?" Her face is desperate for me to say *yes*,
but my body is populated by *no*s. "You don't have to keep
doing this alone, Cham."

I shake my head at her. Way in the back of my mind
a voice is saying *Let her in*, but the anger has piled up
like bricks, and it's hard to get even her genuine kindness
through. I look over at the track, trying to locate my parents among so many chipper bodies. Brendan has been
silent the whole time, the iPad limp in his hands, but now
he raises it. "I should go check on things," he says, breaking
the awkward silence.

"Wait," I say to his back. My brain feels like it's over-heating. He turns around, his face uncharacteristically solemn. "I'm sorry I blamed you. I just figured—"

"Why did you think it was Brendan?" Abigail asks. Her voice is deadly quiet now, which it is every time she's about to burst into tears. I take a deep breath that honestly feels quite shallow. "Why would he know anything?"

I look at the two of them, feeling caught between them or caught in a lie or caught in something I don't fully understand, but it's something I can't break free of. It's stretching me out in every direction, and I don't know where I'll rip first. "He—he found out by mistake a couple months ago," I stammer, my voice strangely high-pitched. "I'm sorry, I know I should've told you, but—"

"He's known for *months*?" she says incredulously. "I just don't get why you could tell him and not me."

I look at Brendan and he looks at me. Our eye contact and the things we know and everything from the last few weeks create a bubble that only the two of us live in. I don't know if Abigail can sense it. I sigh and usher her over to the side of the track. I look behind me at Brendan, who's headed for the snack table in his bright yellow tutu. The answer reveals itself to me at the same time I reveal it to Abigail: "It's just so easy with him. I don't have to compete with anyone else: not Helga, not Hilary, no one." I step out of the way of a woman with a stroller who is *very* determined to end Alzheimer's by power walking. "Because I feel comfortable with him."

Abigail bites her lip, seeming totally confused. I can't see my face, but I have a feeling I look totally confused too. "I don't know, okay? Maybe because one time we laughed about dying and it made the whole thing seem less scary. I'm not intimidated by him, and that makes it easy."

"It's because I'm a loser," Brendan fills in. I hadn't noticed him walking back toward us. "Sorry to interrupt, but Mr. Garcia is looking for you, Abigail." He swings the bag of cups and ponchos he's holding, and the centripetal force sucks me in.

"You are *not* a loser," I say, feeling my cheeks flush. "You're sweet and weird in a great way, and you're like the bag that's strapped to a horse's butt during a carriage ride. You just totally get my shit."

"Cham!" my mom calls. She's looping past us and waving while my dad kind of scowls and kind of waves. She cuts across the track nearly tripping a tall man with a foam brain hat on his head.

"Hey, Brendan!" she says. "And Abigail, nice to see you again!"

My dad gives a halfhearted wave, but honestly, he looks miserable. We all do.

"Mom, Brendan, Abigail, I appreciate the effort, but let's go. Dad, we are getting you out of this hellhole of enthusiasm."

The music is still playing, and the people are still walking, and absolutely everything continues despite my decision to leave. "Come on, Dad." I nudge my mom's hands off his wheelchair. "We're going home."

"Oh, good," he says, rubbing his hands together. "Nice to see you kids!"

"No, we're not, Cham," my mom says. "We signed up for a time slot to walk, we bought tickets, and we are staying." She locks his wheelchair with the metal handles that dig into the wheels.

My dad gives me a look like *For the love of god, get me out of here.*

"No, Mom. This isn't up to you. It should be up to Dad." Brendan and Abigail talk together, then back away quietly. I lean on my dad's wheelchair and undo the locks. "Come on."

My mom sighs and takes her keys out. "What do you want to do, Scott?"

"Well, now that you've finally asked me," my dad says, sounding suddenly less tired, "I'd like to get the hell home already."

～

Inside the house, my mom still has her coat on as she takes her cleaning supplies out. I come over just as she's trying to get revenge on the countertops. "Mom, stop. You're scrubbing the enamel off them," I say.

"Just a little spot here."

"Judy," my dad calls from his room.

"Just a second," she says.

She's going at the poor tiles with her elbows out, and her sponge is starting to tear. I touch her wrist gently. "Mom, come on."

"I'm getting it, Cham."

"Judy!" my dad calls again, louder this time.

"I'm coming, Scott!" she hollers back. "Just one—" In making her way down the cabinet with the paper towel, she notices I'm still wearing my combat boots.

"Cham," she says, her eyes flashing, "why the hell didn't you take your shoes off? I've been cleaning and cleaning and—"

"Mom, you gotta stop cleaning," I say quietly, taking the spray bottle out of her hand. "I'm sorry about my shoes, but it's a mess out there, a rainy, muddy mess, and the cleaner you try to make it, the more obvious it is when the shit gets in." I look out the window at the tears the sky is throwing at us. "The shit always gets in." I pull at one of her rubber gloves. Her hands are cracking open under them, which happens when skin soaks too long in soapy water. "Please, for the love of linoleum. Stop. Scrubbing."

My mom sort of smiles, but it's a smile that couldn't bench-press a tooth. "Someone's gotta keep things in order around here."

My dad wheels in with his shirt half on. "Didn't you

hear me calling?" he says angrily. "I almost fell. Why were you ignoring me?"

"I can't always be there immediately," she says too loudly. I inch toward the stairs, sensing the mood turning. "I'm trying, but I can't always—"

"Well, maybe if you didn't waste time doing things I don't want to do, you could actually take care of me when I need you." He scowls at the floor, then uses the arm that isn't in the shirt to pick at something on the tile.

"Dammit," he mutters after a few tries. Then he licks his finger and wipes the crumb on the counter.

My mom intercepts him. "Don't put that there! Don't you see I'm cleaning?"

"You didn't care that I didn't want to go," my dad says, abandoning the crumb and returning to the sleeve of his shirt. "You forced me into the car. You talked with Cham about me like I wasn't there. I should've stayed here, let you two do whatever walking you wanted to do."

My mom takes her gloves off and throws them on the counter. "Well, what am I supposed to do? I'm doing the best I can here. I'm doing this all by myself."

"So, let me *do* something," he cries. "You never let me do anything."

"Because you can't do anything!" she screams. Her shoulders slump, and she slides to the ground with her face in her hands. My dad pushes his other arm through his shirt, and the only sound in the room is the fabric sliding over his head.

"Maybe I shouldn't have pushed it," she says softly, "and I'm sorry, Scott, if you felt ignored. I want you to have as much say in everything as you can, but sometimes I have to step in and make decisions."

He crosses his arms. "I'm never going to one of those things again. And no more hospital or doctors. I don't care if I have a stroke. I'd rather lie there and die than go through that prison again. They wanted to poison me," he says, his voice rising like he might cry.

I touch my throat, hoping to push the lump in it down, but it's getting bigger and bigger. My mom crawls over and puts her head in his lap. At first his arms are stiff, but then he touches her hair. I turn away and make for the stairs. All the things I haven't felt, every instance ignored, every time I was an asshole when really I was just scared, every time I looked away, comes rushing up my esophagus. This is what I was afraid of. To see how it hurts and then to feel it: from my dad, from my mom, from myself. I want to hide in my room if I'm going to cry, because if I start crying I might not stop. But at the last minute I bow my head and squat down next to my parents.

"Hey, Dad?" I say, but my voice hardly makes a sound. Why is it so hard to show the people we love the most how much that is? Why is it so hard to show how scared we are and just the vastness of it all, how much there actually is inside me, and all of us? *It's like there's a whole universe in there.*

I wrap my arms around him, resting my cheek on the back of his sweater. His arm jerks a little under mine, and I can't keep it in anymore. Everything from the last few years and the last few months and the last few days condensates. I cry like the first day I was born. The tears lead to more tears, and eventually I get into some deep belly crying and hiccuping.

"I'm sorry, Dad," I say, voice muffled in the soft fabric. "I'm so sorry."

17

{APRIL}

Days 'til graduation: 17

HERE'S THE THING ABOUT HIGH SCHOOL. AND TIME. AND herpes. (Okay, everything, I guess.) It doesn't need my help. Even if I stop counting down the days to prom, the days still get closer to prom. Even if I look away while my dad gets sicker, he still gets sicker. Even if I start a rumor that Helga has herpes, she doesn't actually have herpes. (I didn't start that rumor, okay?)

What this doesn't apply to is my college essay. Even with Brendan's help, I can't seem to get past *Dear College Admissions Person*. The e-mail I send to Evelyn is so pathetic there's no need to include it in my senior year time capsule. Let's just say I'm finally using my dad's sickness to my advantage. No need to shake the Magic 8 Ball and ask it if I am going to hell. The answer is yes.

Hey Evelyn,

I'm sorry that my essay is late. Again. I was hoping to turn it in this week, but my dad is dying faster than usual, so I've been trying to help my mom take care of him. I haven't had any extra time to work on the essay, and even though Brendan was a good tutor, I don't think I'll be able to pass it in yet. I know me going to Nicaragua depends on getting it in, but my parents need me right now, and I need to prioritize family over schoolwork. Could I get it to you by the last day of class? Thanks.

Your Worst Student

Text exchange with Abigail during which we brave the awkward aftermath of our sort-of-fight:

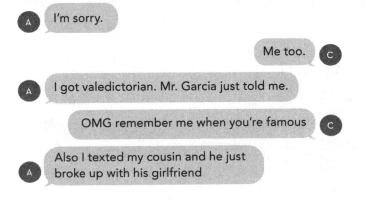

A: I'm sorry.

C: Me too.

A: I got valedictorian. Mr. Garcia just told me.

C: OMG remember me when you're famous

A: Also I texted my cousin and he just broke up with his girlfriend

A: Do you want to take him to prom?

C: Um

C: Not really

C: Don't worry. The universe has my back

C: Lol jk it lives to screw with me

A: Poor Chamaroon

A: You're coming over this weekend and we're making progress on your essay.

A: I'm not going to Nicaragua without you.

A: You owe me for lying

A: I can't believe you made it seem like your parents were weirdos and that's why you couldn't have friends over

A: and actually you just didn't want people to know your dad was sick lmao

C: ok it sounds crazy when you write it out like that...

A: if you ever want to talk about anything i'm here

C: thx

A: come over soon for that essay?

WANTED: A MEDIOCRE PROM DATE

If you're a very good dancer but not a better dancer than me, you should ask me to prom before it happens in two weeks! I'm a cool girl, like comfortable with myself and stuff, and my dentist once said I was "cute," so I guess you could say I'm a catch. One time I had four cavities filled without Novocain, and I run a six-minute mile without walking, so I'm also kind of a badass. Not that I'm bragging. My GPA is a lot of C minuses, but my best friend says it's a blessing to be below average. I like paper flowers as opposed to real ones because real ones always die and that depresses me. My breath smells like an Altoid except when I'm chewing. Please don't apply to take me to prom if you'd rather look at your cell phone than look at constellations. I am a firm believer in wishes and love and wishes that lead to love. I'm making one right now. I've had one boyfriend so far, and he asked not to be mentioned in this ad, but his name is Gene and you should not ask him about me. He's the one with legs on the track team who once asked me to prom quite publicly and then changed his mind. This is the ad to replace him.

Xs and Os (but not on the first date),
Chamomile

Just in case a prom date falls out of the sky in the next seventeen days, I go to Willa's Closet on Saturday. It's been a long morning doing boring things like ordering my cap and gown so that I don't attend graduation in knee-high combat boots and underwear. I was going to see if my dad wanted to go for a walk now that the weather is better, but he was Skyping his sister about the Brain Degeneration Walk (not a happy conversation, especially since my aunt ended up being there alone). I want to be here with him now, but I don't really know what that looks like sometimes. Cue a little shopping break.

"You're back," the same girl from before says as I open the door. It jingles shut and I breathe in the smell of secondhand stuff, which has a sort of sweet rejected quality to it. "Still looking for a prom dress?"

I sigh. "Who knows."

"Bad day?"

"Yeah, like twenty on top of each other."

"Try some shopping therapy," she suggests, and I look over at the mannequin in the window. She's still wearing the lacy white dress.

"I wanted that one. I love the lace around the collar and the sleeves. But shopping isn't going to help me." I lean on the counter and fiddle with the essential-oil testers.

The salesgirl is looking at me as she runs her finger along the rim of her big hoop earrings. "Would you like to vomit-speak about it?"

I take a large whiff of patchouli, decide I'm not interested in smelling like a hippie's underarm, and rest my elbows on the counter. "I might fail English 'cause I can't write a freaking college essay and my boyfriend broke up with me and my dad is dying and I don't think I can go with everyone to Nicaragua after graduation because, well, lots of reasons that mostly have to do with my dad dying and I just really need a sign from the universe." My head is too heavy. I make a pillow with my hands to rest my forehead.

"Oh, girl." She frowns, then gets off her stool. "I'm Izzy." She extends her hand. "Who are you?"

"Cham." My voice is muffled by the glass.

"Cool. You're a senior?" I lift my head and nod. "Don't worry, it gets better after high school. You don't have to see the same people every day and be spoon-fed the same bullshit and pretend something like a dance you get a corsage for could possibly be the best night of your life. Once you stop being forced to be a zombie, you stop acting like a zombie. You fucking wake up."

I blink at her. "But prom is the last dance of high school. It's not *not* a big deal. It means we made it."

She shakes her head. "None of those things actually mean anything. We grow up at weird, unexpected times." I shift back and forth and she laughs. "Oh no, I hope I didn't crush your high school dreams. Shit, I was trying to cheer you up. All I mean is don't sweat it, any of it: prom, graduation, college. It may not seem like there's anything more important, but trust me. There's a whole world out there." She points beyond the display window, with its lacy white dress and pink cowboy boots and open trunk of scarves and pocketbooks that people gave up on.

"I just need a sign," I say again. "Just one huge sign about what the universe has in store for me or just like how to be a freaking person in the world."

She laughs. "No matter what sign you get, you still have to make up a story about it. The sign is irrelevant. It's how you *interpret* it."

"I don't want to interpret anything. I want to be told what to do." She raises an eyebrow at me. "It's too confusing. Seriously, my brain is populated by question marks. I just wish I had someone to ask."

"You and everyone else." She picks up a cardboard box from the floor and heaves it onto a table, adding little blue circular price stickers to the tank tops and flowy skirts.

I take one last look at the lacy white dress in the window and sigh. "I should go work on my essay so I can eventually go to college and be a member of society slightly more useful than a toilet plunger."

"Hey! Toilet plungers are crucial at handling our shit." She grins and makes a joke sound effect, hitting an invisible cymbal in the air. "You don't want me to launch into my spiel about how college is a big moneymaking machine that obliterates creativity and real thinking and turns us into little capitalist nightmares. I'll spare you from that."

I laugh. "Thanks. Honestly, I just want to lock myself in my room or go for a run or make out in bed until the world ends."

"Ooooh, you didn't mention you had someone to make out with."

"I don't," I say quickly, backing toward the door. "Just got dumped, remember?"

"And yet," she says, following me with her pointer in the air, "you said 'make out' like you had a little pair of lips in mind. High school's almost over. Last chance, last chance," she chants. "Does this person have a prom date?"

"Don't know, not asking." I back into the door and it opens with a jingle. "Attempting my college essay now and also scoping out toilet plungers."

"Do your thing, girl," Izzy cheers, holding up a hideous vacation T-shirt with pairs of drunk flamingos covering it. She slaps it with a price sticker. "Go after your own shit."

～

"Well, well, well," Abigail says, opening her front door. "Look who came crawling back to me!"

"Oh, shut up, Abigail." I push her into the house playfully. "I'm not *that* desperate to get this essay done and go to Nicaragua or whatever."

"No, of course not." She takes me into the kitchen and pours me a glass of water. "Come, wet your lips, hydrate yourself in preparation for this amazing essay we are going to write."

"I don't know about that." I take the glass and down the water in four huge gulps.

Abigail pats the countertop. The stools are high and there are six electrical sockets so that she can do her homework without any of her devices dying on her. Some parents really will do anything to see their kid get into college. "Let's start by looking at your old essay," she says, her fingers poised over her keyboard. "E-mail it to me real quick."

"Nope, definitely not." I shake my head so fast the illuminated apple on her laptop doubles. "Let's start fresh."

"You at least have to tell me what it was about so I can know where to go from there."

"No way." I trace my finger on the glass, where cool drops of water are starting to condense. "We gotta just start over."

She glares at me and I glare back at her. My eyes are fully lubricated and good to stay open for the next two and a half minutes if they have to. She blinks first and I cackle. "What did *you* write about?" I ask.

She points to the postcard on her refrigerator that says

¡Hola from Spain! with two cartoons dancing cheek to cheek. "I wrote about me and Hilary's trip to Europe over the summer and how it made me want to study Spanish in college or maybe art history and just eat up the world. I could show you if you want."

She turns her laptop to face me. I rest my chin in my hands and offer to read aloud to her because that at least will guarantee I won't fall asleep.

"Go for it," she says, and closes her eyes like the delicious, overconfident ham she is.

"Ahem!" I say, using my empty water glass as a microphone. "'With just one look upon the garish decorations splayed across the Gaudi House Museum in Barcelona, the clandestine exchanges between patrons experiencing for the first time the eponymous designs, I too suddenly understood the thrill of such outrageous, one-of-a-kind mosaics, and knew that I would not rest until I'd seen the plethora of history and culture Spain had to offer.'"

I look up at her to find she's smiling. With her eyes closed. "What the hell do all those words mean? And who talks like that?"

"It's good, right?"

I listen to the dishwasher laboring over the plates and glasses it didn't get dirty but still somehow has to clean. "I mean, it just doesn't sound like you at all. When you talk about Spain, you talk about the club you got into and how you drank sangria and danced all night long in tall heels that you're probably gonna have to see an orthopedic surgeon about but it was so worth it because for once you found people who want to break it down all night just as intensely as you do."

"Well, duh, but I can't talk about *that*." She flicks me in the forehead. "The point is to come off in a very particular way, like cultured and curious and smart and—oh, come on, Cham, don't make that face."

"I'm not making a face," I say, fixing my face, then breaking into a smile. "Listen, I'm not writing some phony bullshit essay about some life-changing event some rando adults want to hear."

Abigail slides a bottle of nail polish across the counter and unscrews it. It's a pinky-bluish-purple shade of iridescent marvelousness. "What do you want to do, then?"

I think for a second. "I want to make the anti-college essay. It'll be exactly the opposite of that bullshit everyone writes, and instead of writing it, 'cause writing sucks, we will video it."

"Cute but no. We need an A."

"I'm serious! This is a good idea! And we can put it on YouTube or whatever, and college admissions people everywhere will have their minds freaking blown."

"Cham! We have so much work to do—we don't have time to make a video."

I hop off the stool and kneel at her feet, clasping my hands together, my lower lip protruding. "Just one little video. I just want one true thing." As soon as it's out of my mouth, I realize how true it is. Maybe that's why I couldn't get myself to write this damn essay. "Look, we need your old dance costumes, okay? We have to get into the performance of it."

"Cham..."

"Oh, come on! We made silly videos all the time freshman year, remember? There was that one where we put on black lipstick and pretended to haunt ourselves."

She laughs. "Yeah, and the one where we cut masks out of cardboard boxes and just did the stupidest shit and put it on Instagram."

"Yeah! The problem is that in the last year or two everyone's been so caught up in their extracurriculars and college applications and stupid baloney grades that no one just fucks around anymore."

I grab a wooden spoon off the counter and smack the steel pot. Its ringing reverberates off every metal surface in the kitchen: the toaster, the refrigerator, the oven, even the claddagh ring on Abigail's finger with the heart always pointing out.

"I WANT TO FUCK AROUND!" I yell over my own ruckus. "AND THEN I WANT TO TELL THOSE BUTTMUNCH COLLEGE ADMISSIONS PEOPLE ALL ABOUT IT!"

Abigail laughs and shakes her head with her hands over her ears. "You're a nut," she yells. "Quit it before I go deaf."

I put the spoon down. "Come on, we're doing it."

"We are *not* doing it." She crosses her arms.

"Shut up and get the music," I tell her. "Oh, and for props we need that black swan feather mask in your room and blue lipstick and cooked spaghetti."

Her eyes widen. "Um, what the hell are we going to do with all of those things?"

"We're gonna perform a damn good college essay. We're gonna perform one with *heart*," I say excitedly.

She goes upstairs and I swipe a little of that pinky-bluish-purple shade of iridescent marvelousness on my pinkie finger. I haven't actually *felt* excited in a really long time. I was excited about prom and graduation, but that was more of a mental thing. And yeah, I got excited about Gene and hooking up with Gene, but that was a different kind of excitement. What I feel right now is potential: potential to say one true thing, to create one real thing. In a world where everything seems to be a long to-do list where the last thing to do is die, this is a tiny, tiny rebellion. To say what I am, to actually reflect. It's kind of absolutely thrilling. It's also an excellent way to procrastinate.

"Got everything," Abigail says as she clanks down the stairs with her arms full of speakers and costumes. She dumps it onto the floor, and we sift through the stuff together. I settle on the black feather mask with some blue lipstick. Abigail wears metallic wings.

We turn off all the lights except the lamp, which is

acting as a spotlight, and I do my lipstick in the reflection of the toaster. I shake out my hands and legs. "We need the perfect song."

"Your essay, your choice."

"Okay, when I was a kid, my favorite song was this." I take out my phone, sync it to the speakers, and turn the song on for her.

"What is it?"

" 'Obvious Child.' "

"What's obvious?"

"No, the song," I say, and laugh. "It's called 'Obvious Child.' "

"Ooh, I like these drums," she says.

"They're good, right?"

"Oooh, yes, I like this a lot. Wait," she whispers in my ear as we stand side by side, looking into the camera. "What are we going to say? I got so excited to put on a costume and dance that I completely forgot what we should say."

"Um, it's gonna come to us," I say, because suddenly I'm sure of it. "We're just gonna dance and sing and say exactly what it's like right now. You know, everything we didn't put in our essays."

She replays the song. "I really hope my parents don't come home."

"Same."

The drums start again, and Abigail drops it low on every other thud. I drop it low too, just not nearly *as* low.

While the drums get faster and faster, she adds some shaking of the lower half of her body. I circle around her because I definitely won't be attempting anything like that.

"Hello, College Admissions Persons," I start. "I just want to clear the air because a lot of people are sending you a lot of bullshit right now. Tonight, on the eve of the day before the day that her college essay is due, Chamomile Myles would like you to know about the real her."

"Why are you talking in the third person?" Abigail giggles.

I blow the camera a blue kiss. "Despite what a million people are saying in their essays to you, what it means to be seventeen is this."

I point to Abigail and close my eyes and let the music pulse through me and say just exactly what comes to mind. "Seventeen is that message in the bottle you wrote yourself when you were a kid asking, *How cool is it with boobs? What weird places have hair now? Are you tall?* Seventeen is a lot of nights scrolling through feeds, figuring out who's luckier than you are. Seventeen is breakfast food at every meal—"

Abigail laughs and hisses, "What the hell are you talking about?"

"Just go with it, Abigail, come on! Your turn!"

I wave the camera in her face and duck out of view.

She clears her throat, then says tentatively, "Seventeen is driving in a car...and the music is loud enough to make your ears scream....and nothing isn't possible in this car with this person and you." She gets louder. "And the world is not an oyster, it's a trampoline, and your next jump will launch you to the moon—"

Now I cut in. "Seventeen is a million questions about love, and searching every book and movie for an answer. Seventeen is being very certain you will be nothing like your parents. It's a text to a random number who's known you all along, a lot of texts, actually, usually at three AM."

Abigail laughs. "Seventeen is a dream we're all awake for."

"It's all these reasons to run away from home, but then Mom makes pie, and actually your favorite socks just came out of the wash, and really there is always tomorrow to flee to your freedom."

"It's worrying about not being invited to things like sleepovers and parties and bowling nights and movie dates." I look at Abigail. I didn't know *she* worried about those things.

I pause, then say more seriously, "Seventeen is being very aware of this thing called other people's eyes and what you look like in them and who you really are when you're alone at night and your phone just died. Seventeen is a lot of mornings cursing alarm clocks and wanting so much to tell someone something, but no one's invented the vocabulary for it yet, so it sits in your throat like a bolus of FUUUUUUCKKKK!"

"FUUUUUUCKKKK!" Abigail yells back.

"Seventeen is the suspicion that an emoji understands you better than your own parents. It's having to write a stupid college essay, when instead of trying to answer fake questions, you could actually be asking *real* ones."

The drums wind down and Abigail waves hurriedly at me. I put my face very close to the camera. There's no way we're sending this to Evelyn, but it matters even if no one sees it but us. "Seventeen is Cham about to turn eighteen and she's officially asking the universe what the hell she's supposed to do. She will donate a boob if she has to, just show her a sign, a flash of brilliance, a heartbreaking work of staggering genius. It could be a freaking tampon applicator, *something* so that she knows. Because she wants to know." I lean in closer so it's only my blue lips filling the screen. "She's ready."

18

Days 'til graduation: 11

FOR MOST OF SENIOR YEAR, I COULDN'T WAIT TO CHARGE OUT the doors of the Gill School and flash the world because I did it. I graduated high school. Now that it's actually happening, though, it's less of a tits-out situation and more of a shit-my-plaid-skirt situation. Everyone's talking about college and gap years and a summer spent backpacking the edge of the freaking universe, but do any of them have a dad who may or may not live through the summer?

The good news is that as long as I don't think about the end, it's marvelous. The teachers in all my classes besides English have officially stopped bothering to teach. The window of opportunity to educate has closed, and every senior is standing behind it, smiling and waving. (Okay, some people are making obscene hand gestures. Others are perfecting a good old pants-down-ass-up mooning.)

English is another story, of course. I sent Evelyn the video Abigail and I made of my college essay, but she hasn't said anything about it, which is either a great sign or a dismal one. I've put it out of my mind because we've gone into full-blown final-project mode. The cool thing is that Evelyn gives us class time to work on it, which, let's be honest, means do anything *but* it. The less cool thing is it's due in a week, and Cham's Personal Philosophy is currently a three-word document: *Cham's Personal Philosophy.* It's in a really nice font, though.

"How have you written so much?" I ask Abigail in class on Friday as she scrolls through what could be an ebook's worth of work.

"I keep thinking about the A I'm going to get so I graduate high school without a single B." *Gag me with a compostable spork.* "You just have to get some words down. Even if you hate thinking about philosophy and life and stuff, just write *something* down. It gets easier after that."

"I *have* written—"

"Titles don't count. No matter how long you spend trying different fonts."

I pause and pick at something under my chair that could be gum. Brendan sits on his desk, paging through a copy of *Caligula.*

"Actually, I don't mind thinking about this stuff at all,"

I say. "I kind of like it. I just don't want to do anything more than think about it."

Abigail looks behind her. "How have we not talked about the fact that Brendan was *at your house*." She adds knowingly, "I bet getting out of high school is going to be really good for him."

He sees us looking at him and stands up. I feel something weird when he walks over. Like nervous? Nah, probably just hungry.

"Hey, Abigail, hey, Cham," he says. I look up and he meets my eyes. I look away quickly and attempt a garbled sound that I swear is a greeting. Abigail looks at me like *Excuse me?*

There's a tapping on my desk and I turn around. "Can I talk to you in the hall?" Evelyn asks. "We're about to transition to silent thinking time, but I wanna chat a bit before then."

"Okay," I say.

Abigail does the sign of the cross over her chest, and I follow Evelyn out of the room.

The posters in the hallway are different now that school is almost over. The GET YOUR TICKETS TO PROM signs have been replaced with GET YOUR CAP AND GOWN signs. Apparently, you have to buy tickets to go to your own graduation, which is one of eight thousand reasons why I've decided I'm not going. When they hear about the buy-your-own-tickets scam, I'm sure my parents will understand. For sure.

"I got your e-mail," Evelyn says as she closes the door

and traps me in the large open space of the hall. "I'm sorry to hear that your dad is sick."

"Thanks."

"I can definitely extend the deadline on your essay when you're having such a hard time at home, and I'm glad to hear you got some tutoring on it, but the video won't work."

"Darn," I say. I can see over Evelyn's shoulder into the classroom. Brendan's got a fortress of books stacked on his desk.

"Get a *written* version to me by the last day of class, okay?" Evelyn says, obstructing my view with a subtle shift of her body. "I don't want you to miss out on Nicaragua."

I turn toward the door, hoping that's all she wanted to talk about. "Thanks, I appreciate it."

She looks at me with those shovel eyes that threaten to probe your depths and churn up all your funky soil. "How's your final project coming? Have you started your outside research?"

"Um."

"Never mind, don't answer that. Do you know what you'd like your statement to be?"

I look down at my feet: two combat boots nearly covering two rather sallow-looking socks.

"I don't know," I say, gazing down the hall to where a pair of freshmen have clambered up the stairs and are starting to make out. "Literally, I have no idea."

"Get to class," Evelyn calls to them, then smiles at me with a shake of her head. "Living in the questions is good."

Why do teachers always speak in sentences that don't make sense?

"How about if for now you don't worry about forming a cohesive project. Just write down whatever questions you have, no matter how small or seemingly silly."

"Like just write down all my questions?" She nods. "Sure, I can do that." That's the most manageable thing she's asked of me all year.

"Good! I've been thinking about what you said about high school and beyond high school and the moon. I like that you went there, Cham," she says as I subtly inch toward the classroom door, the noise inside having gotten louder and louder as Evelyn's been out here talking to me. "A lot of people just want to get a good grade, and they're afraid of offending me or something, but sometimes I think you have to be a little offensive to really learn something." She pauses and reconsiders. "Well, maybe not. All I'm saying is that a lot of philosophy came out of realizing just how strange normal life is. Keep thinking. And don't forget to be researching an outside source too, okay?"

"Sure," I sigh, glaring up at the sign reminding seniors to get caps and gowns ordered before graduation. "Likelihood that I'll pass your class?"

A particularly loud laugh reaches the hallway, and Evelyn opens the door. "Quiet down, everyone," she says, then turns to me. "Just give it everything you can, okay? I know you want to go to Nicaragua."

"Right, yes, of course."

Because I definitely want to be stuck in a foreign country for six weeks with my ex-boyfriend and no way of knowing if my dad is dead.

"You got this, Cham. I believe in you."

"Thanks," I say, lingering in the hallway and suddenly not wanting to leave. "I'm not totally positive what there is to believe, but I appreciate the faith."

Dear Universe,

1. Does this shirt make my boobs look flat?
2. Should I really wear sneakers while running, or are bare feet the soul of moving?
3. What the hell do I do now that everyone's moving forward and my dad's health is moving backward and I'm moving at 8.0 on the treadmill, clocking mile after mile, but never getting any farther than my own basement?

⌁

Days 'til graduation: 6

"Here, Cham, don't forget your papers and your deposit when you go to school," my mom says after dinner one night during the last week of school. She hands me a large packet covered in red ink that swears she won't sue the Gill School if I get killed by the spirit of volunteering.

"Oh, thanks."

"I talked to Mr. Garcia," my mom says, getting the Swiffer out of the hall closet and sweeping with a bit of a swing to her hips. "Seems like Nicaragua just depends on this English assignment. You can do it, sweetie. Want me to help you?"

"Uh, that's okay." I dart around her, not wanting to interrupt this romantic moment between her and the mop. "Where's Dad?"

"In his room, I think."

I walk in and he's in his wheelchair in the corner, holding *Motorcycle Maintenance*. His glasses are on and he's squinting at the text.

"Hi, Cham," he says, voice clear and eyes bright.

"Hi, whatcha doing?"

"Giving this old book a try again. I feel good today, but—" He shakes his head. "It's too…" He pauses and taps his finger against the book. "Mmm, I'm not processing things like I used to. Anyway, enough about me. How are you?"

"Mom gave me my paperwork for Nicaragua," I offer.

"Nicaragua?"

"The volunteer trip thing."

"Oh, right." He frowns and looks out the window. I doubt he *does* remember about Nicaragua. "I don't know if I want you going alone to a foreign country where you don't know the language. I only have one daughter."

"That we know of," I say, and smile wickedly.

"Chamomile Myles."

"Sorry." I pick a piece of lint off my sweater. "You know, Dad, I don't *have* to go to Nicaragua. I could stay here."

"So it *is* dangerous?" he asks.

"What? No. I promise, the chaperones have our asses covered."

"Don't swear, Cham, it's not becoming."

"Sorry," I sigh. "I just mean with your motorcycle accident and everything, I didn't know if you wanted to spend some time together this summer or something."

He locks and unlocks his wheelchair, then looks up at me blankly. He's not getting that I just want his permission to leave, but of course that's not what I want at all. He'd never *ask* me to stay. So what am I really asking? And who?

"Cham," my dad says, wheeling closer to me. "Why would you want to sit around with your old man and watch Netflix for the whole summer?" He looks over at the TV like *Can you believe this girl?*

"We don't have to just watch TV," I say, suddenly frustrated and wishing I hadn't brought this up at all. "I could read to you about the boring art of motorcycle maintenance. I was probably supposed to read that like two months ago for school anyway."

"Don't tell me that, Cham," my dad says, picking the book up off the table, then putting it back down at a slightly different orientation. "You loved learning so much as a kid. You know you skipped kindergarten?"

I gasp. "You mean I taught myself how to finger-paint?" He laughs, and I try to say what I mean, which I guess is that time isn't infinite, not for any of us, but it seems even more finite for him. What comes out is "I'm serious, Dad. I could stay."

He wheels toward me and pretends to plow me over with his chair. "For me? Nope."

My mom pokes her head in, cleaning bucket in her rubber-gloved hand. "What's going on in here?" she asks, searching the room for dust, lint, and hairballs.

"Nothing. Cham was just packing her Nicaragua bag," my dad says. "Can you bring Mace on an airplane?"

"Sure," I say eagerly. "I'll just hide it in my machete case."

The two of them laugh, and then my mom prods me with her bucket.

"Don't you have an essay to finish?" She pushes me out of the room, and my dad says something about me "finishing high school on a strong note," and before I can escape, it's just me, my mom, and the unfinished essay in my room.

I take my laptop from my desk and hold it like a baby. Maybe if I coddle it properly, the Word document will grow up to be a strong, healthy essay.

"I overheard you talking to Dad," my mom says, leaning

against the door to my room. "That was sweet of you to offer to stay, but you know we'd never want you to. You have a whole future ahead of you."

"I know," I say, sinking onto my bed. "But it's not that simple."

The silence between us holds a lot of silences that have come before. I feel a boulder in my throat. "I think I forget that he's not just what's happening to him," I say.

She sits on the edge of my bed with me and she kisses my forehead, moving a frizzy curl aside. "I know, baby. I know."

Suddenly I have so many flavors of bitter and sweet in my mouth that I can't really taste anything, just coffee and honey, but much more than coffee and much more than honey. "Remember how he played Elvis Christmas songs every day one summer?" She nods. "And how he never remembered Valentine's Day until the day after, so we always got double amounts of discounted chocolate?"

My mom laughs and puts her arm around my shoulders. "I miss how he used to tell the same joke when I sang. 'Don't quit your day job, Judy!'"

I giggle and lean into her more. At first all I smell is organic bleach and lavender, but then I get a hint of her perfume too. I close my eyes and say, "He doesn't do that stuff or like the same things anymore, and I'm mad about that sometimes or I miss him." I wipe my eyes. "I just want him to cook pancakes for dinner and drive the car around in the afternoon. I want to argue with him about using the push mower over the big gas-guzzling lawn mower. I want him to be the one locking the doors because, no offense, but you never remember."

"We get attached to people as they are, but people change," my mom says, running her fingers through my hair.

"I know." I take a deep breath, but there's still more in me. I guess when you don't say anything for a long time, there comes a time when you have a lot to say. "I want to remember that he's still all those things, but he's also neighbors in the tree and shaking hands and broken bowls because he's not *not* his sickness either. Do you know what I mean?"

My mom nods. Her eyes are closed. Outside my window the stars are nailed to the sky and looking very sturdy up there, like completely unmoving dots of light. Her voice softens to nearly a whisper.

"And then at some point he's beyond all of these things, which you know already, because we all are." She yawns and holds me tighter. "At least that's what I believe."

19

ON MY LAST NIGHT OF HIGH SCHOOL, I STAY UP ALL NIGHT WITH Abigail's copies of all the books we were supposed to read for English. She still has her sticky notes in them, and she gave me her class notes, so basically I'm going to do better than I possibly could've done on my own. I also have my dad's copy of *Zen and Motorcycle blah blah blah* because Evelyn's project description said *DON'T FORGET TO USE AN OUTSIDE SOURCE!* I'm probably just gonna Google a bunch of quotes from it, but maybe I'll read it someday. Or absorb it through osmosis. Or take up motorcycling. Just kidding.

STATUS OF COLLEGE ESSAY: 18 percent complete

TITLE: The Sicknesses We Have

Spoiler alert: It's about how my dad is sick and humans are sick, but talking about it anymore is going to *make* me sick.

Anxiety level: Get Xanax @now.

Status of class project: A little nonexistent, though Evelyn wrote on the top of my project description *Live the questions!* So at least that gave me a vague starting point.

Current materials: Like six thousand questions that range from *Why is my left nipple starting to grow a black hair?* to *What happens when we die and get eaten by wolves?*

My projector is humming, but the stars aren't visible because all the lights in my room are on. I'm surrounded by a case of Red Bulls, with my English materials splayed out on the floor. My strategy was to finally read *Caligula* with the hope that Camus King-of-Misery-and-Nothingness would inspire my personal philosophy and give me a passing grade in English. At an unknown wee hour of the morning, I finish the last page with itchy eyes, then throw the book to my floor on top of piles of things I've accumulated over the last week, or perhaps my whole lifetime.

"Are you serious?" I ask my projector, then call Abigail ASAP. I'm so tired that I'm *not* tired, just terribly awake and agitated.

"Cham, it's so early," she groans when she answers.

I drain my sixth Red Bull with a loud slurp and bounce

up and down on the edge of my bed. "I'm sorry, but why did Evelyn spend so long on Camus? Camus freaking sucks."

"I was having a dream about half men, half turtles. Can I please resume it?"

"There are like a billion more important questions we could be asking than whether life is worth living!"

There's silence on the other end. My alarm clock professes the time in neon blue lights: *Way Past Cham's Bedtime.*

"Jesus, Cham, there's like ten hours until class. What are you going to do?" Abigail asks. "And if you don't know, can I please resume my mutant male turtle dream?"

I drag my time capsule out from under my bed and run my fingers over its glow-in-the-dark stars. "What do you mean, what am I going to do?"

"About English class and prom and Nicaragua and college and everything?"

Uh, wait in my room with a box of canned goods in case the world ends and I'm still waiting for an answer to fall out of the sky?

"I really don't know," I say, throwing the empty can of Red Bull by my foot into the mausoleum with its friends. After a second, I pick it up and add it to my time capsule. "As for prom, I'm just waiting for a couple to break up, and I'll go with whoever is the most heartbroken-slash-desperate for a date."

"You and me and Hilary could go together," Abigail offers, her voice groggy.

"Thanks," I say, but they never offered before, and it feels too late now. I get back into bed and roll over to look at the stars through my window.

"That still doesn't explain English class." Abigail yawns loudly, creating a lot of static in the phone.

"It's okay, I'm gonna wing it."

"Wing it?" she says loudly, suddenly sounding awake. "What if she fails you, and you can't go to Nicaragua?"

At least I wouldn't have to choose which world to let go on without me. I rub my eyes and pinch my left butt cheek, which has been going numb for the last hour. "Well, then nature can take its course and rearrange its shelves, and I'll still be moseying down the tampon aisle trying to find God."

She laughs. "What the hell are you talking about?"

I put my pillow over my face and breathe in its dead goose-iness. "Sorry, I'm literally so sleep deprived and so caffeinated."

Abigail sighs. "I'm worried, Cham. It feels like you've been so distant."

"Yeah, things are just kinda weird."

"Nicaragua might be good for you." Silence. "Why are you so against it anyway?"

I'm so tired that I don't care when the truth comes out. I remove the pillow from my face. "Because I can't be out of reach if something happens with my dad. I can't go off on this big adventure while his world is getting smaller and smaller."

I hear her sharp intake of breath. "Oh, right, shit, I'm so sorry I didn't put that together."

I wipe my eyes, which are not tearing up but rather producing salt water for shits and giggles. "It's okay," I say. "I didn't put a lot of things together." Brendan's words come to mind and I decide to latch onto his reasoning. It's less painful than my personal one. "Besides, I don't know why we have to go on a disguised-vacation just to 'do good.' There are enough people suffering right here. Everyone's doing it so they have something to tell college people. It's a little bit disgusting."

"Isn't it better to help someone for kinda shitty reasons than not to help someone at all?"

I pick up the straw I just rolled over, remove a piece of lint from it, and blow air into my hand. "I guess? But maybe if we didn't go on these fancy trips and stuff, we'd be forced to help the people we know who need it the most. You know, the people we're always turning away from who are right here."

There's a throat-clearing noise on her end. Then—

"Shit, Cham, I'm sorry."

I close my eyes and rest my chin on my pillow.

"I didn't mean to say it like that." I sigh and itch my eyes. "I guess I'm kinda delirious. What time is it?"

She groans. "Three forty-five."

More silence. "I'm gonna try to sleep for the next two hours. See you soon?" I say to Abigail. "And text me about coordinating outfits. I won't be that idiot who actually wears her uniform on the last day."

"Of course," she says. "Next time I see you, we'll be so close to the end!"

"So close," I agree. "Night, Abigail."

"Night, Cham."

I hang up hoping that over the next few days I can train the fear in my voice to sound like excitement. It's finally actually *really* happening. Graduation. Life. Every. Freaking. Thing.

Even after I hang up and brush my teeth and pet the objects in my senior year time capsule, I can't sleep. I end up staying awake all night watching the stars move. Not that I can see them moving, but they *are*, and that's reassuring.

Dear Universe,

I'm sorry for interrupting you with my presence. Again. I'm just wondering if you could have my back on this one. I had a massive chin zit three weeks ago and a period stain you could see from space, and also they ran out of tacos on Tuesday, in addition to all the shit that's already happened to me this month. I'm not blaming you for any of these things, but if you could just like show up for me during my last English class so I can graduate and like achieve my potential or something, I'd greatly appreciate it.

～

It's a tradition at the Gill School that on the last day of school seniors get to go uniform-free. On this fateful culminating day that it's finally happening to *us*, the weather is unseasonably warm, like climate change is breathing all over us. Abigail, Hilary, and I opt to wear the shortest jean skirts we own. It's a bit of a screw-you to all the years we had to do the knee-length nunnery getup, but I'm a little concerned I'm gonna have a pube slip.

It's a day that's full of lasts: the last lunch, the last time I poop in the second-floor bathroom during Calc, the last time I take anything from my locker, which happens to be a mighty tuna fish sandwich reeking of life past its expiration date. Every hallway is full of a loud giddiness, then occasionally some squealing that turns into tears. Most of the day actually feels like a show I'm watching; the characters' lives are progressing, and they're finally getting everything they want! But as the episode winds down, I remember I'm still where I started, but with a fresh drool stain on my person.

"Holy shit, last class ever," Abigail says as we walk into English with our arms linked, my knee-high combat boots in sync with her platform wedges.

"Amen, hallelujah."

We sit down in our usual spot for the last time that it's ours. Beyond us the hallway is loud and muggy. I have a feeling it can't wait to get rid of us seniors so it can have some peace and quiet.

"Last day, last day, last day," Jared chants as he walks through the doorway. The rest of the class trickles in behind him with the sound of the bell. I think today we deserve a trumpet.

"Yes, seniors, this is it," Evelyn says, standing in front of us and admiring our various last-day-of-school looks: sunglasses on backward, shirts tied with hair-elastics because real crop-tops aren't allowed, even on the last day. "Here you are in your final class before you head out to parts unknown. I know you're eager to discuss the new-found responsibility accompanying this freedom, but we'll save that for prom." She grins and rubs her hands together. "Won't you want to take a break from the dance floor and hang out with your supercool teacher while continuing to ponder the meaning of life?" The only sound in the room is the two flies getting it on in the corner windowsill. "Come on, guys, I'm messing around! Let's have a little fun!"

"I'll have more fun when I'm not so nervous about this project presentation," Abigail says matter-of-factly. I try to exchange a look with her, but she's too busy rehearsing her presentation under her breath to an audience of none.

"Okay, fair enough," Evelyn says with a sigh. "I'm excited

to hear what y'all have come up with, and I know you're on the edge of your seats too. Who wants to start?"

"I will," Doug says, hopping up quickly. The sunglasses fall off the back of his head.

"Great! Take it away!

He jogs to the front of the room, and someone in the back gives him a cheer. "What makes life worthwhile," he says, pausing dramatically, "starts and ends with the sneaker. Running."

Damn, why didn't I think of that?

"There's nothing in the world like running next to my teammates, feeling the wind through my two-inch locks, and moving my hot bod." People laugh and he flexes a calf muscle. Evelyn makes a *tsk*-ing sound but lets him go on. And for the next few minutes he does, his concluding statement being that the mighty sneaker couldn't do anything without its trusty partner, the *other* mighty sneaker. "So, that's it, running is my philosophy." He does a few high knees, then takes a bow. "Adidas, if you're watching, please sponsor me."

We clap and he bows and sits back down in his seat in a much more relaxed fashion than before.

"Shit, that was good," Abigail whispers, looking at her notes worriedly. "Do you think I have time to change my project?"

"What's that, Abigail? You want to go next?" I say loudly.

Evelyn looks over at us and points to the front of the room. "May as well get on up there, Abigail."

"Twat," Abigail hisses at me, but I know she'll thank me later.

Once poised at the chalkboard, Abigail tucks her hair behind her ear, pulls her jean skirt down, and begins. "*Aretē*," she says, picking up a piece of chalk and writing the word out, "refers to the highest human potential, the best that we can be." *Oh, how I'll miss the sound of chalk on slate.* "It's a principle that dates back to ancient Greece and the writings of Plato, Homer, and other cool philosophers...." Evelyn makes an affirming sound that must be the closest a teacher gets to an orgasm. The more Abigail name-drops philosophers, the more my chest swells with pride. Abigail's presentation is *good*. Yes, it's a little bit masturbatory for the valedictorian to argue that what makes life worthwhile is reaching one's highest potential, but I have nothing against a girl feeling herself.

"That was great, Abigail," Evelyn says, with a vigorous round of applause. "Which brilliant philosopher-in-training do we have next?"

For the next forty-five minutes, I labor to keep my head out of my ass so I can listen to what people have to say. And I'm not being a suck-up, I swear. (It's a little late for that anyway.) It's just kinda cool hearing about what rocks people's socks. Travis finds fulfillment in the present moment, Josie says something about family, and Danika has a whole philosophy around a deep connection with animals. *Maybe my dad would like a service dog? Or maybe I just want a puppy.*

Toward the end of class, Marquis lugs his tuba up to the front and inflicts a solo on us. He proceeds to sit down without any explanation of his personal philosophy. Someone starts slow clapping, and the rest of the class follows suit.

"Very unique, Marquis," Evelyn says, then checks the clock. "We have two people left. Brendan or Cham, who wants to go first?"

"I'll go," Brendan says.

"What he said," I agree.

Brendan walks up my row, no tutu on today, the *one* day we don't have a uniform. When he passes me, he flicks my shoulder. I bite back a smile, relieved the year is ending, because I don't know how to fit Brendan into this world when he seems to be part of another. (My personal history will show you I'm not very good at mergers.)

Brendan faces us at the front of the room, with a triceratops staring mournfully from his T-shirt and lamenting, *All my friends are dead.*

"Camus is one of my many dead friends," he starts, and there's a little bit of laughter. "He's very dead. Way dead. But even if he weren't, he'd be far away. I would never have known him...and he probably wouldn't have wanted to meet me." He gives me a wry smile. "But that doesn't matter. We're still friends because he wrote some-thing I needed to read, and I read something he needed to write."

I stare at Brendan shamelessly because everyone else is. He's presenting, okay? I get a free pass to take in the curl that's fallen out of his bun, and the way his dinosaur T-shirt fits snugly around his arms.

"Maybe it's cheesy," Brendan says, "but writing things down condenses what it means to be a person in the uni-verse. When someone else reads that writing, a friendship is made." He takes *Caligula* out of his pocket and flips through the pages. "If Camus hadn't written and pub-lished his...*unique* perspective, we wouldn't have had the *pleasure* of reading and discussing the meaninglessness of life ad nauseum." He rolls his eyes slightly, and that gets a round of laughter from nearly everyone.

"Caligula wants the moon because it's out of his world. I think we all want that. When we connect with the honest written word, we can reach what's in one another's worlds." Brendan looks right at me. "And maybe, just maybe, we can find the moon."

I hold his gaze, and then realize that I'm holding his gaze. I look down, my heart racing.

"So yeah," he says with a shrug. "My philosophy is to read books, or at least *parts* of them."

Abigail claps loudly, and the rest of the class joins her. Evelyn beams as Brendan takes his seat. "Wonderful," she says once the applause has died down. "Really wonderful. Just what an English teacher wants to hear." She looks at the clock and then at me. "Ten minutes left in senior year. You ready, Cham?"

I pat my crown of frizzies down on my head. "*So* ready."

I walk toward Evelyn's desk, careful not to take long strides in my mini skirt. I'd hate to expose myself and have my lasting legacy involve a pube. Before starting my presentation, I say a prayer to the stain on the ceiling that looks like a piece of toast with Jesus on it: *Bombs away*. I know it's not a *prayer* prayer, but I kinda wanna go out with a splash.

"Anytime you're ready, Cham," Evelyn says.

"I just have to swallow my vomit," I say. People laugh and that makes me relax a little. "Okay," I say, feeling my armpit sweat seep and spread out halo-style into my shirt. "After staying up all night and consuming enough Red Bull to fill up an SUV, my philosophy is this." I look at Abigail and smile mischievously. "I don't have a philosophy."

It becomes very quiet in the room. Even the flies in the corner stop mating. Everyone's eyes mirror confusion back at me. "I know that doesn't bode too well for my grade on this project or my ability to go on Senior Volunteer Trip, but I don't have a clue about what makes life worthwhile." I look down at my combat boots, which give me both strength and blisters, depending on their mood. "Instead of making something up, like I tried to do for my college essay, I just want to finally own up to this in front of all of you fine people: I don't know shit. My personal philosophy is a foreign language no one's ever spoken yet."

I walk over to Abigail's desk and take a sip from her water bottle. "If I do know one thing," I say, wiping my mouth and grinning apologetically at Brendan, "it's that Camus truly sucks." Evelyn's eyebrows shoot up. "Sorry, but c'mon, guy. Do better. I can think of a million people who had a shittier life than you, but they still managed to find something meaningful." My dad's face comes to mind. "Some things happened to me this year," I continue. "Like my dad was in the hospital, and some of you might remember a certain lunch where I whipped Tater Tots at a certain someone's head...."

Even Doug is laughing. I smile and indiscreetly hold my arms up so my pits will dry.

"The end of this year really sucked, but it made me realize I've kind of been sleepwalking through life. This whole year I was obsessed with prom and graduation and just getting out of here. I bullshitted assignments that were supposed to be meaningful and—C'mon, don't look at me like that! I know you guys fudged your college essays." I'm getting a lot of blank stares in return. *Assholes.* "Anyway, instead of bullshitting this project too, I want to tell you guys the truth. I don't want to be asleep anymore. I want to find out what makes life worthwhile. Like the dude in *Zen and the Art of Motorcycle Maintenance* kind of says, the real cycle you're working on is the cycle called yourself."

I start to feel a little teary, and my voice wobbles. "In conclusion, I don't have a philosophy. I also don't have a college essay. I'm sorry, Evelyn. And I hope you all have fun in Nicaragua without me. What I do have is this moment in time where I ranted at you guys about two assignments I basically didn't do."

Abigail's looking at me like I'm living her nightmare, but it's the opposite for me. "The crazy thing is, I feel like for the first time in the history of school, I *learned* something."

"Woo!" Brendan yells from the back. My face gets hot as pizza sauce.

"Camus sucks. Evelyn, you're dope, and you guys," I say, looking at the clock and the fifteen seconds remaining in this era of our life, "we fucking did it."

20

Days 'til graduation: Still 4

THE SUN REFUSES TO GIVE ITSELF TO ANYONE ELSE. AT 2:05 IT shines strictly for us as we count down the seconds 'til the last bell, then burst out of the school and into the parking lot.

"Hell-freaking-yeah!" Abigail yells in my ear, the warm air filling us up as the sounds of people cheering mingle with the sounds of cars blasting music. Everyone's mood is overflowing, and I'm standing in the middle of it, taking notes.

When Hilary comes over to us, we get into Abigail's car and blast the music like everyone else. We don't drive anywhere. We just occupy the parking lot once and for all. They commandeer the playlist and I commandeer the back seat, head leaning against the open window. No matter how tightly I grip the seat, I keep drifting farther and farther from everyone else in this world, and what alcohol they're getting for the after-prom party, and whose house everyone's meeting at to take group pictures before all the *other* group pictures at *actual* prom. Everyone has a date and a plan and a purpose. They have a place in this world, whereas I suspect I've left the world entirely. The next time a satellite goes by, I will take a selfie and caption it *Girl in her own outer space waves to something far, far away.*

"Hey, guys!" I yell to Abigail and Hilary. "Turn down the music for a sec!"

"Ugh, no fun, Cham," Abigail says, but pauses it.

"I gotta go," I tell them, leaning forward and peeling my thighs from the seat.

"What? Why?" Abigail asks. They turn around and look at me. Travis raps on the roof of Abigail's car and she cheers.

"I have so much to do before prom," I say, "like coax some lost soul into being my date." I hop out of the car.

"But you can do that with us at Abigail's," Hilary offers.

I shake my head. "It's way too many things, and it'll be easier if I'm home. I'll text you guys later, okay?"

"Okay," Abigail says with a little bit of concern in her voice.

"It's gonna be fine! Just gotta hammer out all the prom details: date, dress, et cetera." I wave to them through the windshield and pull my skirt down. "Talk to you soon."

"Okay!" Abigail calls, and suddenly the music is at full volume again. I put my phone to my ear and pretend to be on a very important call as I cross the parking lot. It seems like everyone is wearing a T-shirt with their college on it, 70 percent of them in State colors. Hurrying past the entrance to the Gill School, I realize I don't ever have to go in there again. I'm done with high school, and now that it's over, I have nothing *left* to do. Except draw my shades, turn my projector on, and hide in my universe.

—✒—

SHOULD YOU TAKE YOURSELF TO PROM?
(A QUIZ FROM THE UNIVERSE)
ANSWER YES OR NO:

1. Most of your conversations happen in your head with someone/something that doesn't exist.

2. If alone, you feel in danger of being totally kidnapped by a dismal expanse of nothingness, leaving behind only your supercool knee-high combat boots because that's all you're really worth. And they've been resoled three times.

3. You like dresses, but only if no one's looking. Otherwise it's too stressful, what with the wind and utility holes and stuff.

4. Your favorite song to slow dance to is the ballad of your loneliness and inadequacies, mezzo forte in E major. Also everything Elvis.

5   You think bobby pins and hair spray should actually be used to blind boys and keep their mouths shut. Just kidding. You love boys. Need boys. Hate all the boys you know (kind of) but firmly believe there's one out there who doesn't have a douche-y haircut and loved his mom before rap songs made it cool.

6. You've been asked to prom, then un-asked to prom.

7. You considered taking your dad in his wheelchair but then remembered this is not a sappy rom-com where the girl "learns a lesson." This is you, and you never learn a damn thing.

ANSWER TRUTHFULLY: DID YOU ANSWER MOSTLY *YES* TO THIS QUIZ? THEN DO NOT ACTUALLY GO TO PROM WITH YOURSELF, BECAUSE YOU SHOULDN'T SUBJECT YOURSELF TO YOURSELF AT ALL. ☺

Text exchange with Abigail, Hilary, and me with twenty-two hours and twenty-two minutes left 'til prom:

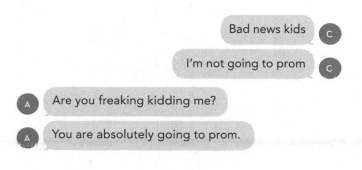

Bad news kids — C

I'm not going to prom — C

A — Are you freaking kidding me?

A — You are absolutely going to prom.

In fact I'm not. C

A IN FACT YOU ARE. YOU ARE GOING TO DANCE WITH ME AND HILARY AND IT IS GOING TO BE A-FREAKING-MAZING.

Nope. C

Prom is just a lot of makeup and uncomfortable clothes and taking pictures. I want to do something real tonight. C

A BUT IT'S FUN!!!

Idk I'd rather just hang out C

Exchange personal philosophies with the dust bunnies under my bed C

BTW I bombed English class C

soooo ttyl Nicaragua C

A Did Mr. Garcia say that?

No, but I didn't do my essay C

He probably doesn't wanna break the bad news before prom C

A Come to prom and we'll figure your summer out after. I bet we can talk Mr. Garcia into letting you come.

Nah not feeling it C

FaceTime me from the dance floor C

It'll be like I'm there except better cause I won't be there!!!

lol jk I'm done being an ass

you guys have fun and we'll do something special the three of us after graduation OK?

Hellllooooo?

Texting into the abyss here...

To avoid the smothering pressure of dealing with the post–high school oblivion, I've pledged to stay in my room until I'm thirty. It's only when my mom calls through my closed door that I realize my mistake in hiding someplace that basically has my name on it.

"You're not tweezing your eyebrows in there, are you, Cham? Don't change yourself for prom. I think the asymmetry is really—"

"Ahh, Mom!" I yell as she opens the door and a fierce ray of hallway light exposes me. "Stop it, I'm not going to prom."

"What do you mean, you're not going?" she asks, taking in the whole Cham-in-her-universe situation I've got going on: lights off, projector on, antenna up, and waiting for an extraterrestrial life-form to claim me as their own. "You can't *not* go."

I sit up and squint at her. She smells like organic lavender bleach. "In fact, I can. I am *not* going to prom."

"Cham, you have to go," my dad says, wheeling in behind her.

"No, it's so fake." I run a hand through my bedhead and estimate the nest in my hair to be perfectly sized for a squirrel. "It doesn't have anything to do with our friends, which is basically all I got out of high school. It's just a photo op, and I don't wanna waste my time on things like that. You can't do meaningless stuff your whole life. That's pretty much what I learned in English this year."

My dad frowns. "I always thought the Gill School was a little out there. Is it too late to send you to high school somewhere else?"

"Very funny, Dad." I smile when I realize he's joking. Today's looking like a good day.

"Just because Gene isn't your date anymore doesn't mean you should miss out on such a big night," my mom says sympathetically, as if all this has to do with a boy. "It's a milestone."

"Yeah, but just 'cause the yearbook lays out certain moments for us to be world-rocking or whatever doesn't mean they are."

"But they could be," she prods.

"I'm still not going."

My dad parks his wheelchair in front of my dresser and holds up his hands. "Well, *I'm* still going."

I summon some patience. "You're not going to prom, Dad, remember? You did that a long time ago. Ice ages ago, probably."

"No, I mean, in life." He looks me in my eyes. "There's no cure, but I'm still going."

My head almost makes a 360-degree movement. My mom studies him carefully too, the only sound being the gentle hum of the projector pretending to mind its own business, when really it's hanging on our every word.

"What do you mean, Dad?" I ask carefully.

He settles into his wheelchair. "They can't fix it, this Parkinson's or whatever, but I still get up and have coffee and get on with it."

He runs a hand through his salt-and-pepper hair. "You can't waste time thinking about the bad stuff. It's depressing."

I don't know what to do with myself so I stand to get a hairbrush. My mom sits down against the wheel of my dad's chair and rests her head on his knee.

"Careful you don't rip your hair out," he says as the teeth of the brush tear through the knots in my hair.

I give up and put my hairbrush back on the dresser. "I just can't take everyone being all pumped about Nicaragua now that my summer's looking like a sinkhole."

"You're young and you should go dance," my dad says. "Come here, we can turn the go-my-man into the go-my-girl."

He chugs his arms and hums a mix of a couple of Elvis songs. I hum along unenthusiastically and do a few arm chugs myself. The mirror confirms that I look like an old-fashioned, clinically depressed train.

My dad laughs so hard he chokes, and my mom slaps him on the back. "You know you can always stand around the punch table," he offers. "You don't *have* to dance."

I shake my head. I want them to leave so I can sort out my senior year time capsule. Or throw it away. "Thanks, Dad," I say, moving toward the door with the hope that they'll take the hint. "But I'd rather stay here and cut my toenails."

"You'll regret it forever if you don't go."

"Come on," my mom encourages. "Forget about your English grade and Nicaragua and college and marriage and kids and midlife crises and retirement homes and nursing homes and crematoriums. Just go enjoy your last night before you graduate from high school!"

I look over at my closet and try another way to get them off my back. "Even if I wanted to go, I don't have a dress."

"I happened to see one that reminded me of you," my mom says, hopping up. "It was in the window of Willa's Closet, and I got it on my way home." She disappears into the hallway and comes back holding up a short bright blue dress with layers and layers of shiny ruffles. "Ta-da!"

"Wow, Mom," I say slowly. "That is a really, really unique dress. Thanks so much." I take it from her and hold it up to myself in the mirror. Honestly, it's like I'm being eaten by an eighties-themed pastry.

"Oh, it's perfect," she says, clapping her hands. "We'll leave so you can put it on."

Upon squeezing myself into the most unfortunate piece of fabric that's ever been on my body, I poke my head out of my room. I hear my parents' voices downstairs. "It's really beautiful and I appreciate it, but I'm still not going," I yell. "Prom is just a dance. I can dance anywhere, anytime."

I'm about to take the dress off and hide until graduation when the doorbell rings. "Oh god, if it's Abigail and Hilary trying to get me to this dance—"

I run down the stairs. When they see me in this dress, they will understand that I can't go. In a way, my mom probably just saved my life.

"Hi, Mr. and Mrs. Myles," Brendan is saying as my mom opens the door. He's wearing a pale blue suit just like Elvis's. I try to dart back to my room, but he's already seen me. I reach the bottom of the stairs, and a smile accidentally takes over my face.

"Hey, Cham," he says, pulling a big white balloon in behind him and closing the door. It grazes the ceiling when he comes in.

"Uh, what's that?" I ask, crossing my arms over my chest

in a failed attempt to hide my runaway ruffles. "And what are you doing here?"

"We'll be in the other room, kids," my mom says. I've never seen my dad wheel anywhere so fast.

Brendan steps toward me and holds out the balloon. "I'm bringing you the moon," he says. "I mean *a* moon, to hold you over while you look for yours." He hands me the string, and our fingers touch.

"Wow." I look up and pull the balloon to me. It's twice the size of a usual helium balloon, with a silvery-white face. "Well, that's—" I start, but I don't know where I'm going with this exactly. In fact, I'm a little bit speechless.

"I know it's not the real moon," he says, putting his hands in his pale blue pockets. "But it was the biggest balloon they had at iParty."

It drifts above our heads. I tug the string and the balloon comes toward my face. For a second I think I could actually be holding the moon, which is big and scary but also thrillingly unknown and seemingly infinite.

"Anyway, I'm on my way to prom," he says, pointing at his tie. "Do you want to go with me?"

I blush and look down at his dress shoes, starting up a stuttering conversation with their black laces. "Wow, um, I, it's just—"

"Not *with me* with me," he says quickly. "Just like do you want to *carpool* with me?"

"Oh, I knew what you meant," I say, laughing and hoping it's loud enough to drown out my disappointment.

"Go to prom, kids," my mom calls, careful to stay out of sight.

"Come on," Brendan says, taking the balloon from me and tying it to one of the coatracks. "Prom itself can't be worse than the pictures of prom you'd be torturing yourself with if you stayed home."

I put my hands on my hips. "How do you know I don't have big plans?"

He bites his lip and says facetiously, "That dress *does* seem to be for a *special* occasion."

I punch him in the arm and he laughs. "Well, I do have a whole summer to plan out now that I can't go to Nicaragua," I say. "Not to mention the rest of my life."

"Are you sure they're not gonna let you go?" he asks.

"Pretty damn positive. You heard my presentation, and I just couldn't bring myself to write the essay." For a second I feel like crying. I was on the fence about going before, what with my dad and everything, but now that I *can't* go, it feels like I've been cut out of my whole future, or at least any hope of a future that resembles anyone else's. Above us the balloon sways back and forth before making up its mind to occupy one little random piece of space close to the ceiling.

"Well, all the more reason to go to prom, then,"

Brendan says, nodding toward his car parked in the driveway. "This might be the last time except for graduation that you ever see these people. Unless you go to State," he adds thoughtfully.

At that my eyes start dribbling. I wipe them quickly, but it's too late. He's already seen.

"Oh no," he says gently. "I'm sorry, I didn't mean to—"

"It's not you," I sniffle, wiping my face and engaging the floor in a staring contest.

"I didn't know you wanted to go to Nicaragua so badly," he says.

I run my fingers through some of the ruffles. "I don't really." I lean my forehead against the doorway. "It's just everything. Everyone's moving on and going to college and whatever while I'm stuck here in limbo. If I go to prom, I'm just going to feel even more like a freshly hatched alien. Everyone else is in that world, and I'm in this world. And they can't wait for me, and I can't catch up with them."

Brendan looks at me steadily. "How about this: We go to prom and convince Mr. Garcia to let you go to Nicaragua. Then at least you'll have a little bit longer to be part of everything."

I wipe my nose. I *guess* I could go, but not because I *want* to. Me going is kind of a selfless act to appease my friends, my parents, and, okay, future Cham, who might find herself a true idiot for not going.

"Okay." I tug on a particularly egregious ruffle at my hip. "We just have to make one stop first."

—⁓—

According to the hours posted online, Willa's Closet is open for another fifteen minutes. Luckily, our town is small enough that you're never more than ten minutes away from where you want to go, even when the traffic is particularly "heavy."

"Here?" Brendan asks as he slows through the center of town and stops between the pizza place and the bank.

"Yep, perfect." I dash out of the car, blue ruffles of my dress swishing together. "There you are," I whisper. My darling white dress is front-and-center in the fingerprint-smudged window, waiting for somebody. *My* body to be exact. As fun as it sounds to go through life pissed about the only As I ever got, maybe if I fake it 'til I make it, my boobs will actually grow on me one day (not literally, although that'd be some great karma). I open the door to find—Iggy? Izzy? Izzy.—looking very intently at her laptop, where a sticker says PROUD TO BE A COLLEGE DROPOUT next to one that says NACHO PROBLEM.

"Hey, sorry to interrupt," I say, leaning on the counter and accidentally invading her personal space. "Even though it won't fit, I gotta have that dress."

I point to the window and she eyes me up and down,

one blue ruffle at a time. "Do your thing, girl. Anything's better than what you have on."

She hops off the stool and heads for the window display. "You going to prom?" she asks.

"Yeah, changed my mind last minute," I say, following her past the racks of clothes. "I wasn't going to, 'cause it's all about pictures and dates and uncomfortable shoes. But then this guy I like, I mean as a friend, offered me a ride, so…"

She unbuttons the dress from the mannequin's plastic back and hands the white lace fabric to me. "Good for you. Life's too short not to go to prom."

"Uh, last time I was here, you were shitting on prom." I follow her to the dressing room and strip down in the tiny space.

"Just 'cause something's stupid doesn't mean you shouldn't do it," Izzy calls through the closed door. "Honestly, it's so much *better* that way. It frees you up to do your own goddamn thing. Now lemme see."

I zip the dress up and open the door. When I look down there are miles and miles of material across my chest, just hanging there like *Please love me*. "I'm having a bit of a boob situation, which I'm sure could be fixed with two balloons and a bicycle pump, but I'm trying to be *accepting*."

"Don't worry," Izzy says. "I'll be right back." She heads toward the front of the store and calls out, "Is the guy with the vigorous dance moves in the car out front your date?"

"Not my date," I say quickly, attempting to down-size the nest in my hair from squirrel babies to chipmunk babies. "He's just my ride, and he wasn't even supposed to be that. He just showed up at my house." *Also, he brought me the moon.*

"Well, that's good timing. Here, use these," Izzy says, coming back with four pieces of thin black duct tape. "Gather up the material and tape it like an X."

I stand in front of the mirror hesitantly, then do it. I mean I can't really look more ridiculous than I do with saggy ghost boobs. At first it's awkward pulling the fabric up then down, but finally I've effectively taped two Xs on my chest.

"Ooooh!" she says, nodding in approval. "X-tits might be the next big thing."

I grin. "Gotta admit, I actually look *good*. In a lived-through-a-horror-movie type of way."

"Which you did," she says, patting my shoulder. "But I'm done shit-talking high school. Now pay up."

I rip the tag off the back of the dress and she walks over to scan it at the computer. As my card goes through I look at Brendan, jamming out alone in his car. It's like he's hold-ing his own private prom between the seat and the steering wheel.

"All yours," Izzy says, handing me my card.

"Could I have the tag too?" I ask. She gives me a puzzled look, but the existence, location, and contents of my senior year time capsule are entirely private, thank you very much. I hold out my hand and she gives it to me with a shrug and a smile. "Glad you got your sign from the universe. That dress looks great on you."

"What?" I ask. She points through the glass door at Brendan, who does a particularly violent head-shake-thing. "Oh, no," I correct her. "A boy is not my sign."

" 'Cause there's no such thing as a sign," she says in a stage whisper that I ignore. She flips the lights off and takes out a key chain. "Wanna hear a Jesus joke?"

"Not really?"

She opens the door for me and we stand on the sidewalk in the late-afternoon light. "So a man is drowning and asks Mr. God to help him," she says, locking the door with a few clicks. "Shortly after, this boat comes by with a crew offering the man a ride. The man refuses and says that God will save him. Not long after that, the man drowns and goes to heaven. He asks God, 'Why didn't you save me?' God responds, 'You idiot, I sent you a boat.'" She looks at me expectantly and I laugh. "Just saying," she says with a wiggle of her eyebrows.

"Okay, thanks, I'll make sure to tell my dad that one."

The sun is low in the sky, illuminating Brendan's silhouette. Izzy puts a felt hat on and waves. "Well, off ya go, Cinderella."

"Okay, see ya," I say, looking down and realizing I'm still in my orange running sneakers. *Classic.* She disappears down the street looking like she has someplace to go. I feel a little jealous for a second. But then I realize that I do too.

21

Days 'til graduation: Still 2

WE'RE STANDING BEFORE A PALACE FIT FOR SUBURBAN GOLFERS and us, the most recent almost-graduated class of the Gill School. On the clean-cut fake green lawn, a sprawling building with big glass windows is framed by decorative trees. Pink and white lanterns hang from them.

"It's kind of beautiful," I say to Brendan, looking up at the main entrance to the country club, where a banner with silver lights spells out GILL SCHOOL PROM.

"It is, isn't it," he says, then looks down at our feet. "Cool sneakers."

"Shut up," I say, and push him toward the door.

As we walk, I kick up some of the red flower petals covering the stone walkway. Through the big glass windows we can see everyone in their suits and gowns and corsages and boutonnieres, taking pictures, talking loudly. I look at Brendan again, and my face gives way to a smile. "Everyone looks good. This whole place does."

"Prom Scrooge satisfied?" he asks, admiring one of the lanterns hanging in a nearby tree.

"I'm just saying the decorations are pretty and we all look a lot better in fancy clothes." We both flash our tickets, and a man in a suit opens the big glass doors for us. "Welcome to Gill School prom," he says, politely avoiding my X-tits. "Hope you have a great night."

"Thanks," Brendan says. I step behind him a bit, suddenly embarrassed to be walking into the huge bright room together. What if people think we're *together* together?

Get over yourself, shit huffer.

Inside it smells like so many types of perfume and cologne. The sun is casting golden shadows around the room as if to say, *No filter required!* We slowly make our way across the blue oriental rug toward various cliques' group photos.

"There you are!" Abigail calls. She and Hilary ditch the photo they were in to throw themselves at me: Hilary's hair is freshly dyed, and the cool blue with her dark green dress has this magical mermaid effect.

"You guys look so beautiful," I say, touching the silk of Hilary's dress.

Abigail fake-sobs into my neck. "I think I might cry."

Her hair is in a ballet bun on top of her head, and her red dress drapes off her shoulders. "Look at your badass grungy bride dress, Cham. Is that *tape* over your boobs?"

"Yep."

"Good for you, darling," Hilary says, eyeing Marquis behind us, who's tied a bow tie to his tuba and is currently dancing with it. I wonder how long her British accent has been in effect.

"You look so handsome, Brendan," Abigail says as she turns to him. Then she elbows me in the side. *Not* subtly.

"You're looking handsome too. You *all* are," he says, and his eyes linger on mine.

"Can you take a picture of the three of us?" Abigail asks, handing her phone to him.

We make a beeline for one of the large flower arrangements on the other side of the room. It's a fustercluck of orchids and lilies that we squeeze ourselves in front of. At the last minute I switch places with Hilary so I'm in the middle, and I link my arms in both of theirs. "You guys," I say, feeling suddenly sentimental, as if it's years from now and I'm looking at the picture we're about to take, senior year time capsule resurrected. "Look at us. We look freaking hot *and* we're graduating from high school in two days. Aren't you excited?"

"Um, yes, I've been waiting for *you* to be excited," Abigail says, insisting we take one picture with our middle fingers up. "I can't wait until they're done Breathalyzing us so I can dance ass-up for like six hours."

"Okay, smile," Brendan says, taking a step back and nearly landing on the train of Rose's pink lace gown. "And one not flipping the camera off? There, I think I got it." He hands the phone to Abigail.

"Okay, now one of you two," Hilary says, pushing me into Brendan.

I feel my cheeks burn, and then I literally almost say out loud, *Get over yourself.* I don't want to be one of those people who's embarrassed their whole life to like what they like.

"I guess I could be bothered to take one picture," Brendan says, standing next to me. He puts his arm around my waist, and I feel how warm he is: a 98.6-degree human.

"Smile!"

"Thanks for the ride," I whisper up at him. "And the moon."

"No problem," he says, leaning away once the picture's been taken. I sort of wish we'd take another.

To our left the front doors open, and there are voices and heels clacking as more people walk in. I turn around to find Danika and Doug, then Gene and Helga. As our eyes latch, the egg of my heart cracks and it makes a rotten breakfast. His head comes up to Helga's shoulder with her heels on, and he's matched his orange bow tie with her orange sparkling gown. Suddenly I feel homemade in this dress. And not in a cute Etsy way.

"Hey, Cham, you look great," Gene says with a *We're such good friends* smile.

I smile back, but like are you kidding me? Just because we're in nice clothes doesn't mean we have to be nice. As Gene walks away to stand in line to be Breathalyzed, it occurs to me that when we weren't making out or running, there wasn't much else between us. I feel sad about it for a second, but maybe all first loves are like that. Maybe you have to love someone on the surface at least once in your life so that when you love someone beyond that, you know the distance you've traveled.

"Oh, come on," Abigail whispers, watching my face. "Nine point eight out of ten high school relationships end. Did you really think yours was the exception?"

I punch her in the arm and burst out laughing. "Wow, you're kind of a dick, huh?"

"I'm just saying you can move on now," Abigail says, waving us toward the diminishing line of people waiting to go inside. "Come on, I gotta get to the dance floor."

She and Hilary go ahead, and Brendan smiles at me. "Well, have fun with your friends!"

"Aren't you coming?" Abigail asks, turning around. Brendan looks at me.

"He's coming," I say, catching my reflection and nodding certainly in the big mirror with the vase of roses in front of it.

Brendan shrugs and turns toward the regal-looking wooden doors. "Looks like I'm coming."

—⟋—

Our senior prom is in a big, bright room with a polished wooden dance floor that looks out onto the sprawling green golf course. In the right-hand corner a DJ sets up her table while a catchy, warm-your-ass-up dance tune plays in the background. "Wanna bet who's gonna be the first to do it on the golf course tonight?" Abigail asks, standing in front of the doors that lead to a romantically lit balcony.

"Mr. Garcia," Brendan says, and we all laugh.

"You guys," Abigail says suddenly as we half marvel at the place and half marvel at everyone all dressed up. "I'm literally crying."

"No, you're not," Hilary points out.

"But I *could* be." Abigail walks toward the tables in the back of the room, all set for dinner with white tablecloths and floral centerpieces. We follow slowly, taking in the fanciness of everything. It's a little weird how weird it's *not* to hang out with Brendan and Hilary and Abigail. I thought it'd be awkward, but it's kind of like we've been doing this all along. Or maybe the illusion of separate worlds is just that: an illusion.

"Oh, right," Hilary says, glancing down at one of the cards on a place setting near us. "They make you eat dinner with your date."

Brendan cranes his neck toward the other side of the room. "I think that's the table for singles. Yep, there's my name. See you guys soon."

"Okay," I say, feeling a little tug inside me as he walks away. *How soon?*

"Here we are, Abigail," Hilary says, pointing to one of the tables in the middle, with its fake candle all lit up because can we really be trusted not to burn this place down? No, we cannot.

"Okay," Abigail says, "now we gotta find Cham and switch it with whoever's next to us."

I scan the tables carefully. The white tablecloths are pristine, but not for long. "Oh no, guys." I point to a chair a few tables down.

"Oh, shit," Abigail says, moving a few wooden-backed chairs aside to get a closer look.

"Of course," I groan, following her to my seat of doom. "The place settings were assigned a while ago, back when Gene got the tickets." I look up at the ceiling. "Why do you insist on screwing me like ten times over, Universe?"

"Uh, you talking to yourself, Cham?" Hilary asks, prodding me with a nearby fork.

"No, I'm talking to the *universe*." I look at them and my eyes widen. "Wait, could this mean that Gene and I are meant to—"

"No!" they shout. I look behind me. Across the room, Gene and Helga are crossing the dance floor, looking for seats among the dinner tables too. "Well, this is gonna be awkward," Hilary says.

I smooth my dress and summon the power of my X-tits. "It doesn't have to be. I think I'll just trade with Helga because in addition to graduating from high school, I'd like to graduate from giving a fuck."

"Woo!" Abigail says, pushing the chairs in and turning around. "That's the Cham I've been waiting for."

I take my name card off the plate and walk steadily toward Gene and Helga. They stop holding hands when they see me, which I guess is considerate, but we're also kinda past that point. "Hey, Helga," I say, looking up at her glitter-sprayed hair and really wishing I'd done more than provide a home for baby forest animals in mine. "Do you want to switch dinner seats with me?"

I hold up my card and point past the DJ to where Doug and Danika are already taking the seats next to Gene's card.

"Thanks," Helga says, "That'd be great, except I was late buying my ticket, so I don't know if I have a place card anywhere to switch with you." She looks over her shoulder, seemingly scanning the place settings to find herself.

"It's okay, I'll drag up a seat somewhere." I hand her my place card, which says CHAMOMILE because we're mature now. We use full names.

"Thanks, Cham," Gene says, and I kind of hate how grateful he looks. Like it's a prom seat, not a kidney. "Maybe catch you on the dance floor."

"I wouldn't be caught dead on the dance floor," I say. "Not because of you," I add quickly, as I register the look on his face. "Just like in general. Okay, toodles." I turn on the heel of my orange sneakers. *Toodles?*

By the time I cross the brightly lit room, almost everyone is seated for dinner. Waiters are coming out with baskets of bread and pitchers of Shirley Temples because when Gill School goes out, it goes all out. Crossing the room in my sneakers while everyone else is wearing heels, I feel like I'm going to cry again. Even if I *do* talk my way into Nicaragua, it's just postponing the inevitable. As they go off to college and who knows what else, I'm going, where, home?

In the lobby I stop by the table with the fancy cucumber-and-mint water for a drink. Nothing says *special occasion* like water with leaves in it.

"Happy prom night, Cham," Evelyn says, coming up behind me as I pour myself a glass. She's wearing a purple dress with a silver bow tie, and it's an improvement over the yellow Curious George suit. Still, she's not exactly the first person I want to see.

"Happy prom night to you too," I say wearily, lifting the glass to my lips and preparing my palate for some very gourmet water. I have a feeling this is gonna be awkward, since she probably has to fail me and all.

"How's it going so far?" she asks, plucking a carnation

from the vase at the end of the table and sniffing it before putting it back.

"Well, I just gave up my seat to the girl my ex-boyfriend is now attending prom with."

She laughs and I chug the rest of my water, begging the burp in my throat to stay put. We're silent for a few seconds, but it feels like a few years. I look around at the decorations in the lobby: the bouquets of flowers, the photo booth in the corner with the props. "You know, Cham," Evelyn says. "I've been thinking about your presentation. I admire your honesty." *Admire it enough not to fail me?* "I was also thinking that there's a place to go for people with questions."

"Lemme guess, Google?"

She laughs. "I'm talking about philosophy."

I blink at her. "Does it have a physical address I don't know about?"

She places her cup down on the polished wooden table and sighs. "I'm going to ignore your sass. Look, some people turn to philosophy because they want to, and some people turn to it because they need to. I needed it, and maybe you do too." I look down at my orange sneakers clashing with the blue oriental rug and fix some of my boob tape. Maybe an X-marks-the-tits-spot is all my boobs have ever needed. "Here," she says, reaching into her purse and handing me a book. "No one really talks about how scary graduating is.

I appreciate your acknowledging that in your presentation yesterday. It takes a lot of courage to admit what you don't know. It reminded me of something I read in here, and I thought you might want to check this book out."

"Thanks." I take it from her and examine its cover. The pretty cursive font fills most of the navy-blue background. "For giving a shit," I add.

"One more thing before I forget…" She wipes a bit of condensation off the fancy water container. "The whole reason I came over here was to say I enjoyed reading your essay scraps." *What essay—?* I start, then shut my fat mouth before I even open it. "For that, combined with your presentation, you'll be getting a passing grade from me, which means you're good to go on Senior Volunteer Trip." She smiles at me and pats me on the back. "I wanted to tell you in person before you get the e-mail from Mr. Garcia."

"Well, thank you," I say as my tiny brain tries to process its future. I turn the book over in my hands.

"Just wondering, though: You had so much there. Why didn't you finish it?"

I help myself to another glass of water, even though it probably doesn't come as a shock that vegetable water tastes like garden runoff. "Same reason I couldn't start it for so long, I guess. I'm not ready yet." I study the painted wall behind Evelyn's head. There's something soothing about the repeating pattern of flowers, so pretty and unspecific. I tear my eyes away to look at her, then down at the book, which is the less intimidating of the two. "Finishing the essay means finishing high school, preparing to move on to something else, literally applying to the next thing. I don't know what that is yet, and it feels fake to pretend."

"Fair enough," she says, studying me. I imagine I'm quite a sight in the lobby of this country club, with my nesty hair, white dress, and orange sneakers. We're quiet for a moment, and at first she looks like she's going to say something, but then she salutes me. "I'm gonna go back inside and make sure no one's launching spitballs through their soda straws. Or fornicating under the table."

"Ew," I laugh. "I'm gonna examine the bathroom wallpaper until dinner is over."

"Enjoy the night, Cham."

"Thanks, you too." As she walks away toward the regal doors that separate us from the dance floor and the dinner tables and the rest of the night, I have a tiny feeling I might miss her. *Might.*

Safely inside the heavily Febrezed bathroom stall, I gather my dress up, put the toilet seat down, and make myself comfortable. I address the ceiling with the fiercest face my eyebrows can muster.

"Universe, help me. I'm freaking terrified." I sink into the toilet and wait for lightning to strike. "I have not applied to college. I don't even know if I *can* go to college. And now that I can go to Nicaragua, I have to decide about it, which is just like shitfuckgoddamn. Just tell me what to do. Please?"

I push the door of the tampon receptacle in and out, making a squeaky, clanking song of impatience. "Universe?" I whisper tentatively. "Don't be a mega-asshole."

After a few minutes, I start reading the book Evelyn gave me. Honestly, this guy Rilke is boring as hell, but not as boring as waiting for the universe to get its shit together and grace me with its presence. I turn one of the pages and see that Evelyn's underlined a whole passage. I read it, and then I read it again.

"Universe, you weird and wonderful thing," I say once I've read it a few times: *Live the questions.* Like Brendan said in his presentation, it's as if this old, long-dead dude is talking to me, and as I read, we are becoming friends.

The bathroom door opens, its hinge so well oiled it hardly creaks. I close the book quickly.

"Cham?" Abigail's voice floods the bathroom. I get off the toilet and peek under the door. There are her snakeskin heels, pausing outside my stall. "Ew, get out of there, Cham!"

"Germs are my friends."

"Chamaroooon!" Hilary sings as the door opens again. I wait for her plastic, totally see-through heels to stop in front of me. "We see your sneakers in there."

"Hi, friends," I say, butt cheeks regaining feeling after so long on the toilet seat. "I wasn't hiding, I swear. I was *researching.*"

"Researching what?" Abigail asks, pounding on the stall door so hard it rattles.

"My poop's horoscope."

Abigail sniffs the air theatrically, and her heels take her toward the mirror. "It doesn't smell like you're pooping, and, ew, why didn't you tell me my lips have melted into my chin?"

"You're beautiful, Abigail," I say, flushing the toilet, just in case it wanted a reset.

"We got bored at dinner without you," Hilary says as I open the door. She's leaning against the counter, and the mirror is reflecting her cool blue hair back at me. "Here, we brought rolls."

She passes one to me and I pop it in my mouth. "You angel, you prebuttered it."

As I chew this squishy, salty treasure, I sift through the prom kit on the counter: a basket full of bobby pins and spray-on deodorant and mouthwash and condoms. In the mirror, Abigail is licking her finger and attacking her chin with a cotton ball. I want to tell them about Nicaragua, but just because I can go doesn't mean I should.

"Okay, all fixed," Abigail says, applying a fresh coat of lipstick with her face a centimeter from the mirror. "Let's go."

"I'm not leaving until I have a sign from the universe," I tell them. I back toward the woven basket of hand towels with my arms crossed. "I will stay in this bathroom until my teeth fall out, and then I will get the denture creator to come in here."

"Shut up, Cham," Abigail says, rolling her eyes in a very unsympathetic way, considering *her* dad isn't dying. "You don't have to decide your whole life right now. You're gonna miss prom if you try to do that. Actually, you'll probably miss your whole life if you do that. Just let go for one night and shake your tight little runner's ass."

They push me through the bathroom door. The lobby is loud with the sounds of prom transitioning from dinner to dancing.

"Come on, Cham," Abigail says, linking her arm in mine as we head toward the loudening music. "It's time to dance like we danced in my kitchen that night, even though Evelyn refused to acknowledge our brilliance. And don't act like you're all above high school." Abigail starts to swing her hips. "You're one of us, whether you like it or not."

"You're killing me, Abigail," I say as she and Hilary drag me toward the photo booth.

"Quick stop here first," Hilary says, pulling back the curtain. There are props and a bright light, and facing the black curtain is a camera that has a button on a foot pedal.

We put on the fake mustache and the huge glasses and hold up the square frame that says *Gill School's Senior Prom*.

"Three…two…one," the photo booth tells us. Then

clicks. *Seventeen is wanting something more and finally being able to go after it, even if you have no idea what the freak to call it.* "Quick, switch it up," Abigail says. I grab the mustache from Hilary, and she takes the frame from Abigail, and we stick our tongues out. *Seventeen is dancing barefoot with the people you know way too many things about, because dress shoes hurt and heels hurt and at the end of the day high school hurts enough.*

"Okay," Abigail says, throwing the cardboard mustache on the floor. "Now for the dance." She turns toward the doors containing all the sound and color and sequins and sweat and, holy shit, Mr. Garcia's dance moves.

"Wait," I call, running after Hilary and Abigail and taking them by the arm. "One more, but no props this time." I arrange us in the small black booth, Abigail in the middle. "Just your default face, please." We get perfectly still and I try to look straight-faced into the camera, but as soon as the timer starts, we all burst out laughing, and the camera sound effect clicks.

"Come on, Cham," Abigail says, zipping across the oriental rug, past the fancy water station and the various bouquets, toward the wooden doors. "You can move faster than that. Look at those terrible sneakers."

"Coming," I call, running to squeeze between Abigail and Hilary. The fabric of our dresses overlaps—white and green and red and probably other colors our retinas don't register.

Seventeen is just a word someone made up that doesn't mean anything at all without us, I realize as we approach the doors and all the familiar and unknown things behind them. I hug my friends before we're too sweaty to stomach each other, and they give me a taunting look.

Abigail puts her hands on her hips while Hilary leans against the metal door handles. "Now go find Brendan," Abigail says.

"What?" I ask innocently.

"Oh, come on, Cham," Hilary says. "You obviously have a crush on him."

I widen my eyes. "Do not."

Abigail gives me a stern look. "You lying little shit," she teases.

I retape my left boob X, then burst out laughing. "Fine, wish me luck."

Abigail slaps my butt and opens the door for me, the sounds and smells of prom washing over me like a high school–themed tsunami. "Godspeed."

22

Days 'til graduation: Still 2, but minus a few hours

I HAVE WORMS IN MY STOMACH AS I WALK INTO THE BIG, BRIGHT room, just huge, fat springtime worms that have been crawling out of the cracks of the earth lately and now are crawling out of me too. I *hate* walking into rooms by myself, especially ones that are loud and fancy and full of the entire senior class. I wouldn't wish that sort of emotional trauma even on Helga. After a few moments of anxiously looking at all the tables where everyone is finishing up their dinner and clanking their silverware and taking selfies with the asparagus stalks, I find Brendan at a table in the back. I walk over with my hands sweating, grateful for the first time all night to be in sneakers and not heels.

"Can I talk to you for a sec?" I ask hurriedly, speaking to his bow tie because it's less intimidating than his face. *Slow down. Deep breaths.*

"Well, well, well, if it isn't Prom Scrooge!" he says, turning in his seat and twirling a pink rose in his hand. "Sure, we can talk, but only if we promise to stay absolutely miserable."

"Shut up." I laugh and pull him up from the table, hitting him with his napkin.

As we cross the room toward the lobby, a few people look up as we pass. I realize I might look carefully styled by a punk-rock six-year-old, with the white dress, black-taped Xs over my boobs, and highlighter-orange sneakers. But if the only sane response to an insane world is insanity, I guess I'd rather be crazy than live life fast asleep with my eyes open.

My confidence drains in the lobby, which is a stark contrast from the loudness of the room back there. *What the hell am I going to say, and why did I think this was a good idea?* I stop by the table with the fancy water for a drink, feeling all my fucks rushing in.

"That's how you know you made it," I say a little too loudly to Brendan, taking a sip and passing him a cup too. "When your water has food in it on purpose."

He holds his cup up to me, looking handsome in his pale blue suit. "It's official. We did it." I hear him swallow, and the voices inside the room change as dinner is cleared and the DJ starts the dance music. Man, it is stressful to be a standing, breathing person. I take an inhale I hope he can't hear.

"Do you want to take a walk?" he asks me at the same time I say, "I was lying earlier."

"Oh," we both say, and laugh. I run a sweaty palm over my hair frizzies and look out the glass doors, where the sky has darkened. The lanterns in the trees are even prettier now, and though the wind has blown most of the petals off the walkway, they still look beautiful piled against the building.

"Yeah," I say, deliberately avoiding our reflection in the mirror to our left. "A walk sounds good."

It's the cool, damp weather that's the worst for my hair, but I try not to think about that as we walk toward his car. The stone walkway gives way to a parking lot, and the trees with their lights get fewer and fewer the closer we get to the golf course. His dress shoes make a clicking noise against the pavement, and every few strides our fingers touch by mistake, sending my atoms haywire. We stop outside his car and I take in the lights and the sounds of the country club behind us.

"Jacket?" Brendan asks, opening the car door and offering me a blue fleece.

"Please."

I put it on and look up at the sky. I'm starting to become very aware of my skin, and every inch of it that's making contact with the air.

"So what were you saying," he asks, "when I so rudely interrupted you and suggested this cold walk?"

"Um…" *Shit shit shit.* I glance at his bow tie, then back up at the dark, clouded sky, wishing I could locate just one star. *Time to graduate, Chamomile. Time to fucking graduate.* "I was lying earlier," I squeak, then look him in the eyes and steady my voice. I poke his arm, which seems decidedly uncool and even less sexy. It becomes a weird caress and I manage, "I was hoping you were asking me to prom."

A smile twitches on his lips and I wonder about them— how they move, what they feel like.

"I *was* asking you to prom," he finally says. The wind carries the sound of his voice around the whole parking lot. I'm glad I'm the only one to hear. "I just didn't want to come on too strong."

My heart falls upward, which is something my heart has never done before. It's becoming very hard to make eye contact—I can't look away, but if I keep looking into his eyes, I don't know that I'll stay in one piece.

"Well, okay, that's good, 'cause here we are at prom." I point awkwardly toward the giant sign now hanging sideways, then consider pulling the fleece over my head. Instead I tug at its zipper. A foghorn sounds someplace far from us, an alert that the dense air is hiding something. *It's here, right here.*

"Um, I like you," Brendan finally says, fiddling with the flower pinned to his shirt. "At first I thought you were kind of an asshole, and maybe I still do, but...you're really beautiful, Cham. Even when no one's looking."

The way he says it, I know he doesn't mean *You're so hot.* I used to love it when Gene said that, but this stirs something different in me, like there's a whole universe inside me.

"I, um...I like you too," I say, stepping a tiny bit closer to him.

He lets out a breath that he might have been holding all night. "Well, that's a relief."

I smile dumbly. He smells like some combination of deodorant and shampoo that I've never smelled before. It's exciting, the prospect of learning his smells. He leans toward me. Every star is behind him. I know it, even though I can't see it.

"Can I kiss you?" I ask, finally looking up into his eyes. They're so many shades of brown. I'm self-conscious, petrified.

"I *suppose* so," he jokes, then leans against his car and pulls me toward him.

At the last second, I pause. Our faces are so close together that there are just a few atoms between us and how we are now and what we could be. I giggle in my head because my heart is racing and he can probably hear it and my breathing seems loud too. I stop thinking about it, just close my eyes and go in the direction of him. Immediately our teeth clank together. Both of us jerk back.

"Ow!"

"Sorry." I giggle, relieved that it's dark in this parking lot. We try again, and this time our noses kinda hit each other in a weird way.

"Third time's a charm," he says, and it is. We get it. The softest parts of our faces connect, creating this slow, deep, twisting kiss that really shouldn't be called a kiss, since it feels like so much more than that. He runs his hands through my hair, drawing me closer. I put my arms around his neck as I fall for him. It has to do with gravity. Our gravities.

"I meant to tell you," he says, abruptly pulling away and smiling at me shyly.

I quickly adjust my X-tits as he opens his car door and then hands me a folder. One hand is still touching mine while the other holds out a manila envelope. "I put together some of the stuff we talked about."

"What do you mean?" I ask, taking the envelope from him.

"Pieces of your essay."

He lets go and I undo the tab, then peek inside. "I don't understand."

"I mean, I sent Evelyn all the stuff you said that day in your room. It wasn't a coherent essay or anything, just a lot of notes, but I wanted Evelyn to know that you worked really hard on it."

"Wow," I say. I consider taking the pages out, but then I reclose the envelope. I haven't had anything to add to the box under my bed in a while. Now I do. And someday I have a feeling this will be worth remembering.

"This is really nice, Brendan." I hold the envelope to my chest and look up at his face. His eyes are sweet and familiar behind his dark lashes. "Thank you."

He takes my hand and gives it a gentle squeeze. "Just in case you ever want to write a college essay sometime, you'll have some notes to work from."

"Yeah," I joke, "'cause I'm totally dying to do that right now." I hold the envelope for a second longer, feeling its weight before I hand it back to him and he puts it on the hood of the car. I cross my arms, feeling the dampness starting to sink into my bones, and the weight of this moment in time, all the things that are ending. I take a deep breath.

"I was getting so tired having two separate worlds. But when you came to my house a few months ago, that started to change. You were the thing in between." I pull his fleece tighter around me. I'm starting to shiver. "I'm glad you are."

He fixes the jacket and brings me closer to him. "That's

goot," he says, then cocks his head at himself, laughing nervously.

I laugh too. "What?"

He closes his eyes and hangs his head. "I was starting to say 'good,' but then I said 'great' and—"

I kiss him then pull back grinning. I don't want separate worlds. I want one big, humongous universe that can fit all of me in it. *I want you in it.* I fall back to his chest, so close that if either of us moves the tiniest bit, our lips will brush and ignite everything again. And one of us is bound to move. We have to. He brushes a curl off my face. "So what now?"

"Let's stay out here a bit longer," I say, looking behind me toward the big room with all its windows. Multicolored lights are flashing, and people have started dancing, and the thick beat of the music reaches us even in the parking lot. "I know we're missing prom but I think a girl's gotta make her own world in this world."

Brendan smiles and takes my face in his hands. My cheeks are flushed and I feel a warmth all around me. Not like I peed myself; like the population of my universe just increased by one. "Well, then if it's okay with you," he says, leaning toward my lips, "I'd like to be in yours."

We fall back against the car. "I'll have to submit your request," I say, softly running my finger over his lips.

He laughs and he doesn't get it, but that's okay. I do. I stand on my tiptoes. Soon we will go back to the dance.

The night will end and we will graduate and there will be choices to make. But right now our breath is forming its own sweet atmosphere. Our eyelashes are touching. He's tall enough that kissing him is like kissing the sky. And the next thing I know, I am.

Epilogue

Dear College Admissions Person,
This essay has been a bitch to write. Can I say that?
If not, this whole system is bullshit. Oops. There I
go again. I'm sorry, I just want to express myself, the
real me, and that includes a few colorful swear words
and also probably a few words that *aren't* words.
Is that okay? I'm gonna forge ahead without your
permission.

   As I was saying, this essay has taken me a while to
write, like a year, or I guess my whole life, if you think
that every moment is a culmination of all the moments
that came before it and each one is indispensible. I

do. It's taken me so long because I didn't know what I wanted to say. I just knew I wanted to mean it.

All the people I know applied to college because it's the next right thing to do. They wrote essays and collected their extracurriculars and responded to a prompt using excellent vocabulary words and badass grammar. That didn't work for me, mostly because I didn't do extracurriculars and I always screw up the rules of grammar. Also, I wasn't sure I wanted to go to college. I wish it had to do with my principles, like *I don't want to be a drone who does the next right thing!* But actually it just had to do with my dad being sick. And not being able to leave him behind while he's fading away, but still feeling left behind by everyone who was moving on. Does that make sense? I was feeling stuck like a bee in amber. All I had were questions. And that's still true. Now I want to devote my life to the questions. I have to.

While I was sitting on the toilet at a particular momentous dance, feeling real sorry for myself, I read something a dead friend of mine wrote in a book. Tl;dr: *Answers are overrated. Live the questions.* I don't know if that's true, but I guess you could say it's another question I have.

Here's the thing, College Admissions Person: Even if you do not accept me to your institution of higher learning, even if I change my mind last minute and decide not to send this application in, I will still find a way to ask questions and keep asking more questions.

Last summer my dad and I read this book together about motorcycles. It was boring as hell, but it got me thinking: Anything can be college, you know? Taking classes at State and chugging beers or driving a motorcycle across the country. Even going for a run can be college, and it is for me a lot of the time. I lose touch with my feet and my legs, and there's more sky and more horizon. Everything is closer but also more infinite. It's like wading through stars beyond the ones we usually see, stars that are part of unsolved universes, secret places I want to know. As long as I keep asking questions, I have a feeling that one day I'm going to get close enough to know the nature of these alien familiars—the unknown things that I suspect have really been with me all along. I hope you'll accept me so I can explore mine. (Mostly I hope *I* can accept me, but that's a topic for another essay.)

I've attached the questions I have, and I'm sorry that they're not specific to you or your college. I'm used to writing letters to a very special entity, and it's too late to change my target audience now.

Dear Universe,

1. Does this shirt make my boobs look flat?

2. Should I wear sneakers while running, or are bare feet the soul of moving?

3. If freedom comes after high school and transcripts and SATs, what's a girl to do with the opposite of freedom? The stuff that comes with growing up and sickness and death?

4. Can you ever bring two worlds together once and for all? Or is it a constant kneading of earth and ocean and atmosphere?

5. How many licks to the center of a lollipop?

6. Is that me I'm seeing, or is this selfie stick facing the wrong way entirely?

7. What if some questions don't get punctuation marks?

8. What if I think he's an exquisite specimen of boy and you pushed us together for a reason?

9. What if I didn't really love that other boy—I just loved his skin on my skin?

10. Is one type of love just a branch of dermatology?

11. Could it be that the square root of who I'm going to be is {me right now} × {all my adventures} × {alchemy}?

12. Do I have spinach in my teeth?

13. How do we love the people we love so much we don't always know how to love them?

14. And what does it all mean—this cardboard box covered in stars, full of things like pictures and notes? The kisses and the crying and the bellyaches from laughing, eating candy, running?

15. Do you even know how expansive you are and how infinite and petrifying?

16. Do you know that I'm coming?

17. Are you ready for me? Are you listening?

Of course you are. I've been here all along.